THE X-FILES™

CREATED BY
Chris Carter

Skin

Ben Mezrich

HarperEntertainment
A Division of HarperCollinsPublishers

HarperEntertainment
A Division of HarperCollins*Publishers*
10 East 53rd Street, New York, N.Y. 10022–5299

Printed in the United States of America

First printing: May 1999

Library of Congress Cataloging-in-Publication Data

Mezrich, Ben 1969–
    Skin : the X-files / Ben Mezrich. — 1st ed.
      p. cm.
    I. Title.
    ISBN 0-06-105041-5
    PS3563.E986S45   1999
    813' .54—dc21   98-49471

Visit HarperEntertainment on the World Wide Web at
http://www.harpercollins.com

99 00 01 02 03 ❖/RRD 10 9 8 7 6 5 4 3 2 1

Skin

X Two hours after midnight, sirens tore through the cinder-block walls, shattering the momentary calm. There was the screech of rubber tires against pavement—the ambulances careening to a stop in the receiving circle—and the steady wail was joined by the shouts of paramedics as they unloaded their cargo. A second later, the double doors crashed open, and the vast room seemed to buckle inward, as a torrent of stretchers streamed across the tiled floor.

"Here we go!" someone shouted, and suddenly the emergency room came alive. Bleary-eyed doctors in white coats and pale-blue scrubs leapt forward, shouting for chem trays and surgical consults. Triage nurses in pink uniforms swirled between the stretchers, trailing IV wires and portable crash carts. At first glance, the room seemed gripped by chaos, but in reality, it was a highly controlled, intricate performance. The nurses and doctors played off one another like professional athletes, acting out their roles in kinetic bursts of harmony.

Huddled in a corner near the back of the ER, Brad Alger watched the unfolding spectacle with wide eyes. Although he had been on duty for less than twenty minutes, his scrubs were already thick with sweat. Red splotches covered the sleeves of his white doctor's coat, and his high-top Nikes had turned a strange, nearly violet color. His platinum-blond hair rose from his head in unruly locks, like a miniature sunburst. There were heavy bags under his glassy blue eyes, and he looked as though he hadn't slept in months.

He rubbed a damp sleeve across his forehead, then quickly stepped aside as a disheveled nurse pushed a crash cart up against the wall next to him.

"Christ," Alger coughed, his voice pitching upward, "it's knee deep in here. I thought the first salvo was bad—but this is crazy. How many ambulances did they say were coming?"

"Twenty-two," the nurse answered, tossing a pair of blood-spattered gloves toward the floor. "Maybe more. At first, they thought there were only nine cars involved in the accident. Now they say it was more like thirteen."

Alger whistled. "Thirteen cars. At two in the morning."

"This your first Friday night?"

She had spiky dark hair and kind eyes. Alger guessed she was thirty, maybe thirty-five. He felt like a kid next to her, and he tried to take the fearful edge out of his voice. "My internship started on Sunday."

The nurse offered a sympathetic smile. "Welcome to New York."

She grabbed a clean pair of gloves from the crash cart and moved back into the fray. For the thousandth time in less than a week, Alger wondered what the hell he was doing there. A month ago, he had been a fourth-year medical student in Cincinnati, Ohio. His biggest worries had been his school loan payments and Kelly Pierce, his most recent ex. He had done a rotation in emergency back in Cincinnati—but he had never imagined anything like this.

The evening had started innocently enough. A few cardios,

2

a handful of recent entrants into the knife-and-gun club, a half dozen respiratory gomers sneaking cigarettes under their oxygen masks. And then the call had come over the emergency room's intercom system. There had been a multicar accident on the FDR Drive; at least ten critical, another two dozen in bad shape. All available doctors had been summoned down from the hospital's other departments, and the emergency room had been put on full trauma-alert.

Alger had made the mistake of asking Duke Baker—the gargantuan, short-tempered chief resident—what that meant in English. The Duke had nearly busted a capillary berating him; the only English spoken in the Duke's emergency room took the form of four-letter words. Trauma-alert meant you tried not to kill anyone before dawn—and in the process, kept the fuck out of Duke Baker's way.

"Brad! Over here!"

Alger felt his pulse rocket as he caught sight of Dennis Crow. Tall, thin, with a shock of dark hair and freckles covering every inch of exposed skin. Crow was one of the four interns who had started with Alger, and the only one who seemed even more out of place. Born on a farm, trained at the University of Wisconsin—and completely in over his head at the big-city ER. In other words, he had the Duke's footprints all over his freckled ass.

At the moment, Crow was standing between two paramedics, at the head of a stretcher on the other side of the ER. The two paramedics were struggling with a convulsing patient as Crow worked an endo tube down the man's throat. Although both paramedics were big and burly, they were having a hell of a time keeping the patient still. One was fighting to get a Velcro restraint around the man's shoulders, while the other was using his weight against the patient's wrists.

Alger grabbed a pair of sterile latex gloves from the cart

next to him and rushed forward. As he navigated across the room, he signaled for a crash cart, a portable EKG machine, and a chem tray. He reached Crow and the stretcher seconds ahead of the equipment and a nurse. He watched as Maria Gomez began pasting the circular electrodes from the EKG monitor across the patient's chest. She was a big woman, with thick folds of fat hanging from around her arms and neck—but her motions were fluid and practiced. Still, her brown eyes showed a spark of concern. Crow and Alger were both interns with less than a week of experience. No nurse in her right mind wanted to stand around and watch two kids playing doctor.

Alger pushed the thought away. He wasn't playing doctor— he *was* a doctor. He focused his attention on the patient in front of him.

Caucasian, maybe twenty-four, twenty-five years old. Tall, muscular, with chiseled, boxy features and glazed, bright blue eyes. A blond crew cut, military style. His shirt had already been cut away by the paramedics, and there was a tattoo on his upper right shoulder, some sort of dragon with red flames coming out of its mouth. No visible signs of trauma, none of the marks of injury that Alger would have expected from a car-crash victim.

He watched as Crow finally got the intubation tube past the man's epiglottis and into his throat. The man's chest swelled beneath the EKG electrodes, and Crow quickly attached an air tube to the top of the endo tube. As the patient's breathing resumed, he settled back against the stretcher, his eyelids rolling shut. Alger turned toward the paramedics. "What have we got?"

The larger of the two answered as he finished fastening the Velcro restraint around the patient's chest. "Found him collapsed, unconscious, in the breakdown lane, maybe twenty feet from the site of the crash. No contusions, no visible signs of trauma. He convulsed twice in the ambulance—and just a few minutes ago he went into respiratory distress."

"Any history?"

The paramedic stepped back from the stretcher. "No ID, no wallet. Doesn't respond to any stimulus at all. He was conscious for a few minutes in the wagon—but we couldn't get him to answer any questions."

"Start him on any meds?"

The paramedic shook his head. "His pulse and BP seemed fine. Like I said, his breathing didn't go down until a few minutes ago."

"What about the EKG?"

"You'll be the first to see it. It was a real grab and dash at the scene. We had another in the same ambulance, in much worse shape. We're not even sure this one was involved in the accident—he might have been a bystander. Certainly doesn't look like he was thrown through a car windshield, or anything like that." He paused. "Okay, you guys got it from here?"

There was obvious hesitation in the paramedic's eyes. Alger felt his face flush red. He couldn't help how young he looked. He nodded, his expression bold. The paramedic turned and headed back toward the double doors. His partner gave Alger a tiny nod, then followed. It was up to the two interns, now. Alger tossed a glance toward the Duke, huddled over a patient on the other side of the ER, then gritted his teeth. He was fresh—but he could handle this.

"All right, let's start with the basics. Airway, Breathing, Cardio."

He knew he sounded like an idiot to the experienced nurse, but he had to begin with what he knew—and that meant the ABCs of medicine. He watched the man's chest rise and fall, and knew that Crow had done a good job with the intubation. Then he turned toward the EKG—the cardiac monitor—and focused his eyes on the small screen on top of the waist-high steel cart.

"Holy shit," he whispered.

Crow followed his gaze, his eyes widening. The screen was covered with frantic green lines. "He's all over the place! It looks like his heart's doing cartwheels! Is that V-fib?"

Alger stared at the screen, then shook his head. The man wasn't in arrest yet—but he was certainly close. Alger had never seen anything like it before. One second, the monitor showed an elevated cadence—and the next second a prolonged skip. One second he seemed to be in normal, sinus rhythm— and the next second he was bouncing through a combination of arrhythmias. Alger had no doubt that if the paramedics had seen such a bizarre EKG reading in the ambulance, they would never have handed this patient over to two interns. They would have brought him straight to the chief resident.

Alger turned back to the patient. The man looked calm, still unconscious, but there were visible spasms beneath his skin. His muscles seemed to vibrate in concert with the readings on the screen. No doubt about it, something weird was going on. "Jesus, this isn't good. What's his BP?"

Maria Gomez looked up from the blood-pressure gauge strapped around the man's right arm. "Two-twenty over one-twenty."

"What?"

The nurse looked at the gauge again. She shrugged, her face slightly pale. "Two-twenty over one-twenty."

Alger coughed, his stomach churning. Two-twenty over one-twenty was extremely high. Along with the erratic heart-beat, it was a dangerous sign. The man's circulatory system was completely out of whack, and his heart was enormously overstimulated.

"An acute MI?" Crow tried. "Maybe a pulmonary embolism?"

Alger shook his head. The EKG didn't look like an MI or an embolism. Alger rubbed sweat out of his eyes. *Stay calm. Stay focused.* It was a mystery—but that was the thrill of the ER, wasn't it? Solving the mysteries? "Okay, we need a blood workup, a Chem 7—"

"His BP's rising!" Gomez blurted. "Two-fifty over one-fifty!"

Shit. How could his BP be rising? It was already off the map! Alger cursed. Thrill or no thrill—he knew it was time to bring the Duke over. Any second, this patient was going to arrest. Alger was about to call out across the ER when Crow shouted at him. "Now *that's* V-fib! That's definitely V-fib!"

Alger whirled back toward the EKG screen. The bright green lines had become completely disjointed and frantic, indicating that the man had gone into ventricular fibrillation. His heart was responding to random electrical impulses, and was no longer capable of pumping blood to the rest of his body. In other words, this patient was failing. Fast.

"BP dropping!" Gomez chimed in. "He's crashing!"

Alger leapt for the crash cart, while Crow called the Code. Normally, doctors and nurses would have rushed toward the crashing patient—but tonight there were so many tragedies filling the ER, the Code barely registered. Alger knew that the Duke would make his way over when he realized his two interns were in charge of the dying man—but Alger didn't have time to wait for the chief resident to take over.

He grabbed the defibrillator paddles off the crash cart and slipped them over his hands. He rubbed the conductive fluid over the pads, then scraped them together in a circular motion. He had no choice but to shock the man and pray that his heart resumed a workable rhythm. He had never used the paddles before—but he had watched the procedure a dozen times during medical school.

"Three hundred joules," he declared, trying to keep the

emotion out of his voice. He knew three hundred was a high place to start—but this was a big, muscular guy. Probably worked out every day of his life. "Clear!"

Everyone stepped back from the stretcher. Alger pressed the paddles against the man's bare chest and hit the triggers with his thumbs. The man's body spasmed upward, then crashed back down onto the stretcher. Alger turned to the EKG machine.

Still nothing. He turned back toward Gomez, who was now standing by the defibrillator. "Three-sixty. Stat!"

"Jesus," Crow mumbled. "Where the hell is Duke?"

Alger ignored him. There wasn't anything the Duke could do at this point—either they got this guy's heart started again, or he was finished. Gomez upped the voltage, and Alger readied the paddles. "Clear!"

This time, the man arched a full four inches off the stretcher. His neck twisted back and his arms convulsed beneath the Velcro straps.

"Flat line!" Crow yelled. "He's down! Brad—"

"Again!" Alger shouted back. "Clear!"

He shocked the man a third time. The smell of burned flesh filled Alger's nostrils, and he frantically turned back to the EKG machine. Still nothing. He tossed the defibrillator paddles aside and leapt halfway up the stretcher, placing his palms roughly near the center of the man's chest. The muscles of his forearms contracted as he started the most vigorous CPR of his life. The man's chest felt strangely stiff beneath his fingers, his skin rough, almost leathery. He worked in near silence, the minutes ticking by as he tried to coax the man's heart back to life. He ignored the sweat running down his back, the ache in his arms and shoulders. His mind raced through everything that had just happened, searching for some reason why things had gone so drastically wrong. Was there anything he had missed? Was there anything else he could have done? Did he make the right choice when he went for the defibrillator paddles?

"Well?" he asked, desperate, already knowing the answer.

"Still nothing," Crow responded. "He's gone, Brad. You're just pumping beef."

Alger looked at the EKG screen, then back at Crow. He glanced at Gomez, who nodded. He felt his shoulders deflate, his arms going limp. *Damn it.* It had all happened so fast. He glanced toward the Duke, who was still working on a patient near the front of the room. Either he hadn't heard the Code, or he was handling an emergency of his own.

Alger swallowed, telling himself that he had done everything by the book. The Duke wouldn't have handled the situation any differently. The guy had gone into arrest less than two minutes after he had been wheeled into the ER. The paddles could have saved him—and they certainly didn't kill him. Still, Alger felt awful. *A man had just died in front of him.* He lifted his hands off the man's bare chest and took a step back from the stretcher. *Why the hell had he chosen emergency?* He glanced up at the clock over the double doors. "Time of death—three-fifteen."

He peeled off his gloves as Gomez rolled the stretcher toward the elevator at the back of the room. The elevator was a straight shot downstairs to pathology, then onward to the hospital morgue. There would probably be an autopsy, because of the mysterious circumstances behind the man's death, and maybe the pathologist would be able to tell him what had really happened. But it wouldn't make any difference to the man on the stretcher.

Alger's face went slack as he watched Gomez push the corpse away. His eyelids suddenly seemed as if they were filled with lead. He felt Dennis Crow's hand on his shoulder. "We did everything we could. People die, and despite what the Duke might think—sometimes it's not our fault."

Alger looked at him, then toward the double doors at the front of the room. He sighed as he watched another stretcher skid into the ER.

Twelve hours later, Mike Lifton fought back nausea as Josh Kemper yanked open the heavy steel drawer. The thick scent of dead flesh mixed with the antiseptic chill of the refrigerated storage room, and Mike grimaced, wishing he had never agreed to accompany his classmate on the harvest.

"You get used to it," Josh said, as he pulled the cadaver drawer forward with both hands. Josh was tall, gangly, with oversize ears sticking out from beneath long, stringy brown hair. "It helps to remind yourself how much money you're making. Twenty bucks an hour beats the hell out of pouring coffee at Starbucks."

Mike tried to laugh, but the sound caught somewhere in his throat. He nervously pulled at the sleeves of his green scrubs, rubbing the soft material between his gloved fingers. He could feel the sweat cooling against his back, and he shivered, staring down over Josh's right shoulder.

The body in the drawer was wrapped in opaque plastic with a zipper up the front. Mike took a tiny step back as Josh drew the zipper downward. "Here we go. One stiff, medium rare."

Mike blinked hard, his mouth going dry. Then he ran a gloved hand through his short, auburn hair. He had worked with cadavers before; as a first-year medical student, he had poked and prodded enough dead bodies to fill a zombie movie. But he had never seen a body so *fresh*.

The man inside the plastic bag was unnaturally pale, almost a blue-gray color, with fuzzy blond hair covering his muscular chest. His eyes were closed, and his face was drawn, the skin tight against his cheekbones. Early rigor mortis had begun to set in, and his square jaw jutted stiffly forward, his neck arched back against the steel storage drawer. There were no obvious signs of injury, no gaping wounds or visible bruises. The only distinguishing mark was a colorful tattoo high up on the man's right arm.

"Nice dragon," Josh continued, pointing. "That's about three hundred dollars of wasted skin."

Mike shivered at the macabre thought. He knew that the part-time job with the skin bank was a good way to make money—and great practice if he decided to go into surgery after med school—but he couldn't help feeling ghoulish. His classmate's attitude didn't help matters. It was more than just cynicism bred by experience; Josh Kemper had been born without a deferential bone in his body. During his first year at Columbia Medical School, he had nearly gotten himself suspended for playing catch with a pancreas during anatomy section. No doubt, he was heading straight for a career in pathology.

Mike had always been more sensitive than his classmate. His first day of anatomy, he had nearly fainted when his professor had made the first "Y" incision. And although he had grown stronger over the past three years, he still had a long way to go before he was ready to hold a surgeon's scalpel.

"Aside from the tattoo," Josh continued, unzipping the bag the rest of the way, "he looks pretty good. Both arms, both legs. And the eye bank hasn't gotten here yet. He's still got both peepers."

Mike turned away from the corpse as he steadied his nerves. It's necessary and important work, he reminded himself. The human body was recyclable. And that meant someone had to do the recycling. Heart, liver, kidneys, eyes, skin—someone had to harvest the raw material.

Still, the thought didn't make it any easier. He bit down against his lower lip, trying not to count the steel drawers that lined three walls of the deserted storage room.

"If you're going to puke," Josh interrupted, "do it now. Once we're in the OR, we've got to keep things sterile."

"I'm not going to puke."

"Well, you look worse than our buddy here. Mike, you've got to get used to this sort of thing. It's just a hunk of meat. And we're the guys behind the deli counter."

"You're disgusting."

"That's why you love me. Check the toe tag." Josh started across the storage room, toward a filing cabinet by the far wall. "I'll get the chart."

Mike breathed through his mouth as he circled around the open drawer. *Don't overthink. Do your job.* He reached the back end of the drawer and pulled the plastic bag down on either side. The dead man's legs were long and muscular, covered with more downy blond hairs. His feet were heavily callused, his toenails yellowed like an old man's. Mike wondered if he had suffered from some sort of fungus.

Now you're thinking like a doctor. He smiled inwardly, then searched the big toes for the tag. The skin above his eyes wrinkled as he realized it was missing. He searched the drawer beneath the man's callused heels, but there was no sign of the plastic ID. "Hey, Josh. I don't see the tag."

Josh returned from the other side of the room. He had a manila folder open in his gloved hands. "Sometimes it falls down below their feet."

"I'm looking everywhere. There's no tag."

Josh stopped at his side, cursing. He held the manila folder under his arm and lifted the corpse's feet with both hands. Working together, the two students searched the drawer, but came up empty.

"Fuck," Josh said. "This is just great. Eckleman is such a moron."

"Who's Eckleman?"

"The ME's assistant. He runs the storage room. Tags the bodies, makes sure the files are coded correctly. He's a big fat piece of shit, and he drinks." Josh retrieved the folder from under his arm and leafed through it with gloved fingers. "Derrik Kaplan. Caucasian, mid-thirties. Blond hair, blue eyes. Acute aortic dissection, died in the ICU."

Mike glanced down at the body in the drawer. "Well, he's blond, and he's got blue eyes. But he doesn't look like he's in his mid-thirties. Does it say anything about the tattoo?"

Josh shook his head. "No, but like I said, Eckleman is a moron. Look, this is locker fifty-two. Eckleman blows the tags all the time. Especially when the ER is jumping, and after the accident last night—"

"Josh, are you sure we shouldn't ask somebody? What if it's the wrong cadaver?"

Josh paused, rubbing a gloved finger under his jaw. He glanced toward the elevator in the corner of the room, where a stretcher waited to take the body up to the OR for the harvesting. Then he shrugged. "We've got consent, we've got a body. More importantly, we've got an OR reserved for the next hour. So let's go slice up some skin."

He turned, and headed for the stretcher. Mike glanced back at the dragon tattoo. He hoped his classmate knew what he was doing.

"Watch carefully. I promise, you're going to like this."

Mike bit his lips behind a papery surgical mask, as Josh played with one of the saline bags that hung from the IV rack above the operating table. There was a sudden hiss as the infusion pump came alive. Mike watched, shocked, as the skin covering the dead man's chest inflated like an enormous water balloon.

"The saline empties into the subcutaneous base," Josh

explained, pointing to the three other saline bags that stood at the corners of the operating table. "The pressure lifts the dermis up from the layer of fat underneath. Makes it easier to get a smooth cut."

Mike nodded, repulsed but fascinated. The cadaver's chest—shaved, prepped with Betadine, and inflated with saline—no longer looked human. The inflated skin was slick, smooth, rounded, a sort of beige color Mike had never seen outside of a J. Crew catalog. "Is this going to be bloody?"

"Not very," Josh answered, reaching into the surgical tray by the operating table. "Until we turn him over. Most of the blood has pooled along his back."

He pulled a shiny steel instrument out of the surgical tray, showing it to Mike. It looked like an oversize cheese slicer, with a numbered knob near the razor-sharp blade. "I'm going to set the dermatome for point-oh-nine millimeters. The goal is to get a piece that you can just barely see through."

He leaned forward, placing the dermatome right below the cadaver's collarbone. Mike considered looking away, then dug his fingers into his palms. In a few months he would be doing rotations in the ER, and he'd see things just as bad—or worse.

He watched as Josh drew the dermatome down across the man's chest. A trickle of dark, deoxygenated blood ran down into the chrome table gutters. The thin layer of skin curled behind the blade, and Josh deftly twisted his wrist as he reached the bottom of the cadaver's rib cage, slicing the strip of skin free. He lifted it gently by an edge and held it in front of Mike. It was nearly transparent, a little more than a foot in length.

"Open the cooler," Josh said, and Mike quickly found the plastic case by his feet. The cooler was a white-and-red rectangle, with the New York Fire Department seal emblazoned across two sides. Mike opened the cooler and retrieved a small tray filled with bluish liquid.

Josh put the slice of skin into the liquid, and Mike sealed it shut. The cooler would keep the skin fresh until it could be transported to the skin bank. There, it would be soaked in antibiotic liquid and stored indefinitely at minus seventy degrees Fahrenheit.

Josh went back to work on the man's chest. His strokes were deft and sure, and in a few minutes he had skinned most of the man's chest and abdomen, both arms, and both legs. He left a small circle around the dragon tattoo, which stood out like a colorful island against the whitish pink background of subcutaneous fat.

"Help me turn him over," Josh said, sliding his hands under the man's back. Mike moved to assist him, and together they heaved the body onto its side. Mike noticed a small, circular rash on the back of the corpse's neck.

"Josh, look at that."

Josh glanced at the rash. It was no more than three inches in diameter and consisted of thousands of tiny red dots. "What about it?"

"Was it in the chart?"

Josh finished turning the body over, then went back for the dermatome. "It's nothing. An insect bite. A random abrasion. Maybe we scratched him when we transferred him to the operating table."

"It looks kind of strange—"

"Mike, the guy's already dead. Someone else is out there with a really bad burn, and this guy's been generous enough to sign away his skin. So let's just do our job and get out of here."

Mike nodded, realizing that Josh was right. The man on the operating table had already gone through the ER. The doctors had tried to save his life, and there was nothing anyone could do for him anymore. But because of Josh, Mike, and the New York Fire Department, someone else was going to benefit from his death. Derrik Kaplan was finished—*but someone else needed his skin.*

Mike gritted his teeth, then gestured toward the dermatome in his classmate's hand. "If you don't mind, I'd like to give it a try."

Josh Kemper raised his eyebrows, then smiled behind his mask.

One week later, in the private-care ward at Jamaica Hospital in Queens, Perry Stanton jerked twice beneath his thin hospital smock, then suddenly came awake. Dr. Alec Bernstein beamed down at him.

"Professor Stanton," Bernstein said, his voice affable, "good afternoon. You'll be happy to hear, the procedure was a complete success."

Stanton blinked rapidly, trying to chase the fog from his vision. Bernstein watched the little man with almost fatherly pride. He always felt this way with his burn patients. Unlike the face-lifts, breast augmentations, and other elective procedures that made up the bulk of his caseload, the burn patients filled him with pride.

Dr. Bernstein felt that pride as he gazed down at Stanton. A forty-nine-year-old associate professor of history at nearby Jamaica University, Stanton had been wheeled into the emergency room eight hours ago, a full-thickness burn covering most of his left thigh. A boiler had exploded in the basement of the university library, and huge drafts of superheated steam had literally flayed the skin from Stanton's leg.

Bernstein remembered getting the emergency summons; he had been right in the middle of a liposuction and had scrubbed out immediately. He had surveyed the damage and made a quick call to the skin bank. An hour later he had gone to work on Stanton's thigh.

Bernstein glanced up as a nurse brushed past him and attached a new bag of fluids to the IV rack above Stanton's bed. Teri Nestor smiled at the surgeon, then looked down at the slowly awakening professor. "You're going to be as good as new, Professor Stanton. Dr. Bernstein is the best the hospital has to offer."

Bernstein blushed. The nurse finished with the IV rack, then moved to the pair of large picture windows that looked out on the hospital parking lot, two floors below. She fiddled with the blinds, and orange sunlight glinted off the twenty-inch television screen on the other side of the small private-care room.

Perry Stanton coughed as the light reached his pale, puggish face, and Bernstein turned his attention back to his patient. The cough bothered him; steam could easily damage lung capacity, and Stanton had shown some signs of respiratory distress when he first came into the ER. Stanton was a small man—barely five-four, no more than 120 pounds, with stubby limbs and diminutive features. It wouldn't take much steam to diminish his breathing ability to dangerous levels.

Bernstein had already put Stanton on IV Solumedol, a strong steroid that had helped ease his respiratory distress. Now he wondered if he should up the dosage, at least for the next few days. "Professor, how does your chest feel? Any problems breathing?"

Stanton coughed again, then shook his head. He cleared his throat, speaking in a slightly slurred voice. "I'm just a little dizzy."

Bernstein nodded, relieved. "That's because of the morphine. How about your thigh? Are you experiencing any pain?"

"A little. And it itches. A lot."

Bernstein nodded again. The morphine would keep the pain to a minimum, as the temporary transplant helped the burned area heal enough to allow a matched graft. The itching was a little uncommon, but certainly not rare.

"I'll up the morphine a bit, to take care of the pain. The itchiness should go away on its own. Now let me take a look at the dressing." Bernstein leaned forward and gently pulled Stanton's smock up, revealing the man's left thigh. The area of the transplant was covered by rectangular strips of white gauze. The gauze started just above his kneecap and ran all the way to the inguinal line, where the thigh met the groin.

Bernstein gently lifted a corner of the gauze with a gloved finger. He could just make out one of the small steel staples that held the transplanted skin in place. The skin was whitish yellow, and clung tightly to the nerveless subdermal layer underneath. "Everything looks fine, Professor. Just fine."

Bernstein pulled the hospital smock back down over the gauze. He decided he could ignore the itchiness, unless it got worse. Bernstein was slightly more concerned about something he had noticed a few hours ago, when he had checked on his sleeping patient for the first time since the transplant procedure.

"Professor Stanton, would you mind turning your head to the side for a moment?" Bernstein walked to the top of the hospital bed and leaned forward, staring at the skin on the back of Stanton's neck.

The small, circular rash was still there, just above Stanton's spine. Thousands of tiny dots, a blemish no more than a few inches in diameter. Some sort of local allergic reaction, Bernstein supposed. Nothing dire, but something he would have to keep his eye on.

Bernstein stepped back from the hospital bed. "You try and get some more sleep, and I'll have Teri up your morphine. I'll be back to check on you in a few hours."

Bernstein gave Teri the morphine order, then headed out of

the private-care room, closing the heavy wooden door behind him. He turned an abrupt corner and entered a long hallway with white walls and gray carpeting. At the end of the hallway stood a coffee machine beneath a large scheduling chart.

He paused at the coffee machine, taking a Styrofoam cup from a tall pile by the half-filled pot. He poured himself a cup, noticing with a sideways glance that the hospital seemed quieter than usual, even for a Sunday afternoon. He knew there were three other doctors wandering the private-care hallways, and at least a dozen nurses. But at the moment, he was alone with his coffee, his patient, and his thoughts.

He took a deep sip, feeling the hot liquid against his tongue. Not hot enough to burn, to sear skin and cauterize vessels, but hot enough to spark his synapses, to send warning messages to his brain. A little hotter, and his brain would send messages back: Escape the heat before it has a chance to damage and destroy. A little hotter still, and there would be no time for messages. Perry Stanton probably never felt the steam—even now, his pain had nothing to do with the burned area, which had no surviving nerves. It had to do with the steel staples that held the temporary graft in place. But in a few weeks, the staples and the pain would disappear. The professor would leave Jamaica Hospital with little more than a scar and the memory of a wonderful plastic surgeon.

Bernstein smiled, looking up at the scheduling chart above the coffee machine. Then his smile disappeared as he ticked off the rest of his afternoon. A lift at four, a breast consult at five, a liposuction at five-thirty. All elective procedures. Bernstein sighed, taking another deep sip of coffee.

He was about to refill when a sudden scream ripped through the hallway. Bernstein's eyes widened as he realized that the scream had come from Perry Stanton's room.

He whirled away from the coffee machine. As he rushed

down the hallway, the scream still echoed in his ears. A female scream, filled with terror. Bernstein had never heard anything like it before.

He reached the end of the hall and turned toward Perry Stanton's room. The heavy wooden door was still shut, and there were sounds coming from the other side: the splintering of wood, the crash of breaking glass, the thud of heavy objects slamming to the floor. Bernstein swallowed, glancing back down the hall. He could hear voices from around the next bend, and he knew that a dozen nurses, techs, and doctors would be there within the next few seconds. But from the sound of things, Perry Stanton and his nurse might not survive that long.

Bernstein was about to step forward when something hit the door hard, near the center, and the wood buckled outward. Bernstein jumped back, terror rushing through him. The door was made of heavy oak; what could have hit it hard enough to buckle the wood? He stared, waiting for the door to crash open.

It never happened. Seconds passed in silence; then there was the sound of running feet, followed by a loud crash. Bernstein overcame his fear and dived forward, his hand reaching for the knob.

The door came open, and Bernstein stopped. He had never seen such devastation before. The metal-framed hospital bed had been bent completely in half, and there was a huge tear down the center of the mattress. The television set lay on the floor, its screen cracked and smoking. Both picture windows had been shattered, and shards of glass littered the floor. My God, Bernstein thought, what could have done this? Some sort of explosion? And where was Perry Stanton? Then Bernstein saw the IV rack embedded halfway into the plaster wall to his left. His head swam, and he took a slight step forward.

His foot landed in something wet. He looked down, and a

gasp filled his throat. There was a kidney-shaped pool of blood beneath his shoes. It took him less than a second to follow the blood back to its source.

Teri Nestor was lying halfway beneath the warped hospital bed, her legs twisted unnaturally behind her body. Both of her arms looked broken in numerous places, and her uniform was drenched in blood. Bernstein was about to check her vitals when his gaze slid up past her contorted shoulders.

His knees weakened, and he slumped against the nearest wall, covering his mouth. Still, he could not tear his eyes away from the sight.

It was as if two enormously strong hands had grabbed Teri Nestor's skull on either side—and squeezed.

2

 Fox Mulder pressed a soggy hotel towel against the side of his jaw as he lowered himself onto the edge of the imitation Colonial-style bed. Most of the ice had already melted through the cheap cloth, and he could feel the cold teardrops crawling down the skin of his forearm. He lay back against the mattress, listening to the bray of the television in the background, letting the monotonous voices of the CNN anchormen mingle with the dull throbbing in his head. *A wonderful end to a wonderful afternoon.* He ran his tongue around the inside of his mouth and grimaced at the salty taste. Dried blood, mixed with the distinct, gritty flavor of processed cow manure. Well, he thought to himself, it could be worse. *The bastard could have had good aim.*

Mulder closed his eyes, massaging the ice-filled towel harder against the knot of muscle just below his lower gum line. He could still see the shovel flashing toward him, and the crazy glint in the Colombian's eyes. A few inches higher, and the shovel would certainly have cracked his skull open. Mulder only wished his partner, Dana Scully, hadn't cuffed the man so quickly after he had wrested the weapon away. A good, long scuffle would have given Mulder a chance to pay the Colombian back for the blow. And for the wild-goose chase that had led them to the deserted barn in the first place.

Still, Mulder had to admit, it wasn't entirely the Colombian's fault that he and Scully had spent the last two weeks wandering through upstate New York on what should have been a DEA assignment. Carlos Sanchez couldn't have known about the reports of mutilated livestock that had trickled in to the FBI over the past few months, or about the resulting case file that had been dropped on Mulder's cluttered desk in the basement of the Hoover Building—partly because the case's bizarre focus seemed to fit with Mulder's obsession with the unexplained, and partly because no other agent wanted to investigate a bunch of dead cows.

Sanchez couldn't have known about these things—because in truth, the case had had nothing to do with mutilated livestock. Mulder should have known from the beginning that the case had not been a bona fide X-File. Thirty-two cows with scalpel wounds across their abdomens was a cliché, not a paranormal mystery.

Mulder had not seen the clues until too late. When Scully had discovered evidence of old stitches beneath the wounds of the most recently mutilated cows, he should have begun to suspect something. Then, when he and Scully had determined that all the mutilated cattle had originated in the same breeding ranch just outside of Bogota, he should have made the final connection.

But it wasn't until he had stumbled into the abandoned barn on the back lot of Sanchez's farm that he had realized the truth. He had stared at the eviscerated carcasses piled high in the center of the barn, and the bloody, sealed bags of white powder drying in the hay—and the lightbulb had finally gone on. Bandez had been using the cows to transport cocaine into the U.S. The abandoned barn was a drug depository, with distribution routes leading straight down I-95 into Manhattan.

Before Mulder had finished digesting his discovery, Sanchez had come at him with the shovel. A minute later he had been lying on top of the Colombian in a pile of dried manure, while Scully made the arrest. He had nursed his aching jaw in silence during the winding ride back to the hotel, avoiding Scully's eyes. He hadn't needed to see her expression—he knew what she was thinking. Yet another debunked mystery, a mirage with reason at its core. Of course, it was her job to think that way. That's why she was there in the first place—to expose the scientific, rational truth behind Mulder's supposed enigmas. Sometimes even her silence was as subtle as a shovel to his jaw.

He heard the shower go on in the adjacent room and groaned, lifting himself back to a sitting position on the edge of the bed. His athletic, six-foot frame ached from a combination of exhaustion and frustration. He ran his free hand through his dark hair and tried to chase the fog out of his tired hazel eyes. It was almost time to leave. He and Scully had a long drive back to the airfield in Westchester, and if they were going to catch the last commercial flight back to Washington, they would have to break more than a few speed limits along the way. Of course, that was one of the perks of having federal plates and FBI badges. *Somebody else handled the speeding tickets.*

Mulder removed the soggy towel from his jaw and let it drop to the ugly beige carpet. The cramped hotel room stared at him, four white plaster walls glowing in the light of the twenty-inch television set. Aside from the television, the room contained a redwood dresser that was supposed to look like an antique, a desk with a fax machine and a telephone, and a closet Mulder had filled with blue and gray suits. Mulder's travel bag was under the desk, and his gun and badge were next to the phone, the straps of his shoulder holster trailing down behind the fax machine, swinging in the refrigerated breeze from the baseboard vents. Home on the road, another variation on a theme. Mulder and Scully had been there a thousand times before.

Mulder was about to get up and start packing his suits when something on the television screen caught his eye. He paused, momentarily forgetting the throb in his jaw. A reporter with frosted blond hair was speaking into a microphone as she wandered through what looked to be a hospital hallway. Behind her was a spiderweb of yellow police tape. Even through the tape, Mulder could make out the disaster scene in the room on the other side of the hallway; the torn, blood-spattered mattress, the IV rack sticking straight out of the wall, the destroyed, overturned television set, the shattered picture windows—and most disturbing of all, the strange indentation in the center of the half-open wooden door. It was the indentation that had caught his attention in the first place—because it seemed somehow familiar. Something he could almost place.

"The sheer violence of yesterday's tragedy has shocked local authorities," the CNN reporter droned into her microphone, "and a boroughwide search for Professor Stanton is presently in full swing. Still, this is little comfort to the family of nurse Teri Nestor . . ."

The picture on the screen changed as the reporter continued on, and Mulder found himself staring into a pair of intelligent blue eyes. The man in the enlarged photograph looked to be about fifty years old, with thinning brown hair and slightly oversized ears. Even from the cropped photo, Mulder could tell he was a small man; the angled tips of his shoulders barely made an impression through his professorial tweed jacket, and his neck was thin and roosterlike, devoid of muscle.

As the CNN reporter dribbled out sketchy details about the

diminutive professor and the horrible murder of the young nurse, Mulder's thoughts swept back to the moment in the barn when the Colombian swung at him with the shovel. He remembered the violent glint in the Colombian's eyes. Then he looked again at Professor Stanton's photo. He was still staring at Stanton's kind blue eyes when the picture on the television changed again.

This time he was looking at a close-up of the destroyed hospital room. The mattress, the IV rack, the broken television set, the shattered windows—and the marred, half-open door. He took a step closer to the screen, hunching forward, his eyes focused on the strangely shaped indentation in the wood. Suddenly, he realized what he was looking at.

An imprint of a human hand, set a few inches deep into the heavy oak. Palm wide-open, fingers splayed outward. Mulder's eyes widened, as a question struck him. *What kind of force would it take to make an imprint of a hand in a heavy oak door?*

He turned and looked at the open door to his hotel-room closet. As the CNN report ended and the frosted blond reporter was replaced by an overweight sportscaster, Mulder crossed to the closet and placed his hand flat against the cold wood. He gently slapped the door, keeping his fingers stiff. Then he slapped it again, this time hard enough to send shivers back into his elbow. He lifted his hand and looked at the wood. Nothing, of course.

His mind felt suddenly alive; this was the feeling he hadn't gotten with the mutilated cows, the driving sensation that had earned him the nickname "Spooky" in the basement hallways of the Hoover Building. To anyone else, the scene held nothing more than a pair of kind blue eyes, a demolished hospital room, and a mark on a wooden door. But to Fox Mulder, it was like cocaine in his veins. These unexplainable details carried the scent of an X-File.

He quickly moved to the small desk in the other corner of the hotel room and reached for the phone. He dialed the number for the New York FBI office from memory, and spoke quietly to the operator, detailing the request he wanted forwarded to the NYPD homicide division in charge of the Stanton investigation. Then he replaced the receiver and made sure his fax machine was in the autoreceiving mode.

He crossed back to the closet door, pausing along the way to retrieve the soggy towel he had dropped on the floor by the bed. He wrapped the towel around his open right hand and stood facing the unmarked wood.

He shut his eyes, drew back—and slammed his right hand into the center of the door. There was a sharp crack, and Mulder grimaced, the muscles in his forearm contracting. He pulled back and saw fractures in the surface of the wood, expanding outward from the point of impact. The cracks were noticeable—but nothing like the deep indentations he had seen in the CNN report. And even with the towel, his entire arm ached from the collision with the wood. He tried to imagine each finger in his right hand hitting with enough force to leave a dent.

A sudden knock interrupted his thoughts, followed by a muffled female voice. "Mulder? Is everything okay?"

Mulder quickly crossed to the hotel-room door and undid the latch. Dana Scully was standing in the narrow hallway, her rust-colored hair dripping wet. She was wearing a dark suit jacket open over an untucked white button-down shirt, and it was obvious she had dressed quickly. Her usually precise and formal appearance seemed momentarily frayed—from the drops of water that glistened against the porcelain skin above her collarbone, to the concerned look in her green eyes. Although her hands were empty, Mulder could see the bulge of her holstered Smith & Wesson service revolver under the left side of her jacket; no doubt, had he delayed answering the door, she would have entered the room barrel first. "What's going on in here? It sounded like someone was brawling with the furniture."

Mulder smiled. "Not the furniture. Just the closet door. Sorry if I interrupted your shower."

Scully stepped past him into the room. She smelled vaguely of honeysuckle, and there were still flecks of shampoo caught in the lilting arcs of her hair. She stopped in front of the closet door and took in the cracked dent in the center of the wood. Then she glanced at the wet towel still wrapped around Mulder's right hand. "That's an interesting way to ice a swollen jaw."

Mulder had almost forgotten about his injury. The swelling and the pain no longer seemed to matter. "Scully, how often do patients try to kill their doctors?"

Scully raised her eyebrows. Her body had relaxed, and she was working on the top two buttons of her white shirt. She stopped in front of the television set, the glow reflecting off her high cheekbones. "Mulder, we need to get packed and on the road if we're going to make it back to Washington tonight."

Mulder shrugged, then returned to his line of thought. "A patient wakes up from an operation, vulnerable, drugged up, exhausted—and the first thing he does is erupt in a violent rage. How often, Scully? Rarely? Almost never?"

Scully was looking at him intently. She recognized the familiar gleam in his eyes. But Mulder could tell—she didn't know where it was coming from, or why it had to happen here, in the middle of nowhere. It was late, she was tired, and per-haps a little frustrated from the long days they had spent on a case that had turned out as mundanely as she had expected. Certainly, she was ready to get back home to her apartment and what little life she had beyond the enveloping reach of her job. "What are you getting at, Mulder?"

Before Mulder could answer, a high-pitched warble reverberated through the room. The fax machine coughed to life, and Scully turned, startled. She watched as the pages began to slip quietly into the receiving bin. "Did someone kill a doctor?"

Mulder followed a few paces behind as she crossed to the fax machine. "Not exactly. A nurse named Teri Nestor. But he did more than kill her. He destroyed his recovery room. He shoved an IV rack through the wall. Then he put his right hand two inches into a heavy oak door."

Scully lifted up the first three pages and began to leaf through them. Mulder could see her analytical mind going to work as she read the preliminary forensic evaluation he had requested from the homicide investigation. As for himself, he didn't need the details to get himself inspired; his obsessive curiosity was already aroused. "They had the man's picture on CNN, Scully. A small, gentle-looking professor. The kind of guy who gave me better grades than I deserved in college because he didn't want to hurt my feelings."

Scully continued to read the pages coming out of the fax machine, as she spoke from a corner of her pursed lips. It was obvious she had little interest in a case that had seemingly materialized out of nowhere. "People kill for many reasons. Sometimes they kill without reasons. And we both know that size doesn't matter. The human body can perform miracles of violence—when properly provoked. Drugs, fear, pain, adrenaline; all of these things can incite impressive acts of violence. And all of these things are closely associated with hospital stays. This looks like a local homicide investigation, not a federal case—"

Scully paused midsentence. Mulder noticed the sudden creases that appeared on her forehead. He looked at the page at the top of the pile in her hands and saw what appeared to be some sort of medical chart. The page was split into a dozen categories, with lists of numbers and long paragraphs of medical terminology. Mulder had only a rudimentary knowledge of medicine, and the numbers and paragraphs made little sense to him; but Dana Scully was an experienced physician. Before joining the FBI she had completed a residency in forensic pathology and had an expert's grounding in biology, physics, and chemistry. It was the initial reason she had been chosen to act as a foil to Mulder's fantastic quests. It was also part of the reason she had grown into much more than a foil; her rational, systematic approach often functioned as the perfect complement to Mulder's brash and impulsive investigative style.

"What is it?" Mulder asked, trying to read her unreadable eyes. He had requested the entire NYPD case file, and he had no way of knowing what Scully had stumbled upon.

"It's the preliminary autopsy report on the murdered nurse," Scully responded. "There's obviously been some sort of error."

Mulder waited in silence, as Scully continued reading the report. Finally, she looked up from the pages in her hands. "According to this autopsy report, Teri Nestor's skull was crushed with the approximate force of two vehicles moving at more than thirty miles per hour."

Mulder felt a chill move down his back. His instincts had been correct. Despite Scully's reservations, he had a feeling they weren't heading back to Washington just yet.

3

Two hours later, Dana Scully watched her own reflection shimmer against the steel double doors of a carpeted elevator, as glowing circular numbers ticked upward above her head. Mulder was standing a few feet to her left, testing his jaw with his right hand as his left foot tapped an incomprehensible rhythm against the elevator floor. Behind him, a medical student in blue-green surgical scrubs leaned heavily against the back wall, his eyes half-closed from exhaustion. Scully knew exactly how he felt. *The whole world dancing on your shoulders, and all you want to do is sleep.*

She threw a glance at Mulder, noticing the energy behind his features, the bright glint in his hazel eyes. Scully was amazed at her partner's stamina; it was already close to ten, and they had both been on their feet since 6:00 A.M. Scully felt ready to collapse—and she wasn't the one who had been hit in the face with a shovel less than eight hours ago.

Then again, she knew how Mulder's mind worked. The minute he had turned his focus toward the potential X-File, everything else had vanished. He had barely spoken about anything else during the long drive into Manhattan, and Scully had been forced to shelve the follow-up paperwork on the Bandez drug-distribution ring—at least for the time being. Inside, she doubted that she and Mulder would be sojourning in Manhattan for more than a few days. The findings reported in Teri Nestor's autopsy file were alarming—but Scully had no doubt there would be a simple, scientific explanation.

"Miracles of violence," Mulder intoned, continuing the suspended line of conversation they had begun in upstate New York. "Interesting choice of words, Scully. You think Perry Stanton is a miracle worker?"

"It was a figure of speech," Scully responded, keeping her voice low to prevent the med student in the back of the elevator from overhearing. "I merely meant that the human body is capable of amazing feats of strength. I'm sure you've heard the stories of mothers lifting cars to save their babies, or karate experts breaking bricks with their bare hands. There's no real magic involved; it's actually a matter of pure physics. Angles of impact, leverage, velocity. At the right speed, even a drop of water can shatter a brick."

"Or a skull?" Mulder asked, as the elevator slowed to a stop.

Scully shrugged. She had been mulling this over for the past few hours. Her initial shock at the details of the Stanton case had subsided, and she had already begun to analyze the situation as a scientist. "Perry Stanton is significantly bigger than a drop of water. The autopsy report, on its own, is inconclusive. I don't know how her head was crushed with such force—but I do know that it's within the realm of physics."

Before Mulder had a chance to respond, the double doors whiffed open, and Scully stepped out into a long hallway with shiny white walls. Mulder followed a few feet behind, his hands clasped behind his back. "Physics didn't kill Teri Nestor. Neither did a karate expert or a woman protecting a baby."

They turned an abrupt corner and continued down a similar hallway, moving deeper into the recovery ward. The air carried a familiar, antiseptic smell, and the sounds of hospital
machinery trickled into Scully's ears: the steady thumping of
respirators, the metallic beeps of EKG monitors, the vibrating
whir of adjustable hospital beds. The sounds sparked a mixture of emotions in her; she had spent much of her adult life
inside hospitals—first during the years of her medical training,
then more recently during her near-fatal battle with cancer. As
a scientist, she found comfort in a setting guided by the rigid
laws of cause and effect. At the same time, she couldn't help
but associate her surroundings with her past illness; as she
passed the closed doors of a half dozen private rooms, she
wondered how many patients were struggling in silence a few
feet away, praying for the light of just one more morning.

"Here we are," Mulder interrupted, pointing. "The scene of
the miracle."

Scully squared her shoulders as they approached the group
of uniformed officers standing in front of yellow police tape.
She counted at least three men and two women, all wearing
NYPD insignia. One of the officers was interviewing a nurse in
a pink uniform, while two others spoke to a young woman in
jeans and a white, paint-stained T-shirt. The officers looked up
as Scully and Mulder advanced the last few steps. Scully
quickly slipped her ID out of her jacket pocket. "FBI. I'm
Special Agent Dana Scully, this is my partner, Agent Mulder.
We're looking for the detective in charge of the Stanton case."

The nearest officer looked Scully over with dark eyes. He
was a large man, perhaps six-five, with scruffy black hair and a
puggish nose. He gestured with his head toward the yellow
tape. The door behind the tape was half-open, and Scully
could just make out the hand-shaped indentation in the center
of the wood. She kept her eyes on the indentation as she

stepped gingerly through a break in the police tape. As she held the tape up for Mulder, he whispered his own evaluation into her ear. "I'd like to see the physics behind that, Scully."

Scully shrugged. "Give me a computer, a forensics lab, and a week—and I'm sure I could show you, Mulder."

They paused in the room's entrance. Scully's gaze was drawn first to the huge sheets of yellow paper taped over the shattered picture windows. To the right of the windows was a contorted steel shelving unit, in front of which sat the upended, demolished television set. The warped hospital bed sat in the center of the room, the torn mattress sticking straight out of the deformed steel frame. Two men in white jumpsuits were leaning over the mattress with handheld vacuums, collecting hair and fiber evidence. Behind the hospital bed, another man focused an oversize camera on the IV rack still embedded in the wall. His flash went off like a strobe light, making the scene even more gritty and at the same time surreal, like a Quentin Tarantino movie. Scully was surprised to see the forensics people still collecting evidence so long after the incident, another testament to the bizarre nature of the crime. The degree of damage was exactly as Mulder had described it from the CNN report. It certainly didn't look like the work of one man.

Scully felt Mulder's hand on her shoulder and followed his eyes to the floor just in front of where they stood. The chalk outline started somewhere beneath a corner of the bed frame, twisting violently through a circular patch of dried blood. *Teri Nestor's blood.*

"Judging from the suits, I presume you're the two FBI agents your Manhattan office warned us about," a gravelly voice erupted from behind the contorted shelving unit. Scully watched as a heavyset woman in a dark gray suit stepped into view. She was quite tall—perhaps six feet—with wide, muscular shoulders and frizzy dark hair. She had a clipboard in her gloved hands, and there were dark bags under her dull blue eyes. "Detective Jennifer Barrett, NYPD."

Scully made the introductions, noting the strength of the detective's handshake: *Those were paws, not hands.* Barrett towered over her concise, five-foot-three frame, and though the detective looked to be in her late forties, she had obviously spent a lot of time in the gym. Her intimidating size was aggravated by her unkempt hair and the largeness of her facial features. Scully wondered if Barrett suffered from some sort of genetic pituitary problem; she could tell from the look on Mulder's face that he was thinking along similar lines.

Scully broke the silence before it became awkward, and after a few pleasantries, turned the focus toward the case at hand. "It's our understanding that Perry Stanton is the only suspect in the murder. Is that based on the forensic evidence?"

Barrett nodded, gesturing toward the two jumpsuited men still huddled over the mattress. "From what we've gathered so far, Stanton was alone with the nurse when the murder took place. According to the plastic surgeon—Dr. Alec Bernstein— they were in the room for less than five minutes, with the door shut, when the violence started. Hair, fiber, and fingerprint surveys concur with Bernstein's story. Nobody entered the room through the door—and the windows are more than twenty feet above the parking lot."

"A long way up," Mulder commented from a crouch in front of the door. "And an equally long way down."

Scully glanced at him. He had his hand out in front of the indentation in the wood, his fingers mimicking the deep marks from a few inches away. Scully turned away from him and watched, as Barrett crossed to the shattered windows. The detective pulled up a corner of the yellow paper. "The way down's a lot easier than the way up. The trick is in the landing.

Stanton got lucky and hit some shrubs at the edge of the park-ing lot. We found torn pieces of his hospital smock in the branches, along with more of Teri Nestor's blood. Our man-hunt is progressing rapidly through the borough—but so far, we've been unable to pick up his trail."

"So the professor woke up from an operation," Mulder said out of the corner of his mouth. "Tore up a hospital room. Crushed his nurse's skull. Then fell out of a second-story win-dow into a shrub. And he's still managing to evade a police search?"

Mulder had aimed the question at Scully, but it was obvious from the red blotches spreading across Barrett's face that she had misinterpreted Mulder's tone. She turned away from the window, crossed her thick arms against her chest, and set her mouth in an angry grimace. A heavy Brooklyn accent suddenly dribbled down the edges of her consonants. "Hey, you want to bring in your own forensics people? I'd be happy to hear an alternative story. Because the media's already crawling up my ass on this one. We've got the pathologist redoing the autopsy, we've had the fingerprint team in here a dozen times—and it's still coming up the same. One perp, one dead nurse, one man-hunt. And I don't care how fancy you fibbies think you are—you're not going to find anything different."

Scully stared at the woman, stunned by her altered tone. Frustration was one thing—but this was outright hostility. Barrett obviously had issues with control and a temper to match her size. *Not a pretty combination.* Scully decided to intervene before Mulder could aggravate her further. "We're not here to get in the way of your manhunt, Detective Barrett—just to assist in catching the perp. As for Professor Stanton—is there anything in his history that could explain the sudden outbreak of violence?"

Barrett grunted, her anger slowly diffusing. "Model citizen up until the transplant procedure. No priors, not even a speeding ticket. Married sixteen years until his wife died last February. Teaches European history at Jamaica University, volunteers two days a week at the public library in midtown—an adult-literacy program."

"No history of alcohol or drugs?" Scully asked.

"An occasional glass of wine on weekends, according to his daughter, Emily Kysdale, a twenty-six-year-old kindergarten teacher who lives in Brooklyn. According to Mrs. Kysdale, her father is a shy but happy man. He is most content in the basement library of the university—which is where he got burned in the boiler accident."

"Certainly doesn't fit the psychotic profile," Mulder commented. He was standing by the horizontal IV rack, trying to gauge how deeply it was embedded in the wall. "According to the police report, he is five-four, weighs one hundred and eighteen pounds. Scully, how much do you think this IV rack weighs? Or that mattress?"

Scully ignored Mulder's questions for the moment. She couldn't tell whether he was baiting the detective—or merely curious. She nodded toward the clipboard in Barrett's hands. She recognized the hospital-style pages under the heavy metal clip. "Is that Stanton's medical chart?"

Barrett nodded, her eyes on Mulder as she handed over the chart. "The plastic surgeon—Dr. Bernstein—has gone through this with me a few times already. He says there was nothing medically abnormal about Stanton—and nothing that he thought would have provoked a psychotic episode. But something I've learned working homicide in New York for the past twenty years—people crack for no good reason."

The chart was six pages long, full of scrawled medical descriptions and evaluations. Stanton had arrived at Jamaica's emergency room with a full-thickness third-degree steam burn on his right thigh. He had also been complaining of difficulty breathing, and had been given IV Solumedol, a strong steroid. After his breathing had stabilized, he had been prepped and wheeled into an operating room. Dr. Bernstein had performed an escharotomy—cutting away the damaged skin around the burn to prepare it for transplant—and had then attached a section of donor skin over the burn site.

The procedure had gone off without a snag; Stanton had awakened in the recovery room, complaining only of mild discomfort. If all had gone well, the temporary graft would have remained over the area of the burn for two weeks, at which time Stanton would have received a permanent matched graft from another part of his body, most likely his lower back.

Although Scully wasn't a plastic surgeon, there didn't seem to be anything about the transplant procedure itself that would have caused Stanton's violent reaction. But there was something in the chart that struck Scully as a possible explanation.

She moved next to Mulder and showed him the indication on the chart. "Stanton was given a fairly large dose of Solumedol, Mulder. It's an extremely potent steroid. There have been numerous documented cases of patients reacting violently to steroids—sort of an allergic neurological response. Rare, but definitely not unique."

Mulder looked at the IV rack bisecting the air between them. "Steroidal rage? Scully, he was given the Solumedol before the transplant procedure—but didn't explode until hours later."

Scully shrugged. "It doesn't have to be an immediate reaction. The neurotransmitters build up in the nervous system. The procedure itself could have aggravated his body's reaction—and when the anesthesia from the operation wore off, his psychosis detonated."

Mulder looked skeptical. "Wouldn't Dr. Bernstein have mentioned the possibility to Detective Barrett?"

Barrett was watching them from the window, her arms still crossed against her chest. She coughed, letting Scully and Mulder know she was still in the room. "I'm sure I would have remembered if he had. He's performing a laser surgery at the moment—but you can interview him again when he's finished."

Scully nodded. Mulder seemed dissatisfied with Scully's quick answer to Stanton's psychosis. As Scully watched, he pulled a pair of latex gloves out of his jacket pocket and slipped them over his fingers. Then he placed both hands gingerly against the IV rack. Barrett watched him with a smirk on her oversized lips.

"It's in pretty good. I tried for twenty minutes. I doubt *you'll* be able to do any better."

Mulder smiled at the challenge, then leaned back, using his weight against the rack. The muscles of his arms worked beneath his dark suit, and his face grew taut, sweat beading above his eyebrows. He tried for a full minute, then gasped, giving up. "I guess neither of us gets to be king."

There was a brief pause, then Barrett laughed. The sound was somewhere between a diesel engine and a death rattle. Scully was glad that Mulder's charm had broken through some of Barrett's hostility. As long as they were going to have to work together, it would help if they could interact in a civil manner. Scully cleared her throat. "As long as we're waiting for Dr. Bernstein—you mentioned Stanton's daughter? Perhaps she can bring us up to speed on Professor Stanton."

Barrett nodded. "Out in the hallway. The pretty thing with the finger paint all over her shirt. She's been here since her father was brought into the ER yesterday morning. She won't go home until Stanton is safely apprehended. Be careful with her; she breaks easily."

Scully inadvertently glanced at Barrett's huge hands. She

wondered if Mulder was thinking the same thing. *In hands like those—who didn't break easily?*

"This is all too much to take. You have to believe me, he could never have done this. Never." Emily Kysdale stared into her cup of coffee as the cafeteria traffic buzzed behind her bowed shoulders. Mulder and Scully had chosen the relative anonymity of the cafeteria over the recovery ward, to give the young woman a chance to speak without the obvious presence of the uniformed police officers.

Emily was shaking horribly, and Scully could see the goose bumps rising on the bare skin of her arms. Scully felt the immediate urge to reach across the steel cafeteria table and touch her, to let her know that it would be all right—but she resisted. The truth was, it wasn't going to be all right. Emily's father had murdered a woman about the same age as she, a woman with a child and a husband. Even if the violence was caused by an allergic reaction, or a mental illness, or an uncontrollable fit—it was murder.

"Mrs. Kysdale," Mulder said, his voice quiet as he lowered himself into the seat next to Scully, "we need to ask you a few questions. I know this is hard for you, but we're trying to help your father."

Scully could feel the emotion behind Mulder's near monotone. She knew her partner better than anyone in the world, and she could guess at the thoughts running through his head. Emily was an attractive, fragile woman, with long, brownish-blond hair, a lanky figure, and watery green eyes. Her jeans and paint-splotched T-shirt were rumpled, and it was obvious she had not slept since the incident. Her agony was no doubt triggering something deep inside Mulder—perhaps memories of his own sister. He carried Samantha Mulder like an internal scar, always just below the surface of his skin. The unique circumstances of Samantha's disappearance—and Mulder's belief that she had actually been abducted by aliens—did not disrupt the prosaic and sincere nature of his pain. It was what drove his obsession with the unexplained, and Emily's distress would only solidify his resolve to find the truth—however fantastic that truth turned out to be.

"My father is a gentle man," Emily finally responded, looking directly into Mulder's sympathetic eyes. "He lived for his work, his quiet research. He has never been in trouble before. And he has never complained, never gets angry. Even when my mother passed away."

"Mrs. Kysdale," Scully said, "did your father ever suffer any symptoms that may not have been in his medical chart? Any viral diseases—either recently, or in the past?"

Emily shrugged. "Nothing abnormal. He's had the flu a few times this year. And a bout of pneumonia two years ago. He had his appendix out when I was younger—"

"What about allergies?" Scully was searching, but it was worth a shot. Anaphylactic shock involved the entire neurological system—very similar to a steroid reaction. If Stanton had a history of strong allergies, it might be more evidence for her Solumedol theory.

"Not that I know of," Emily answered. "Dr. Bernstein asked me the same question when they first brought my father into the ER. I had arrived just as they were administering something to help him breathe."

Scully perked up, glancing at Mulder. "The IV steroids."

Emily nodded. "I remembered he had been put on steroids during the bout with pneumonia. He hadn't had a problem with it then, so Dr. Bernstein said it wouldn't be a problem this time either."

Scully leaned back in her chair. She could hear Mulder's shoes bouncing against the tiled floor beneath the table. The new information didn't completely rule out the Solumedol—but it certainly made it less likely. Bernstein probably hadn't mentioned the Solumedol to Detective Barrett because Stanton had been put on it before, without adverse reaction. Still, Scully knew that people could develop sensitivities at any stage in life. Insect bites, shellfish, peanuts—and steroids—had been known to kill people who had never had any problem with these things before. The Solumedol, though more improbable, was still a possibility.

"When you saw your father in the ER," Mulder asked, changing tack, "did anything strike you as abnormal—either in his behavior, or his appearance?"

Emily shrugged. "He had that awful burn on his leg. And he was slipping in and out of consciousness. But when he was awake, he seemed normal."

"And after the transplant procedure—"

"I never got a chance to see him after the procedure. I was in the waiting room when I heard what happened. I couldn't believe it. I still don't believe it."

"Mrs. Kysdale," Scully asked, "is there any history of mental disease in your father's family?"

Emily was momentarily taken aback by the question. When she finally answered, she sounded cautious, as if she realized for the first time that she was talking to two FBI agents. "Not that I'm aware."

Scully paused; as helpful as the young woman was trying to be, Emily Kysdale wasn't going to help them understand the cause of her father's violence. It was obvious from Emily's sudden change of tone: in Emily's mind, Perry Stanton was a victim, not a murderer. Scully could tell from the way Mulder was looking at her that he agreed.

Whatever the reason for his explosion, Perry Stanton was a criminal. The cause of Stanton's act was only important insofar as it established culpability. Even if the cause remained a mystery, it would not change the facts of the case, or Scully and Mulder's mission. Their job was to catch the perp who had killed Teri Nestor—and at the moment, the blame still lay solely on Perry Stanton.

"Mrs. Kysdale, do you have any idea where your father might be hiding? Anywhere the police may not know to look?"

Emily's entire body trembled, and she clenched her hands around the Styrofoam cup of coffee in front of her. She lowered her head, then took a deep breath and seemed to regain some level of control. "They've been to his apartment, his office, all of his friends' houses. They've scoured the university. They've looked everywhere he used to go—even the cemetery where my mother is buried. But I can't help them find him—because the man who killed that nurse isn't the man I know. My father isn't the man they're looking for."

Scully felt a weight inside her chest, as Emily's grief finally broke through her veil of reserve. Mulder had his reasons for empathizing with the woman's pain—and Scully had her own. *Her sister's murder, her own father's death.* She knew what it was like to lose a family member—and that was exactly what had happened to Emily Kysdale. The Perry Stanton she knew was gone.

Scully reached across the table and touched the young woman's hand. Then she rose, thanking her for her help. Mulder paused for a moment, watching the woman cry over her coffee. Then he followed Scully toward the elevator at the back of the cafeteria, which would take them up to the surgical ward—and Dr. Alec Bernstein. After the double doors slid shut, Mulder spoke softly. "I believe her, Scully. Her father isn't the man we're looking for."

"What do you mean?"

"You heard what she said—he was normal when he was

wheeled into the ER. He was normal even after he was given the Solumedol. But he wasn't normal when he woke up after the operation. He should have been vulnerable, groggy, in pain; instead, he was capable of unbelievable violence, of a physical act we can hardly describe, let alone understand."

Scully tried to see the expression on his face, but all she got was his profile. He finished his thought as the elevator slowed to a stop on the fourth floor—the surgical ward. "Scully, something happened during that transplant procedure to change Perry Stanton."

Scully wasn't sure what he meant. "Mulder, the temporary grafting procedure is nearly as common—and certainly as safe—as an appendectomy. And it's mainly localized to the area of the injury—Stanton's right thigh."

But even as she said the words, a thought hit her. The transplant procedure involved Stanton's thigh—but certainly, there was interaction with his bloodstream and his immune system. Perhaps Mulder had a point: It wasn't impossible that Stanton had contracted something from the graft itself. She would have to review the literature—but she was certain she had heard about certain viral diseases being transferred in just such a manner. She believed there had even been cases of cancer being transmitted through grafts—specifically, lymphoma and Kaposi's sarcoma. It was rare, but possible. *The question was, what kind of disease could cause a psychotic episode?*

"Something like meningitis," Scully murmured, as the elevator doors opened. "Or even syphilis. Something that causes the brain to swell and affects the neurological system."

"Sorry?" Mulder said.

"If the temporary graft had been infected with a bloodborne virus," Scully explained, "Stanton could have contracted the disease through the transplant. There are many diseases that could lead to an explosion of violence."

"Scully, that's not what I meant. The violence was beyond the scale of any psychotic episode. Stanton didn't just catch a disease—*he transformed.* Into something his own daughter wouldn't recognize."

Scully knew that the words were more than hyperbole; Mulder's ideas were never limited by the laws of science. But Scully didn't intend to let him lead her toward another of his wild fantasies. At the moment, this was a medical mystery— not a fantasy. *This investigation was on her turf.*

She stepped out into the surgical ward. "Sometimes, Mulder, transformation is the nature of disease."

Scully peered through the glass window with genuine interest as Dr. Bernstein carefully navigated the laser scalpel across the surface of the patient's exposed lower back. The tool was pen-shaped, attached to a long, articulated steel arm containing a series of specially made mirrors. The arm jutted out of a four-foot-tall cylindrical pedestal next to Bernstein. A pedal by his heel allowed him to control the strength and depth of the beam.

"Interesting juxtaposition," Mulder said, his face also close to the window as he surveyed the small operating room. "A five-thousand-year-old art transcended by a five-year-old technology."

Scully watched as the red guiding light traced the edges of the enormous tattoo in the center of the patient's bared back. The red light shivered in the thin white smoke rising from the patient's skin as the outer cells vaporized under the intense, pinpoint heat. The patient was awake, but felt no pain; a local anesthetic was enough to deaden the area of skin beneath the tattoo. In fact, the procedure could hardly be considered surgical. Aside from Bernstein and the patient, there was only one nurse in the small operating room, monitoring the patient's blood pressure.

"I guess nothing is truly permanent anymore," Mulder continued. "Anything can be erased."

"It's a tattoo, Mulder. Hardly the raw material for a philosophical analogy." Scully controlled a wince as the laser seared away a beautifully drawn lion's head, then moved backward through a flowing brown mane. She thought about the image on her own lower back: a snake eating its own tail, the result of a moment of whimsy in a Philadelphia tattoo parlor during a solo field trip a little over a year ago. Sometimes, she hardly even remembered the tattoo was there; other times, she found comfort in the idea that she had found the courage to do something so unlike her perceived exterior. She was a skeptic—but never a conformist. *That was another part of what made her and Mulder work so well together.*

The procedure went on for another ten minutes; when Bernstein was finally finished, he looked up from behind his surgical mask and noticed Mulder and Scully on the other side of the viewing windows. He said something to the nurse, then shut off the laser scalpel and stepped away from the patient. As the nurse moved to wrap the sensitive area of skin in antiseptic gauze, Bernstein yanked his gloves off and crossed to the OR door. He pulled his mask down as he moved into the outer scrub room where Scully and Mulder waited.

"I'm guessing you're not here for a tattoo removal," Bernstein said, tossing his gloves into a nearby trash can as he crossed toward the double sinks at the other end of the rectangular room. He was a tall man, slightly overweight and balding, but with handsome features and remarkably sculpted hands. He was wearing surgical scrubs and matching green sneakers. "So how can I help you?"

"Sorry to interrupt, Dr. Bernstein. I'm Agent Scully, this is Agent Mulder. We're here about Perry Stanton."

Bernstein nodded as he ran water over his hands, carefully

massaging his long fingers. Scully could see the troubled look in his eyes and the slight tremble in his round shoulders. "I'm not sure what I can tell you—beyond what I've already told Detective Barrett. Mr. Stanton was fine when I left him in the recovery room—and when I returned, he had already gone through the window. It was a horrid sight—something I don't think I'll ever forget. Or understand."

Scully could sense the disbelief in his words. He reminded her of the many physicians she had known during her medical training; he didn't quite know what to do with an experience beyond his expertise. Scully tried to make her voice as sympathetic as possible. "It's certainly a mystery, one we're working to understand. Along that line, I noticed that you ordered IV Solumedol to help Mr. Stanton's breathing—"

"Yes," Bernstein interrupted with a wave of his hand. "Detective Barrett called to ask me about the Solumedol after you spoke to her downstairs in the recovery room, and you're right, I should have made it clear to her in the first place. Personally, I don't believe the steroid had anything to do with his violent outbreak. He'd been put on similar steroids fairly recently—a bout with pneumonia, I believe it was three years ago. It's extremely unlikely that he would have developed such a fierce allergy in such a short time."

Scully nodded; she had asked the necessary question and had gotten the expected answer. The Solumedol still wasn't ruled out, but as Bernstein had said, it was an extremely doubtful cause. They needed to search for other answers.

Mulder took the cue as Bernstein turned away from the sink and grabbed a towel from a rack attached to the wall.

"Dr. Bernstein, what about the grafting procedure itself? Do you remember anything abnormal about the operation? Anything out of the ordinary?"

Bernstein vigorously dried his hands. "I've performed hundreds of similar transplants. There were no hitches at all. The procedure took less than three hours. I cleaned up the burn, flattened out the donor skin, and stapled it onto Stanton's thigh—"

"Stapled?" Mulder asked, his eyebrows raised. Scully could have answered, but she deferred to the plastic surgeon.

"That's right. The device is very similar to an office stapler—except the staples are heat sterilized and made out of a specially tempered steel. Anyway, I stapled the skin over Stanton's burn and wrapped the area in sterile gauze. I would have changed the dressing in three days—then removed the graft in about two weeks, when he was ready to accept a permanent transplant."

Scully had explained the procedure to Mulder after reading about it in Stanton's chart, but it was good for both of them to hear it again from the expert. After all, it had been a long time since Scully's surgical rotation, and she had spent only a few months studying transplant techniques.

"So the donor skin is only temporarily attached?" Mulder asked.

"That's right. The temporary graft isn't matched to the patient—because it's intended to be rejected after a period of a couple of weeks. Then we graft a piece of the patient's own skin over the wound. In the meantime, the donor skin decreases the risk of infection, and it helps indicate when the burned area is ready to accept a permanent transplant."

"If the temporary graft isn't matched to the patient," Scully interrupted, "what precautions are taken to make sure the graft isn't carrying something that could infect the patient with a communicable disease?"

Bernstein glanced at her. She could tell from his eyes that he had already given this some thought. Stanton had been his patient—and as unfair and illogical as it seemed, he was partially blaming himself for what had happened. "Truthfully, very few—on my end. The skin is transported to us from the New York Fire Department Skin Bank; the bank is responsible for growing bacteriological cultures, and for checking the skin for viral threats. But they themselves are guided by the medical histories provided by the donor hospital. There are a million things to look for, and it's impossible to cover every possibility. If a donor dies from something infectious, they don't accept his skin. But if he dies from an unrelated cause—and happens to be carrying something, there is a chance that it will be passed on through a transplant."

"A slim chance?" Mulder asked. "Or a serious risk? And could any of these transferred diseases affect a patient's brain? Enough to send him into a violent rage?"

"I would call it extremely rare," Bernstein replied, leaning back against the sinks. "But possible. For instance, undetected melanomas have been known to spread through transplant procedures. They grow downward through the dermis and into the blood vessels, then ride the bloodstream up into the brain. And certain viruses could jump through the lower layers of the epidermis into the capillaries; herpes zoster, AIDS, meningitis, encephalitis—the list is endless. But most of these diseases would have shown up in the donor patient. Such microbe-laden skin would never have been harvested in the first place."

Not on purpose, Scully thought to herself. But people made mistakes. And microbes were often tricky to spot, even by trained professionals. A million viruses could live on the head of a pin—and viruses were extremely hard to trace, or predict. "After the procedure, did Stanton exhibit any symptoms at all? Anything that might hint at a viral or bacteriological exposure?"

Bernstein started to shake his head, then paused. "Well,

now that I think about it, there was one thing. But I can't imagine how it could be connected to such an outbreak of violence."

He rubbed the back of his neck with his hand. "A small circular rash. Right here, on the nape of his neck. It looked like thousands of tiny red dots. I assumed it was some sort of local allergic reaction—like an insect bite, only a bit larger. I'm not a specialist, but I can't think of any serious disease that presents like that."

Scully wasn't sure if the strange rash was connected—but she filed it in her memory. She was trying to think if there was anything else they needed from the plastic surgeon when Bernstein glanced at his watch, then let out a ponderous sigh. "I'm sorry, but I've got an emergency surgery scheduled to start in a few minutes. If you have any more questions, I'll be in OR Four down the hall. And if there are any breakthroughs in the case, please let me know. Teri Nestor was a personal friend—but Mr. Stanton was my patient. I know it's foolish, but I feel like I failed him somehow."

He excused himself and exited the scrub room. When he was gone, Scully turned toward her partner. Though it was now well past one in the morning, she felt a new burst of energy. Based on what they had learned in the past few hours, she felt sure they were moving closer to solving the case. It was an intriguing difference in personality: Mulder grew electric when faced with a mystery—while Scully was excited by the prospect of a solution. "I think it's pretty clear what we need to do next. While Barrett continues her manhunt, we have to track down the donor skin and find out if it was infected with anything that could have caused Stanton's violence. And we have to act quickly—we don't want any more of that harvested skin ending up on other patients."

Mulder didn't respond right away. Instead, he moved to the sink. Bernstein had left the faucet loose, and a stream of drops spattered quietly against the basin. Mulder reached forward, and held his palm under the stream. "Scully, do you really think a virus can explain what happened in that recovery room?"

Scully paused, staring at the back of his head. They had both seen the same evidence, participated in the same interviews—but it was obvious their thoughts were moving in two different directions. *As always.* "Absolutely. Dr. Bernstein corroborated my theory. It's possible that Stanton caught something from the graft—something that could have affected his brain, and his personality. Once we track down the graft, we'll be able to find out for sure. And then we'll know how to deal with Stanton when we find him—and what precautions Barrett's officers need to take in bringing him in."

Mulder shut off the sink and dried his hand against a towel from the rack. "A microbe, Scully? That's how you want to explain this?"

"You have a better explanation?"

Mulder shrugged. "Whenever doctors run into a mystery they can't explain, they blame a microbe. Some sort of virus or bacteria, something you can see only through a microscope— or sometimes not at all. If you ask me, it's a convenient way of thinking. It's a scientist's way of pretending to understand something completely beyond his grasp."

"Mulder," Scully interrupted, frustrated, "if you have a better plan of action, I'm listening."

"Actually, I agree with you, Scully. We need to track down that graft. We need to find out what changed Perry Stanton into a violent killer. But I'm not so sure we're going to need a microscope to find what we're looking for."

Scully watched as he moved toward the door. "What do you mean?"

He glanced back at her. "It would take a pretty big microbe to crush a nurse's skull."

As Scully followed Mulder out into the hallway, she failed to notice the tall, angled man watching from the now-deserted operating room on the other side of the viewing windows. The man was dressed in a blue orderly uniform, most of his young face obscured by a sterile white surgical mask. His skin was dark and vaguely Asiatic, his black hair cropped tight beneath a pink antiseptic cap.

His narrow eyes followed the two agents until they disappeared from view. Then he reached into his pocket and pulled out a tiny cellular phone. He dialed quickly, his long fingers flickering over the numbered keys. A few seconds later, he began to speak in a low, nasal voice. The words were foreign, the tone rising and falling as the syllables chased one another through the thin material of the young man's surgical mask. There was a brief pause, then a deep voice responded from somewhere far away. The young man nodded, slipping the phone back into his pocket.

An anticipatory tremor moved through his shoulders. Then he grinned, his high, brown cheeks pulling at his mask. For him, the task ahead was more than an act of loyalty, or of duty—it was an act of nearly erotic pleasure.

His fingers curled together as he followed the two FBI agents out into the hospital hallway.

4

Forty minutes later, Mulder shivered against a sudden blast of refrigerated air as he pursued the ample ME's assistant into the cold-storage room lodged deep in the basement of New York Hospital. It had been a relatively easy task to trace the skin graft back across the Fifty-ninth Street Bridge, but in the process he and Scully had run into the first sign that their investigation was not going to take a simple route—and at the same time, the first strike against Scully's growing belief that the case would soon be explained by a conventional medical query. As Mulder had predicted, Stanton's transformation would not be solved through a quick trip to the New York Fire Department Skin Bank.

"Missing," Scully had said, hanging up the phone as she and Mulder had exited through the Jamaica Hospital ER. "They're unable to locate the six trays of harvested skin from which Stanton's transplant was taken."

The administrator of the skin bank had assured Scully that the FBI would be notified the minute the missing trays had been located. He had also insisted that this was not a matter for alarm; the grossly understaffed and underfunded skin bank dealt with hundreds of pounds of skin on a weekly basis, and mistakes like this were not uncommon. And although he hadn't been able to find the harvested skin, the administrator had been able to give Scully the name and location of the donor corpse: Derrick Kaplan, a current inhabitant of the New York Hospital morgue.

While Scully had accepted the administrator's comments at face value, Mulder had felt his own suspicions rising. He didn't believe Stanton's behavior could be explained by any known microbe—and the missing skin seemed like too much of a coincidence. Still, he and Scully had been left with a lead to follow. While the NYPD continued their search for Perry Stanton, he and Scully would follow the skin graft back to its source.

After Scully had hung up on the skin bank, she and Mulder headed directly to New York Hospital. After a short stop at the front desk, they had located the ME's assistant half-asleep in his office two elevator stops below the ER. Short, unkempt, with curly blond hair and thick lips, Leif Eckleman was exactly the type of man Mulder had expected to find working the basement warren of a hospital morgue. Likewise, Mulder hadn't been surprised to see the neck of a half-empty fifth of Jack Daniel's sticking out of the open top drawer of the man's cluttered desk; alcohol went with the territory. Mulder tried not to pass any judgments.

"The two kids from the med school got here late Friday night," Eckleman mumbled, as he crossed the rectangular room to a set of filing cabinets standing flush against a cinderblock wall. His words were slightly slurred, but Mulder couldn't tell whether it was the alcohol or the fact that he had just been awakened from a deep sleep. "Josh Kemper, and a buddy of his—Mike, I think his name was. Used OR Six, upstairs in the surgical ward. Cleaned it up pretty good afterward. No complaints from the surgeons."

Eckleman pulled open one of the cabinets and began to search through the manila folders inside. Mulder watched Scully amble across the center of the room, her low heels clicking against the tiled floor. Her gaze was pinned to the wall of body drawers that stretched the entire length of the room. Mulder counted at least sixty—and he knew that this was only one of eight similar cold-storage rooms that made up the hospital's morgue. Even so, New York was a big city; hard to find an apartment, and probably equally hard to find a drawer.

"Here it is," Eckleman finally said, lifting a folder out of the cabinet. "Mike Lifton, that was the other kid's name. Both were in their third year at Columbia Med. They signed for your donor at three-fifteen A.M. Derrick Kaplan—Caucasian, mid-thirties, blond hair, blue eyes. Locker fifty-two."

Mulder was already moving toward the wall of drawers. Scully turned to Eckleman as Mulder scanned the numbered labels. "May I take a look at the file?"

Eckleman shrugged, handing her the folder. "Not much to see. Kaplan came into the ER complaining of chest pains, then died in the ICU of an aortic dissection. Had a donor card in his wallet. The skin boys got to him first, because the van from the eye bank got stuck in the mess on the FDR Drive. The big accident, you know. Collected seven bodies that same night, but only Kaplan had the vulture card."

"The vulture card?" Mulder heard Scully ask, as he finally located the steel drawer with the number fifty-two written in black Magic Marker across its cardboard label. "Is that what you call it?"

"You work down here, you get to be fairly morbid. In my opinion, there's nothing wrong with vultures. Damned efficient birds—they don't let anything go to waste. Not so different from the harvest teams, when you think about it."

Mulder wasn't sure he wanted to think about it. He grasped

the handle beneath the numbered label and gave it a gentle yank. The drawer rolled outward with a mild, metallic groan. Mulder paused for a brief moment, then glanced at Scully. She was engrossed in Kaplan's folder. Mulder cleared his throat.

Scully looked up. Mulder pointed, and Scully's face momentarily blanched. The locker was empty. She quickly turned toward the ME's assistant. "Mr. Eckleman?"

Eckleman rubbed the back of his hand against his thick lips. Then he laughed, nervously. "Whoops. That's not good. You sure that's number fifty-two?"

Mulder rechecked the label. "Is there any chance the body was moved?"

Eckleman quickly crossed back to the file cabinet. "Shouldn't have been. But sometimes they get switched around. Especially on the busy nights. And Friday was a busy night. Seven bodies, like I said. And there's always a chance the kids put the body back in the wrong drawer."

He paused as he pulled a handful of files out of the cabinet. He began reading to himself, and Mulder crossed back to Scully, who was still looking through Kaplan's chart. "Anything significant, Scully?"

Scully shook her head. "Nothing noticeably viral. But we need the body to know for sure. Or, at the very least, a sample of his skin."

Mulder felt his adrenaline rising. First the missing trays at the skin bank—now the missing body. Then again, he didn't want to get ahead of himself. He glanced at the flustered, semi-drunk ME's assistant; certainly, the man could have gotten the drawers mixed up.

"I'll check the other six that came in that night, and all of the empties. Odds are, we'll find our boy." Eckleman tucked the files under his right arm and hurried back to the storage wall. He began pulling open the drawers, humming nervously to himself as he worked. Mulder could tell the man was embarrassed. Perhaps this sort of thing had happened before. "Locker fifty-three is all right. Angela Dotter, one of the victims from the accident. Got a steering wheel right through her rib cage. Fifty-four and fifty-five look good, too. And here's another from the accident. Kid can't be more than twenty . . ."

Eckleman paused midsentence as the next drawer slid to a stop by his knees. He began mumbling, half to himself. The stack of files slipped out from under his arm, the pages fanning out as they hit the floor. "What the hell? This can't be right."

He reached forward, and the sound of a zipper reverberated through the room. Mulder moved forward as Eckleman hovered over the toe tag. "Derrick Kaplan. It's him. But this doesn't make any sense."

Mulder looked over the man's shoulder. The corpse was staring straight up, blue eyes wide-open. Mulder heard Scully exhale as she joined him next to the drawer. It was immediately obvious what was wrong with the body.

Derrick Kaplan wasn't missing any skin.

"Damn it," Eckleman said, again rubbing at his watery lips. "The little vultures must have skinned the wrong body."

"The wrong body?" Mulder asked.

Eckleman didn't respond. Instead, he bent down and began pulling open the bottom row of steel drawers: the empties. Each time he stared into another blank box, he cursed, each profanity more colorful and obscene than the last. "Can't blame this on me. No way can they blame this one on me. *I* didn't skin anybody. I wasn't even in here—"

Eckleman stopped, as he suddenly realized that he had reached the last drawer. "Well, son of a bitch. Unless they double-stacked it in one of the other drawers, it's not here."

Mulder looked at the row of open, empty drawers. He

didn't know whether to be frustrated or intrigued. "Can we at least figure out which body is missing?"

"Probably the one that was originally slated for this drawer," Scully answered, pointing at Derrick Kaplan's corpse. "Didn't you say this was supposed to contain one of the seven brought in that same Friday night?"

Eckleman nodded, returning to the stack of folders he had dropped on the floor. His stubby fingers were trembling by the time he found the correct file. "A John Doe. Brought into the ER from the scene of the big car accident I told you about. Also blond, blue eyes—but mid- to early twenties. With a dragon tattoo on his right shoulder."

"Was the John Doe a trauma victim?" Scully asked. "Did he die from injuries sustained in the accident?"

There was a pause as Eckleman read through the file. Then he shook his head. "Actually, no. There were no signs of external injuries. The two interns who worked on him didn't know what killed him. He was scheduled for an autopsy at eight tomorrow morning."

Mulder and Scully exchanged looks. *A missing body, an autopsy less than five hours away.* The trail was getting more circuitous—and, despite their efforts, they still hadn't found an ounce of the original skin.

"I better go report this," Eckleman grumbled, heading toward the door. "Administrator Cavanaugh is going to have my ass for dinner. But I tell you, it isn't my fault. *I* didn't skin the wrong damn body."

Mulder watched him trudge out of the cold-storage room. Then he turned back toward Scully. She was looking through the John Doe's file. "These are big institutions we're dealing with—and it's very late at night. At two in the morning, things get lost. At eight in the morning, they tend to turn up. In the meantime, we have to speak to those med students. If something was transmitted from this John Doe to Perry Stanton—they're the obvious link."

With the John Doe's body missing and Perry Stanton still at large, the two med students were the *only* link. Mulder felt his pulse quicken as he glanced back at the empty storage drawer. Somehow, he found the steel rectangle more foreboding without a corpse inside. It was like digging in a graveyard and finding an empty coffin.

Despite Scully's words, Mulder did not believe the missing corpse was a coincidence. He was certain the John Doe's skin held the key to the tragedy in the recovery room. And he would not accept any explanation that did not expose what had really happened to Perry Stanton—no matter how rational it seemed.

5

 The broken glass glittered like an emerald carpet in the triangle of light, jagged green shards spread out across the black asphalt in the shape of a bloated July moon. Perry Stanton stood beneath a streetlamp at the edge of the curb, his thin shoulders heaving under his torn hospital smock. He could see bottle necks sticking out of the glass like phallic icebergs, the trace of an alcoholic's rage or a fraternity party that had overflowed into the dark Brooklyn streets. Stanton's mind whirled as the shards grew in his eyes, huge green thorns taunting him, daring him, begging him forward.

Suddenly, his mouth opened and a dull moan escaped into the night air. His bare feet curled inward against the sidewalk, and his spine arched back. The muscles in his thighs contracted, and he threw himself forward, diving headlong into the street. His body crashed down into the glass, and he rolled back and forth against the shards, his arms flailing wildly at his sides.

He could hear the hospital smock tearing, the glass crunching under his weight. *But he felt no relief.* The glass did nothing to stop the horrible itching. The shards should have ripped through his skin as easily as it ripped his thin smock—but the terrible crawling continued unabated. It felt as though every inch of his body was infested with tiny, hungry maggots. It was so bad he couldn't keep a single thought in his head, so bad that every command from his brain seemed to echo a thousand times before it found his muscles.

Lying flat on his back in the broken glass, he slammed his palms over his eyes and an anguished wail bellowed through his lungs. What the hell was going on? *What the hell was wrong with him?*

He felt something warm and wet against his closed eyelids, and he quickly pulled his hands away. His eyes opened, and he stared at his bloodred palms. He quickly crawled to his knees, more tears burning at his eyes.

Even through the intense itching, he could still remember the woman's head between his palms. He could still hear the bones in her skull crunching as he had squeezed. He could still see her eyes bulging forward, the blood spouting out of her ears, her cheeks collapsing into her mouth—he could still feel her die between his palms. *Between his palms.*

And worst of all—he could still feel the rage emanating through his body. The rage that had overwhelmed his thoughts and his brain and made him leap up out of the hospital bed. The fierce anger that had started somewhere in the itching: an unbelievable heat, burning downward through his flesh. It had felt as if his veins and arteries had caught fire, his insides boiling under the intense flame.

Then the fiery rage had entered his skull and everything had gone white. He had seen the nurse leaning over him, and it was like looking through someone else's eyes. The rage had taken over, and he had grabbed her head in his hands.

After that, it had all happened so fast. The itching, burning rage had made him destroy everything within reach. And then a single thought had twisted through the agony—*escape*.

His head jerked back and forth as new tremors spiraled through his body. He shook the broken glass out of his smock as he staggered to his feet. *Escape.* Somewhere in what was left of his mind, he knew the command was not his own. It also came from somewhere in the horrible itching. *Somewhere in his skin.*

He had no choice but to obey. When he resisted, the itching only grew worse. He stumbled forward, his bare feet crunching against the glass. He wasn't sure where he was—but he knew he wasn't far ahead of the sirens or the shouts. He couldn't let them catch him. He knew what the itching and the rage would make him do if they caught him. *More skulls between his palms*—

A sudden screech tore into his ears, and he looked up through blurry eyes. He saw the yellow hood of a taxicab careening around the corner ahead of him, the startled driver leaning heavily on his horn. There was a brief, frozen second— then the front fender glanced against Stanton's left thigh.

The cab skidded to a sudden stop. Stanton looked down and saw the mangled hood still partially wrapped around his leg. He stepped back, his entire body beginning to shake. The itchiness swept up through his hips, across his chest, to his face. *No, no, no!*

The driver-side door came open, and a tall, dark-skinned man leapt out. He saw Stanton, and shouted something. Then he noticed his ruined cab. His eyes widened. "Mister, are you okay?"

Stanton's skin caught fire, and his mind turned white. He tried to fight back, tried to stop the commands before they reached his muscles. He tried to picture himself as he was before—gentle, kind, weak. He tried to focus on the image of his daughter, beautiful Emily, and his life before the transplant.

But the thoughts vanished as the maggots crawled through

his skin. He lurched forward, his face contorted. The taxi driver stepped back, fear evident on his face. Somehow, Stanton managed to coax a single word through his constricted throat.

"Run."

The taxi driver stared at him. Stanton held out his hands as he staggered forward. The driver saw the blood on his palms, and realization hit him. He turned and ran screaming down the dark street.

Stanton stumbled after him, the single word still echoing through his brain.

Run. Run. Run!

6

 The sky had turned a dull gray by the time Mulder trudged up the stone steps that led to the arched entrance of the J. P. Friedler Medical Arts Building on the Columbia Medical School campus. He didn't need to look at his watch to know it was close to five in the morning; his muscles had that strange, wiry feeling that meant he was nearing twenty-four hours without sleep. He realized that he and Scully couldn't keep going like this for much longer. But until Perry Stanton was taken into custody, they were in a fierce race with the mysteries of the case.

Just minutes ago, Scully had phoned him with the latest news from Detective Barrett's manhunt. Stanton had wrecked a taxicab somewhere in northern Brooklyn, and the driver had narrowly escaped with his life. The search was now focused on a five-block area, and Barrett was certain they would find Stanton within the next few hours.

Which meant it was all the more important for Mulder and Scully to keep barreling ahead. They had split up to reach the two med students as quickly as possible. Even so, Mulder prayed they would be quick enough. If Scully's theory was right, there was a dangerous, diseased man still raging through the streets of New York. And if Mulder was right—a disease didn't begin to explain the phenomenon they were chasing: *something that could transform a quiet, gentle professor into a vicious killer, with inhuman strength.*

It took Mulder a few minutes to reach the anatomy lab on the third floor of the vast stone building. He was out of breath as he exited the marble stairwell, and he paused for a moment by the double doors that led into the lab, leaning against the wall. He could see the cavernous room through a small circular window in the center of one of the doors. The room was close to fifty yards deep, rectangular, and contained two parallel rows of waist-high steel tables. Mulder could vaguely make out the bulky shapes on the tables; the bodies were wrapped in opaque plastic bags, and there were bright red plastic organ trays on carts attached to the stainless steel blood and fluid gutters that ran the length of each table. Mulder swallowed back a gust of nausea as he pressed his palm against one of the double doors. It was more physiological than mental; he had seen many dead bodies in his career, and he was not squeamish by nature. But the clinical nature of the anatomy lab triggered something primitive inside of him. Here, the human body was nothing more than meat. There was no room for philosophies of life, soul, or even God. Here, humanity was defined by bright red plastic organ trays and stainless steel fluid gutters.

He pushed the door inward and stepped inside the long laboratory. The strong scent of formaldehyde filled his nostrils, and he fought the urge to gag. His gaze roamed over the cadaver tables, jumping from bag to bag. Then he caught sight of his quarry, standing alone near the back of the room, bent over an open body bag. From that distance, Michael Lifton appeared to be tall, gangly, with short reddish hair and youthful features. He was wearing crimson sweatpants and a gray athletic T-shirt beneath a white lab coat. There was a thick book open on the cart at the head of the dissecting table, and Lifton seemed completely entranced by the open body in front of him. He didn't look up until Mulder was a few feet away, and when he did his eyes seemed glazed, far away. His eyelids drooped unnaturally low, and there was a slight tremble in his upper lip. *Was he ill? Or simply tired?* Lifton coughed, as the color returned to his cheeks. "Excuse me, I didn't hear you come in. Can I help you?"

Mulder shifted his gaze from Lifton's face to his bloodied gloves and the scalpel balanced between his thumb and forefinger. "Hope I'm not interrupting. I'm Agent Fox Mulder from the FBI. I tried your dorm room, but there was no one home. Your next-door neighbor told me I could find you here."

Lifton didn't move for a full second. Then he carefully set the scalpel down next to the open book. Mulder read the large-print heading that stretched across the two open pages: PARTIAL BOWEL RESECTION. His gaze slid to the open lower abdomen on the dissecting table. It looked like a bag overflowing with black snakes. Mulder quickly moved his eyes back to the young man's face.

"The FBI?" Lifton asked, his eyes wide. "Am I in some sort of trouble?"

Lifton coughed again, and the sound was course, vaguely pneumatic. Mulder saw beads of sweat running down the sides of the kid's face. It looked like he was running a fever. "Are you feeling all right, Mr. Lifton?"

"Call me Mike. I've got a bit of a cold. And I've been working in here most of the night; the formaldehyde screws with my allergies. What is this about?"

Lifton's hands were trembling, and Mulder could not tell if it was nervousness, or another sign of fever. He thought about Scully's microbe theory. Any minute, she would be arriving at

Josh Kemper's apartment; would he be suffering from the same flulike symptoms as the kid in front of Mulder? Were the symptoms just the beginning of something worse? "I need to speak to you about a skin harvest you and Josh Kemper performed last Friday night."

Lifton took a tiny step back from the dissecting table, his hands falling to his sides. "Did we do something wrong?"

Mulder could tell from Lifton's tone that he was not as surprised by the idea as Mulder would have suspected. "Well, we think you and Josh might have harvested skin from the wrong body."

Lifton closed his eyes, his cheeks pale. "I knew it. I thought something was wrong. But Josh insisted. He said Eckleman probably blew the tags. He said the body was close enough to the chart. Blond hair, blue eyes, no outward trauma."

"So what made you suspect it was the wrong body?"

Lifton sighed, using his forearm to wipe the sweat off of his forehead. "First, there was the tattoo. A dragon, on his right arm. And then there was the strange rash."

Mulder's instincts perked up. He remembered what Bernstein had told him about the rash on Stanton's neck. "What sort of rash?"

Lifton turned his head to the side. He pointed to a clear area of skin, right below his hairline. "Here, on the nape of his neck. A circular eruption, thousands of tiny red dots. Josh told me it was nothing—and it probably was. But if the guy had been in the ICU, it would have been in the chart. A straight shot from the ER, maybe it would have been missed. But not in the ICU."

Mulder nodded. The John Doe had gone straight from the ER to the morgue. Derrick Kaplan had spent time in the ICU before he died. Mike Lifton was a smart kid—but he had allowed himself to be bullied into performing the harvest, even though he had suspected it was the wrong body.

"After you finished the harvest," Mulder continued, "what did you do with the body?"

Lifton looked at him. "What do you mean? We returned it to the morgue, of course."

"To the same locker?"

"Yes. Fifty something. Fifty-two, or fifty-four. I've usually got a good head for numbers, but I've been practicing in here nearly every night this week. Lack of sleep, you know. Screws with everything."

Mulder nodded. He hoped it was just lack of sleep that was affecting Mike Lifton. But he had to cover the bases—to prove or disprove Scully's theory. "We need to get you checked up by a doctor right away. There might be a chance that you caught something from the John Doe."

Lifton's face turned even paler. "What do you mean? Did he die from some sort of infectious disease?"

"We're not sure. That's why we need you to get checked out."

Lifton's entire body seemed to sag as he thought about what Mulder was saying. Then Mulder noticed another tremor move through Lifton's upper lip, followed by a heavy cough. "I think we should get you to an ER right away. Just to be sure."

He didn't know whether or not it was evidence of Scully's theory—but suddenly, he didn't like the way Mike Lifton looked. It seemed as though Lifton's condition was deteriorating as he watched. As the student hastily repacked the open cadaver with trembling hands, Mulder hoped that Scully had gotten to the other med student in time.

Mr. Kemper! Mr. Josh Kemper!" Scully's voice reverberated off the heavy apartment door. "This is Agent Dana Scully of the FBI! The building superintendent is here with me, and if you don't answer the door, I'm coming inside!"

Scully could feel her heart pounding as she waited for a response. She glanced at the short, stocky man in the untucked gray T-shirt standing next to her, and nodded. Mitch Butler began fumbling through his oversize ring of apartment keys. Scully cursed to herself as she watched the super's stubby fingers struggling to find the correct one. *This was taking too long.*

Scully had called for an ambulance when she had first arrived at the Columbia-owned apartment building and found Kemper unresponsive to her attempts to get inside his room, but she knew it would be another few minutes before the paramedics would arrive. She had already lost valuable time rousing the grubby superintendent out of his apartment on the first floor; the trip upstairs to the fourth floor had been insufferably long.

"Here it is," Butler finally exclaimed, holding up a copper-colored key. "Apartment four-twelve."

Scully took the key from him and went to work on the lock. The door came open, and she rushed inside. "Mr. Kemper? Josh?"

The living room was small and almost devoid of furniture. There was a gray couch in one corner, facing a small television sitting on top of a cardboard box. A picture of two dogs wearing tuxedos took up most of the far wall, and dirty laundry invaded every inch of bare floor. Scully was reminded of her own med-school days—when even an hour for laundry would have been a gift from heaven. She had been a kid, like Josh Kemper—just trying to survive.

"How many rooms?" she shouted back toward the super, who was still standing in the entrance, breathing hard from the four flights of stairs.

"Just this one, the kitchen, and the bedroom. Through that door."

Scully headed for the open doorway on the other side of the

living room. She passed through a small hallway and found herself in a tiny kitchen: porcelain-tiled floor, chipped plaster hanging from the walls, a light fixture that looked like it was older than the electricity that powered it. There was an open container of orange juice on a small wooden table in front of the refrigerator. *Otherwise, no signs of life.* Scully rushed across the kitchen and through another open doorway.

She nearly tripped on a pile of bedding, catching her balance against a large wooden dresser. There was a bare mattress in the middle of the room, covered with medical texts and science magazines. *But still no sign of Kemper.*

"The bathroom," she shouted back over her shoulder. "Where is the bathroom?"

"Off the bedroom."

Scully cursed, her eyes wildly searching the cramped space—then she saw the closed door, directly on the other side of the dresser, partially obscured by a sea of hanging colored beads. She shoved the beads aside and yanked the door open.

There he was. Shirtless, lying facedown on the floor, one arm crooked around the base of the toilet, the other twisted strangely behind his back. Scully dropped to her knees and put her hand against the side of his neck. No pulse. His skin felt warm to the touch, but it had a waxy appearance and had turned a blue-gray color. No doubt about it—Josh Kemper was dead. She gently unhooked his right arm from around the base of the toilet, noting the lack of rigor mortis in his joints. She used her weight to roll him over.

His eyes and mouth were open, an anguished expression frozen on his boyish face. His face and bare chest were slightly purple where the blood had pooled beneath his skin. Scully reached forward and pushed an errant lock of blond hair out of the way, then pressed her index finger against Kemper's cheek. The pressure caused a slight blanching of the area beneath her fingertip. When she moved her hand away, the discoloration returned. *Early nonfixed lividity*. That meant he had been dead less than four hours—perhaps three, but no less than two. From the anguished look on his face and the awkward positioning of his body, Scully guessed he had convulsed or stroked out. But there were no obvious wounds to his head or face, so it wasn't the fall that had killed him. It had been something else—something inside his body.

Scully had a sudden thought and tilted Kemper's head to the side. But the back of his neck looked clear. No red dots, no circular rash. Still, that didn't mean it wasn't the same disease that had sent Stanton into a violent fit.

She sighed, rising to her feet. She turned to the sink and turned the water faucet as hot as it would go. Then she grabbed a bar of soap and began working on her hands. She knew she had taken a risk by coming into the room at all—but she doubted it was anything airborne or even contagious to the touch. Airborne viruses deadly enough to kill a man Kemper's age were extremely rare—and if the John Doe had been an airborne carrier, there would have been many more victims by now. That meant it was probably something blood-borne. Those at risk included the interns who worked on him, the two med students, perhaps the paramedics who had brought him in, and Bernstein's surgical team at Jamaica Hospital.

"Ms. Scully?" The super's hack crept at her from somewhere in the bedroom. "Is everything all right in there?"

"Mr. Butler," Scully responded, "I need you to go downstairs and wait for the ambulance. I'll join you in a moment."

Scully listened as Butler's plodding footsteps trickled away. Then she finished washing her hands and pulled her cellular phone out of her breast pocket. Her shoulders sagged as she dialed Mulder's number. He answered on the second ring.

"Mulder, where are you?"

His voice sounded tinny through the phone's earpiece. "The ER at Columbia Medical School."

Scully glanced at the body on the bathroom floor. She could hear sirens in the distance, but she wasn't sure if it was through the phone or through the thin apartment walls. "I take it you found Mike Lifton?"

"Scully, he's not doing so well. When I brought him in, he was complaining of flulike symptoms. Now the doctors tell me he's fallen into some sort of coma."

Scully nodded to herself. The symptoms fit with her earlier hypothesis. A viral threat, something that could cause cerebral swelling. The sort of disease that could also cause a psychotic fit and deadly convulsions. "We're going to have to notify the CDC immediately. They're going to want to track down any-one who's had serious contact with the John Doe. And they'll need to act fast—obviously, the infected subjects' conditions deteriorate rapidly."

Mulder went silent on the other end of the line. Scully wondered if he was still resisting the idea that a microbe was behind the case. Or had the med student's illness finally convinced him that a disease linked all of the elements of the case together? Then again, she doubted he would give in to reason that easily.

Finally, Mulder's voice drifted back into Scully's ear. "So Josh Kemper's pretty sick, too?"

Scully took a deep breath. "He's dead, Mulder. Whatever the John Doe was carrying—it progresses quickly."

"And you think it's the same disease that made Stanton kill Teri Nestor?"

"Yes. Like I said before, it's some sort of microbe that causes a swelling of the brain. And Mulder, whatever Stanton was capable of in that recovery room or out in Brooklyn this morn-ing—I don't think he'll be putting up much of a struggle in a few more hours. This is a fast-acting disease."

Scully heard voices out in the apartment. The paramedics had arrived. "I'm heading back to the hospital with Kemper's corpse. I'll find out what this microbe is, Mulder. And after I do—we're both going to get some sleep."

For once, there was no argument from the other end of the line.

Less than ten minutes later, the EMS team had secured Josh Kemper's body in the back of the ambulance. As the double doors clicked shut and the heavy vehicle pulled away from the curb, a solitary figure stepped out from the narrow garbage alley that ran next to the apartment complex. His glossy, sable hair was hidden beneath a baseball cap, and his lithe body swam beneath a long, tan overcoat. His hands were buried in his deep pockets, with just a hint of white latex showing at the wrists.

He watched the ambulance roll quietly down the deserted street. He could just make out the red-haired FBI agent sitting in the front passenger seat. Her pale cheek was pressed up against the side window, a look of sheer exhaustion in her green eyes.

The young, caramel-skinned man thought about the discovery Agent Scully was about to make. Certainly, it would chase the fatigue out of her pretty features. The young man smiled, carefully removing his right hand from his pocket. He twirled a tiny plastic object between his gloved fingers. The object was thin and cylindrical, the shape of a miniature ballpoint pen. The young man touched a plastic button on the edge of the object, and there was an almost imperceptible click.

A shiver of excitement ran through the young man's skin as he carefully examined the three-inch-long needle that had appeared out of one end of the object. The needle was thinner than a single hair, its point significantly smaller than a single human pore. At certain angles it seemed invisible—too small, even, to displace particles of the early-morning air.

So much more subtle than a gun or a razor blade—and at the same time, so much more effective. The young man closed his eyes, reliving the moment just five hours ago—the tiny flick of his wrist, the unnoticed brush of a stranger in a crowded late-night subway car. Then the second moment ten minutes later, in passing on the stairwell of the Columbia Medical School anatomy lab. A thrill pulsed through his body, and he sighed, wishing he could have watched the results himself.

But despite his love for his work—he had to adhere to at least a semblance of professionalism. His gloved finger again found the plastic button, and the tiny needle retracted. He carefully slid the pen-shaped object back into his pocket and strolled toward a blue Chevrolet parked a few feet down the curb.

The two FBI agents would be returning to New York Hospital. If he hurried, he could arrive just a few minutes behind Josh Kemper's ambulance. He had to stay close to the two agents—on the off chance that they were smarter than expected. If they started to get too close again—the young man smiled, fondling the pen-shaped object inside his pocket. Professionalism, he reminded himself. Still, he could feel the warm, almost sexual anticipation rising through his body.

In his heart, he hoped agents Scully and Mulder were absolutely brilliant.

7

Four hours later, a triangle of harsh orange light ripped Mulder out of a deep sleep. He sat straight up on the borrowed hospital cot in the cozy third-floor intern room, blinking rapidly. Scully came into focus, her red hair highlighted by the high fluorescent beams from the hospital hallway. She was wearing a white lab coat and gloves, and there was a plastic contact sheet in her right hand. The look on her face was somewhere between disbelief and dismay.

"We've found our microbe," she said, crossing into the room and dropping heavily onto the edge of Mulder's cot. She tossed the contact sheet onto his lap. "These are shots of the isolated virus taken by an electron microscope. The sample came from cerebrospinal fluid tapped from a postmortem lumbar puncture on Josh Kemper."

Mulder looked at the contact sheet. He could see a tiny pill-shaped object multiplied a half dozen times in the different-angled shots. It looked so small, so innocuous.

"They woke me with the results from the lab twenty minutes ago," Scully continued. "But I went down there myself to check what they were saying. Because it's pretty hard to believe."

"What do you mean? Scully, what am I looking at?"

Scully took a deep breath. "Encephalitis lethargica. We've matched it up through the CDC's computer link. They're sending a specialist here this afternoon to confirm the diagnosis. But the EEGs and CT scans coincide. There isn't any doubt."

Mulder wasn't sure if he had heard of the disease before. "So it's a form of encephalitis? Isn't that similar to what you predicted—a disease that could cause brain swelling?"

"It is a strain of encephalitis—but Mulder, it's not at all what I expected."

Mulder waited for her to continue. She was staring at the contact sheet in his hands as if the pill-shaped virus might crawl right out into the intern room.

"Mulder," she finally stated, "there hasn't been an outbreak of encephalitis lethargica since 1922. The virus you're looking at has rarely been seen outside a laboratory in over seventy-five years."

Mulder raised his eyebrows. No wonder he hadn't recognized the disease. "How does this virus manifest? Does it fit the symptoms we've seen?"

Scully shrugged. "The disease starts similarly to the more common strains of encephalitis; causing fever, confusion, sometimes paralysis of one side of the body—and in some cases, convulsions, psychosis, coma, and death. But lethargica also induces incredible fatigue, which is why it's sometimes called the 'sleeping sickness'."

Mulder nodded. He remembered Mike Lifton's drooping eyelids and glazed eyes. But Scully still hadn't told him anything that could explain how Stanton could have reacted with such inhuman strength. And there were still other inconsistencies that were not yet explained. "Scully, what about the circular rash on both the John Doe and Perry Stanton? Could that have been caused by encephalitis lethargica? And why wasn't it present on either of the med students?"

"The rash might be unrelated—perhaps a separate infection, one that's more difficult to catch. Remember, the med students did not have the same level of contact with the John Doe as Perry Stanton. Stanton got a slab of his skin stapled onto an open burn."

"That still doesn't explain Stanton's violent explosion. Neither of the med students reacted violently—"

Scully waved her hand. "Viruses can affect different people differently—and especially a virus like this. Lethargica attacks areas of the brain, as well as the meninges, the brain's covering. There's no way to predict how a specific individual might react. During the 1922 outbreak, forty percent of those infected died. This time, we're looking at a much worse percentage—but at least the disease has been confined to two people who had close contact with the carrier. That means the virus hasn't changed its mode of transmission."

Mulder pushed his feet off the side of the cot, stretching his calves. He was becoming more alert by the second. He hoped Scully was as refreshed as he was—because in his mind, the case was nowhere near over. "You mean it's blood-borne. Like HIV."

Scully nodded. "That's right. It's transmitted only by blood-to-blood contact. The 1922 version was also sometimes carried by mosquitoes, or biting flies—but that's extremely rare."

Mulder reached out and touched one of Scully's gloved hands. "Scully, both the med students were wearing gloves. How do you explain the blood-to-blood contact? A swarm of mosquitoes in the ER?"

"Latex gloves aren't a hundred percent protection. And a skin harvest is a messy procedure."

Mulder still thought it was remarkable that both students

had become so sick—so quickly—while the plastic surgery team, which had worked invasively with the harvested skin, had remained healthy. "It doesn't seem right, Scully. Even if the virus links the med students to the John Doe—we don't have any proof of a link to Perry Stanton. If Dr. Bernstein was sick, maybe—but he's not. The only thing that connects the John Doe to Perry Stanton is the circular red rash."

Scully rose slowly from the cot and took the contact sheet out of Mulder's hands. "We won't know for sure until we've got Stanton in custody. I've explained the precautions to Barrett—gloves, surgical masks, limited contact—and she assures me they'll have him within the next hour. By then, the investigator from the CDC will be here to confirm the lethargica, and this tragedy will come to a close."

Mulder ran his hands through his hair. He didn't say what he was thinking—that this tragedy was nowhere near the final act. Likewise, he doubted even Barrett would have such an easy time bringing in a man who had shoved an IV rack a few feet into a hospital wall. Instead, he pressed his fingers against the side of his jaw, testing the stiffness. Then he rose from the cot. "Personally, Scully, I don't think the CDC is going to make this case any clearer. You can follow the lethargica angle as far as it's going to go; in the meantime, I'm going to find out more about our John Doe."

Scully raised her eyebrows. "Mulder, we've already gone through his chart a half dozen times. The interns didn't know what was wrong with him—and until we've got a body and an autopsy, there isn't much more we can discover about his death."

Mulder headed toward the door. "I'm not interested in how he died, Scully. I want to know how he ended up in a medical chart in the first place."

*   *   *

Mulder arrived in the ER just as the trauma team crashed through the double doors. He counted at least six people crowded around the stretcher: the burly chief resident, a surgical consult in green scrubs, two nurses—and at the tail end of the stretcher, two thickset men in dark blue paramedic uniforms. The smaller of the two was holding a bottle of blood above his shoulder as he raced to keep up with an IV tube attached to the patient's right thigh. The larger paramedic had an object delicately braced in both arms; the object was oddly shaped and wrapped in white gauze.

Mulder remained a few feet away as the stretcher passed through the center of the ER, toward the elevators that led up to the surgical ward. He caught a glimpse of the patient between the shoulders of the two nurses: thin, tall, writhing in obvious pain, tubes running out of every inch of bare skin. At first, Mulder couldn't tell what was wrong—then his gaze moved to the tourniquet wrapped tightly around the man's left forearm. He watched as the surgical consult took the gauze-covered object out of the paramedic's arms and lifted a corner of the white cloth.

"It's in pretty good shape," he overheard the paramedic say. "Landed under the track, which protected it from the train. Think you can reattach?"

The consult nodded, then continued on with the stretcher. The two paramedics stood watching as the rest of the group raced toward the elevator. Mulder shivered, then took his cue and stepped forward.

"Luke Canton?" he asked. He had gotten the name from the ER dispatcher. Canton and his partner had brought the John Doe into the hospital on the night of the thirteen-car accident. The dispatcher had described him as one of the best in the city.

Canton turned toward Mulder, looking him over. The paramedic was six feet tall, with wide shoulders, and reddish scruff covering most of his square jaw. He yanked off his bloody gloves and tossed them to the floor. "That's right. This is my partner, Emory Ross."

"I'm Agent Mulder from the FBI. That was a hell of a scene. Is he going to be all right?"

Canton shrugged. His face was grim, but there was something bright, deep in his blue eyes. This was his high—the adrenaline pump of medicine at its most raw. "Lost a fight with a subway car. But if the surgeon's any good, he'll keep his hand."

Mulder noticed splotches of fresh blood all over Canton's uniform. "Covered you pretty good. Was it like this with the John Doe you brought in last Friday night?"

Canton shook his head. "I figured that's what this is about. Heard through the grapevine he might have been carrying some sort of virus."

"It's a possibility," Mulder responded. He knew the CDC would probably be rounding up all of the possible risk candidates by midafternoon. He gestured at the blood on Canton's uniform. "Most likely something blood-borne."

Canton shrugged. "Well, then we're in the clear. The John Doe had no external wounds. No blood at all. Actually, we hardly had any contact with him—other than lifting him into the ambulance and working the Velcro straps. He didn't crash until he was in the ER. We didn't even intubate—the two ER kids took over, and we went back into the field."

Mulder moved his gaze from Canton to his partner, Emory Ross. Neither one looked the least bit ill. "And you're feeling all right? No signs of fatigue or fever?"

Canton smiled. "I worked out for two hours this morning. Hit two-fifty-five on the bench. What about you, Ross?"

Ross laughed. He seemed much younger than Canton, and it was obvious from his eyes that he looked up to his wide-shouldered partner. "I played pickup basketball for forty minutes before our shift started. Didn't score very many, but I got a handful of rebounds."

Mulder felt relief, and a tinge of excitement. He wasn't a doctor, but it sounded as though the two paramedics were not going to be felled by lethargy. Mulder walked with the two men toward the changing rooms located in the corner of the ER, just beyond the admissions desk. "I was told the John Doe was brought in from the scene of a car accident on the FDR Drive?"

"That's right," Canton answered. "Found him unconscious but stable in the breakdown lane, maybe twenty feet from the lead car. We already had one of the drivers in our wagon—a woman with a pretty severe impact wound to her chest—but we decided to risk a second scoop. There were other ambulances on the scene, but the accident was as bad as it gets. Many more bodies than wagons."

Mulder watched as Canton grabbed a passing nurse by the waist. The young woman laughed, wriggling free. Mulder could tell that Luke Canton was well liked. "And he remained stable en route to the hospital?"

"Unresponsive," Canton answered. "But certainly stable. We doubted he was even involved in the accident itself; there were no exterior wounds you would expect from someone thrown from a crash, no bruises or cuts or anything—"

"Except the slight scratch," Ross chimed in as they reached the curtain that led to the changing room. "A circular little thing on the back of his neck. But it didn't look like much—I don't remember if we even bothered to tell the interns when we brought him in."

Canton tossed a glance at his partner, who quickly looked at the floor. Canton looked at Mulder. "It was a crazy night. We had to get right back to the accident for the walking wounded.

I'm sure the kids spotted the little scratch on their own. Anyway, I doubt it had anything to do with why the guy died."

They pushed into the small changing room. There was a row of metal lockers on one side, three parallel wooden benches, a closet full of hangers, and a door that led to a shower room. Canton and his partner moved to their adjacent lockers. As they changed into clean uniforms, Mulder contemplated what Canton had just told him. His thoughts kept coming back to the scene of the accident, where the John Doe had been picked up. If he wasn't thrown from one of the cars—why was he unconscious in the breakdown lane, twenty yards away?

When the paramedics had finished changing, Mulder turned to Luke Canton. "I've already spoken to the dispatcher, and if it's all right with you, I'd like to borrow an hour of your time."

Canton raised his eyebrows. Then he glanced at his partner and shrugged. "If you've got the authority, I've got the hour."

Mulder grinned. He liked Luke Canton's attitude.

8

 The ambulance seemed to float through the three lanes of New York traffic as Luke Canton navigated between the moving bumpers with an expert's grace. Only twice did he have to reach above the dashboard and flick on the colored lights. Mulder watched the chain-link snakes of traffic slither by beneath the high side windows, amazed at how the cars stayed so close together at such high speeds. *Coordinated chaos.*

"It's not surprising when they crash," Canton said, reading his mind. "It's surprising when they don't. You know how many people die every year in cars?"

Mulder had an idea, but said nothing. Canton pointed to a dented pickup truck weaving through the lanes two cars away. "More than fifty thousand. About the same number as die from AIDS. Funny thing. We're quite willing to give up casual sex. But give up casual driving? No way."

Mulder felt his seatbelt tighten as Canton punched the brake, and the ambulance suddenly veered to the right. Mulder watched the guardrail grow closer as they rolled to a stop in the breakdown lane. The lane was actually more like a gully, stretching fifty yards along a curved section of rail. It was half the size of a regular lane, a few bare feet wider than the ambulance itself. Mulder saw a glimmer of broken glass a dozen yards ahead and the twisted remains of a rear bumper in the grass just on the other side of the railing. Other than the bumper and the glass, there were no visible signs of the accident. "Looks like it's been cleaned up pretty well."

"Should have seen it right after the accident. The whole Drive was cluttered with metal and glass. All three of these lanes were closed. The cars looked like crumpled socks. You couldn't even tell the front few apart. Found one woman sitting in the driver seat of the car ahead of her."

Mulder opened his door and stepped down onto the asphalt. The noise from the cars whizzing by was nearly deafening. A warm breeze pulled at his jacket, and the heavy smell of exhaust filled his nostrils. Canton came around the front of the ambulance and pointed to the area directly ahead of them. "The accident scene started here, with the last car up against the railing just ahead. A few more were piled together in the center of the highway, then the bulk of the accident was about thirty yards up. The lead car—a BMW roadster—was upside down and crumpled pretty flat, right in the center of the road."

Mulder slowly walked forward, his eyes moving back and forth across the pavement. He knew that natural exposure to the elements, and the sheer passage of time, had probably erased most of the evidence left behind by the thirteen-car accident. But he also knew that investigative work relied heavily on luck. "Was it possible to determine what caused the lead car to spin out?"

Canton nodded as they continued forward down the breakdown lane. "According to a witness from five cars back, a white van was careening wildly back and forth between lanes, just ahead of the BMW. The back doors of the van popped open, and the driver of the BMW panicked. She bounced off the guardrail, then flipped over. The next car—a Volvo—hit her head-on at sixty-five miles per hour. Then the others just piled on."

They reached the spot Canton had described as the rough area where the first car had spun out. Mulder turned to the guardrail and saw a huge, jagged tear in the heavy horizontal iron bars. Two dark tire tracks led up to the tear, and Mulder could imagine the driver's frantic efforts to stop the BMW. Obviously, those efforts had been too late. "Did the lead driver get a good look at the van?"

"Maybe"—Canton sighed, leaning against an unmarred section of the guardrail—"but she was decapitated by the front axle of the Volvo. Like I said, the only good witness was five cars back. All the police know was that the van was white, some sort of American model, and the back doors were open. There's an APB out on it now, but there are a lot of vans like that in this city."

Mulder nodded. He would talk to the police after he returned to the hospital, but he didn't expect them to have any answers. If the van ran from the scene of the accident, chances are the driver didn't want to be found.

"And the John Doe?" Mulder asked. "He was unconscious somewhere up here?"

Canton walked a few more paces, then pointed to a spot in the breakdown lane. Mulder stopped at his side. The spot was only ten yards ahead of where the lead car had gone out of control. Roughly where the van had been weaving back and forth. *With the back doors hanging open.*

Mulder knelt, looking at the pavement. Of course, there was nothing remarkable. It had been a week. Mulder moved his eyes along the ground, imagining the body sprawled out. "Facedown? Or faceup?"

"Sort of a fetal position," Canton said. "Lying on his side. His head was away from the road."

Mulder felt the pavement rumble beneath his knees as a heavy Jeep roared by in the closest lane. There was a clattering sound, and Mulder watched a Styrofoam cup bounce toward the guardrail. His thoughts solidified as the cup disappeared down the grassy slope on the other side. He rose and walked to the edge of the breakdown lane. He moved slowly along the guardrail—and paused at a spot a few feet away from where Canton was standing.

There was a small dent in the guardrail, just above knee level. Mulder bent down and peered at the dent. Then he looked back toward the highway. "Mr. Canton, how fast did you say the lead car was moving?"

"Probably around sixty-five miles per hour. That's my best estimate, from the damage."

"And the van was traveling at around the same speed when its back doors popped open?"

"That's right."

Mulder nodded. The positioning of the dent seemed about right. If the John Doe's body had fallen out of the back of the van, hit the pavement, rolled into the guardrail, then bounced back a few yards into the breakdown lane—it would have landed right where Canton was standing. The only problem with the theory was condition of the John Doe's body. Both the paramedics and the medical student had corroborated what the interns had written in the chart: The John Doe had showed no signs of external trauma. Mulder could hear the question Scully would ask the minute he told her his theory: How could a man fall out of a van moving at sixty-five miles per hour, dent a guardrail—and receive no external injuries?

Mulder didn't have an answer—yet. But he wasn't ready to discard the theory. The John Doe was linked to Perry Stanton, and Perry Stanton had performed amazing, inhuman physical feats. Wasn't it possible that the John Doe had been similarly invulnerable?

Mulder reached into his coat pocket and pulled out a sterile plastic evidence bag and a small horsehair brush. He leaned close to the dent in the railing and began to collect brush samples. He doubted he'd find anything—but there was always the chance some sort of fiber evidence would show up under analysis.

"What are you doing over there?" Canton asked, watching him. "I said we found the John Doe over here."

"I don't think the body started there, Mr. Canton. I think that was just Mr. Doe's final resting place. It's the journey between that interests me." Mulder was about to drop to the ground and get samples from the pavement, when his brush caught on a small groove in the railing. When he pulled the brush free, he noticed a few tiny strips of white cloth caught in the fine horsehairs. He held the brush close to his eyes and saw flakes of some sort of red powder clinging to the underside of the strips. The powder had a strong, moldy scent—somewhat like a loaf of bread that had been left in a damp cabinet too long. Mulder wondered whether the powder and cloth were related to the John Doe. It was possible that the groove in the guardrail had protected it from the elements. He took a second bag out of his pocket and put the strips inside. Then he crossed back to Canton. Canton was looking at him strangely.

"Why is the FBI so interested in this John Doe, anyway? Was he some sort of serial killer?"

"As far as we know," Mulder said, kneeling down to take more samples from the pavement, "he didn't do anything but die. Problem was, his skin didn't die with him."

Mulder didn't add the sudden thought that had hit him: Maybe it was his skin that was the killer. Not some microbe carried in his blood—as Scully had proposed—but his skin itself. Because that was the real common denominator. Not his blood, not a microbe, not a disease.

Skin.

Forty minutes later, Mulder entered the infectious disease ward at New York Hospital. The ward was really just a cordoned-off section of the ICU; two hallways and a half dozen private rooms with a self-contained ventilation system and specially sealed metal doors. The rooms were designed with various degrees of biosafety in mind: from the highest level of security, with inverse vacuums and specialized Racal space suits—to the more manageable, low-level rooms, with glove and mask guidelines, maintained under strict video watch by a staff of infectious disease specialists.

Mulder was directed to a low-level containment room near the rear of the ward. After donning gloves and a mask, he was led into a small private room. Scully was standing by a hospital bed, arguing in a determined voice. Dr. Bernstein, Perry Stanton's plastic surgeon, was sitting on the edge of the bed in a white hospital smock, a skeptical look on his face. There was an IV running into his right arm, and every few seconds he stared at the wire with contempt. It was obvious he didn't want to be there. And it was equally obvious that he wasn't the slightest bit sick.

"Look," he was saying, as Mulder came into the room, "I can assure you, there was no blood-to-blood contact during the transplant. I was masked and gloved. So were my nurses. I've done similar procedures on HIV-positive patients. I've never had any problems."

"Dr. Bernstein," Scully responded, "I didn't order this quarantine. The infectious disease specialist from the CDC has decided not to take any chances. Your surgical team is the highest-risk group—and this quarantine is just a logical precaution."

"It's not logical, it's pointless. We both know there's no real cure for lethargica. I can understand restricting my surgical schedule until after the incubation period ends. But why keep me and my staff cooped up in these cells?"

Scully sighed, then nodded toward the IV. "The specialist from the CDC has suggested you remain on acyclovir, at least through the incubation period. It has been shown effective in stopping some of the more common types of encephalitis."

Bernstein rolled his eyes. "Acyclovir has been effective only in encephalitis cases related to the herpes simplex virus. Lethargica isn't caused by herpes."

Scully nodded, then shrugged. "Dr. Bernstein, I'm not going to argue medicine with you. Your specialty is plastic surgery. Mine is forensic pathology. Neither one of us is an infectious disease specialist. We should both defer to the expert from the CDC."

Bernstein didn't respond. Finally, a grudging acceptance touched his lips. He glanced at Mulder. "I guess I should do what she says."

Mulder smiled. "Usually works for me. Scully, can I borrow you for a moment?"

Scully followed him out into the hallway. After the door sealed shut behind them, she pulled down her mask. "Mulder, I've got some good news. Dr. Cavanaugh, the hospital administrator, has made some initial headway tracking down the John Doe's body. One of his clerks found a transfer form from Rutgers Medical School in New Jersey. Cavanaugh thinks the cadaver might have been mistakenly sent over for dissection. We'll know for certain within a few hours."

Mulder digested the information. He didn't think it was going to be as simple as that. "I'll hold my breath. In the meantime, I'd like you to take a look at something. Tell me if you have any idea what it is."

He reached into his pocket and pulled out the small bag containing the cloth strips and the red powder. Scully took the bag from him and carefully opened the seal. She looked inside, then scrunched up the skin above her nose. She shook the bag, separating some of the red powder from the strips of white cloth. Then she pressed her gloved fingers together against the sides of the bag, getting a sense of the powder's texture. "Actually, I think I have seen something like this before. From the scent and grain, I think the powder might be an antibacterial agent of some sort. The strips of cloth look like they could have come from a bandage. Where did you get this?"

Mulder's body felt light as his intuition kicked in. Now he was getting somewhere. "The accident scene where the John Doe's body was found."

Scully looked at him, then back at the red powder and the strips of cloth. It seemed as if she was suddenly doubting her own memory. "Before you jump to any conclusions, let me show this to Dr. Bernstein. He's a surgeon—he'll have a better idea of what this is."

They reentered the private-care room. Dr. Bernstein was lying on his back, his hands behind his head. "Back so soon? Have I been paroled?"

Scully handed him the plastic bag. "Actually, we're just here to ask for your opinion. Do you recognize this red substance?"

Bernstein sat up, shaking the bag in front of his eyes. He opened a corner of the seal and took a small breath. Then he nodded. The answer was obvious to him. "Of course. The Dust. That's what we call it. It's an antibacterial compound used during massive skin transplantations. We're talking about patients with at least fifty percent burns, often more. It's fairly cutting edge; very powerful, very expensive. Its use was only recently approved by the FDA."

Mulder crossed his hands behind his back. He felt a tremor

of excitement move through his shoulders. *A powder used in skin transplants.* If it was connected to the John Doe, it was a stunning discovery, and a bizarre, striking coincidence. He cleared his throat. "Dr. Bernstein, how common is this Dust?"

"Not common at all," Bernstein said, handing the bag back to Scully. "I don't think it's used in any of the local hospitals. Certainly not at Jamaica. I spent part of last year out at UCSF, where I first got a chance to try it out. If you want more information, I suggest you contact the company that developed and markets it. Fibrol International. It's a biotech that specializes in burn-transplantation materials. I'm pretty sure their headquarters is nearby."

Mulder had never heard of the company before. He knew there were dozens, if not hundreds, of biotech companies located up and down the Northeast Corridor. He watched as Scully thanked Bernstein, then he followed her back out into the hallway. He could hardly contain his enthusiasm as he told her what he was thinking. "Scully, this is too much of a coincidence."

"Well—"

"A specialized transplant powder found at the scene where the John Doe was picked up," Mulder bulldozed along. "It might mean that the John Doe himself was a transplant recipient. Then his skin was harvested, passing along strange, unexplainable symptoms to Perry Stanton. The red powder—the Dust—might be the key to everything."

Scully squinted, then shook her head. "Mulder, you're jumping way ahead of yourself. You found this powder at the scene of the accident, a spot on a major highway leading out of Manhattan?"

"You heard Dr. Bernstein. This powder is rare and expensive. We need to talk to the people at Fibrol International, find out if we can trace—"

Mulder was interrupted by a high-pitched ring. Scully had her cellular phone out before the noise had finished echoing through Mulder's ears. Only a few people had Scully's number—and Mulder had a good guess who it was on the other end of the line.

"Barrett," Scully mouthed. Her face changed as she listened to the tinny voice in her ear. When she hung up the phone, her eyes were bright and animated. "It's Stanton. An eyewitness saw him entering a subway terminal in Brooklyn Heights. Barrett wants to know if we want to be in on the arrest."

Mulder was already moving toward the elevators.

9

Susan Doppler closed her eyes, the scream of metal against metal echoing through her skull. Her body jerked back and forth—her tired muscles victimized by the rhythmic mechanical surf, as the crowded, steel coffin burrowed through the city's bowels. She had entered that near-comatose state of the frequent commuter, barely kept awake by the turbulent chatter of the rails resonating upward through her feet.

Like many New Yorkers, Susan hated the subway. But the forty-minute ride into Manhattan was a necessary part of her daily routine. A single mother at thirty-one, she could hardly afford cab fare—and there was no direct bus route from her home in Brooklyn to the downtown department store where she worked an afternoon shift. As long as her nine-year-old daughter needed child care and braces, she had no choice besides the underground bump and grind.

Today, the ordeal was worse than usual. The air-conditioning had gone out two stops ago, and Susan could feel the sweat rolling down her back. The air reeked of body odor and seasoned urine; every breath was a test of Susan's reflux control, and her throat was already chalky and dry from her labored

search for oxygen. The car was packed tight, and Susan struggled to keep from being crushed between the two businessmen
seated on either side of her. The man to her left was overweight, and his white shirt was soaked through with sweat.
Worse still, the man to Susan's right was angled and bony, and
every few seconds he inadvertently jabbed her with a knifelike
elbow as he turned the pages of the newspaper tabloid on his
lap.

Still, with her eyes tightly shut and her head lolling back
against the rattling glass window, she could almost pretend
she was somewhere else: a sauna in a city on the other side of
the world; a steaming beach on an island in the middle of the
Pacific; the fiery cabin of an exploding airplane hurtling
toward the side of a mountain. *Anything was better than a
crowded subway in the middle of July.*

Susan grimaced as she once again felt the sharp elbow poking into her right hip. She opened her eyes and glared at the
emaciated businessman. He was tall, spidery, with grayish hair
and furry eyebrows. He seemed completely engrossed in his
tabloid, oblivious to anything but the colorful pictures of
celebrities and freaks.

Susan turned away, frustrated, and rested her chin on her
hand. Wisps of her long brown hair fell down against her
cheeks, framing her blue eyes. Azure, her ex-husband had
called them—back when he had cared. *The prick.* Her eyes narrowed as she chided herself for thinking about him. It had been
over a year now, and he was no longer a part of her or her
daughter's life. Her eyes were *blue*—not azure.

Susan's body stiffened as the subway car wrenched to the
left, the lights flickering. When the flickering stopped, she
found herself staring directly at the man seated across from
her. The sight was so pathetic, she almost gasped out loud.
Only in New York.

The man was hunched forward, his small, football-shaped head in his hands. His jagged little body was barely covered by a filthy smock, the thin material stained and torn and covered in what looked to be flecks of green glass. The man seemed to be trembling—probably crack or heroin—and his thinning hair was slick with sweat. As Susan watched, the man shifted his head slightly, and she could see that his lips were moving, emitting a constant, unintelligible patter. She caught a glimpse of his eyes—noting that they were blue, just like hers. Maybe even a little azure.

She turned away, repulsed. The man was obviously homeless, most likely mentally disturbed. Thankfully, he was too small to cause any problems. Still, Susan was glad she wasn't sharing his bench.

Then the elbow touched her hip again, and she cursed out loud. The spidery businessman finally noticed her, apologizing in a thick New Jersey accent. He folded his tabloid in half, carefully resting it sideways against his knees. As he lifted a corner to continue reading, Susan caught a glimpse of a large black-and-white picture on the back cover of the magazine. The picture was right below a huge headline in oversize type:

PSYCHO PROFESSOR ROAMS NEW YORK

Something ticked in Susan's mind, and she looked up from the tabloid. Her eyes refocused on the little, hunched man sitting across from her. She stared at the torn white smock, a warm, tingling feeling rising through her spine. Slowly, her mouth came open as she realized that it certainly could be a hospital smock.

She remembered the story she had heard on the news that morning. A little history professor had murdered a nurse and jumped out of a second-story window. She couldn't be sure—

but there was a chance that same man was sitting right across from her.

She shifted against the seat, wondering if she should say something. Then a new sound entered her ears—the squeal of the brakes kicking in. They had reached the next stop. The subway car jerked backward, and the little man suddenly looked up. Susan locked eyes with him—and knew for sure. It was the psycho professor. *And he was looking right at her.*

Her jaw shot open, and an involuntary scream erupted from her throat. The professor's eyes seemed to shrink as his entire body convulsed upward. Suddenly, he was on his feet and coming toward her across the narrow car. Susan cringed backward, pointing, as the other passengers stared in shock. There was a horrible frozen moment as the professor stood over her, his hands clenched at his sides. Then the subway car stopped suddenly at the station, and an anguished look crossed his face.

He seemed to forget about Susan as he turned and lurched toward the open doors. His head whirled back and forth as he shoved people out of his way. A heavyset man in bright sweatpants shouted at him to slow down—then toppled to the side as the diminutive professor slammed past. A second later he was out onto the platform.

Susan leapt across the subway car and pressed her face against the window on the other side. She watched the little man reeling away from a crowd of onlookers—then she saw three police officers coming through the turnstiles. Relief filled her body as she realized there was nowhere for the professor to go.

The little man paused, watching the three officers coming toward him. Susan noticed that all three were armed—and wearing white latex gloves. The subway car had gone silent around her, as other passengers jostled for positions at the window.

The three officers fanned out in a wide semicircle, surrounding the professor. The little man made a sudden decision, and spun to his left, heading straight for the dark subway tunnel ahead of Susan's stopped train. One officer stood between him and the oval black mouth of the tunnel. Susan watched as the officer dropped to one knee, his gun out in front of him. He shouted something—but the little man kept on coming.

Susan gasped as she saw the look of determination spread across the police officer's face.

Officer Carl Leary held his breath as the little man barreled toward him. He could see the fury in the professor's wild blue eyes, the sense of pure, liquid violence. He knew he had no choice. In a second, the man was going to be on top of him.

His finger clenched against the trigger, and his service revolver kicked upward, the muscles in his forearms contracting to take the recoil. A loud explosion echoed through the subway station, followed by a half dozen screams from the open subway doors. Leary's eyes widened as he saw the little man still coming toward him. His finger tightened again, and there was a second explosion—

And then the little man was rushing right past him. Leary fell back against the platform, stunned. He had fired at point-blank range. How the hell could he have missed?

He watched as the professor disappeared into the subway tunnel. Then he felt a gloved hand on his shoulder. He looked up and saw the concerned look on his partner's sweaty face. Joe Kenyon had been riding shotgun in Leary's patrol cruiser for two years. They had seen everything there was to see in this crazy city—but, for once, both officers were at a loss for words.

"You okay?" Kenyon finally managed. His thick voice was hoarse from the excitement. "The psycho didn't bleed on you, did he?"

Leary shook his head as he checked the chamber on his service revolver. The barrel was still hot, and he could smell the gunpowder in the air. He counted the bullets, and confirmed that two were missing. Then he shrugged, running a hand through his shock of sweaty red hair. "The diseased little bastard's out of his mind. Came right at me."

"He won't get far," Kenyon murmured, looking back at the subway car. He watched as the other officer herded the passengers out of the stopped train. "I think you winged him pretty good. He'll make it twenty, twenty-five yards at the most."

Leary didn't respond. Kenyon must have been right. He couldn't possibly have missed at such close range. Then again, why hadn't the little man gone down? How could a guy take a hit at such close range and not go down?

He pushed the thought away as he reached for his two-way radio. He was about to call it in when Kenyon pointed toward the turnstiles. "Don't bother with the radio. Here comes Big-Assed Barrett and the two fibbies."

Leary watched the hulking detective and the two well-dressed agents as they strolled onto the platform. Then he turned back toward the dark subway tunnel.

Whether he had winged the little bastard or not—Perry Stanton wasn't going to get away. *Not this time.*

10

Scully watched in clinical disgust as a rat the size of a basketball ran headfirst into the stone wall to her right, bounced off, then scurried beneath the iron tracks. She turned her attention back to the dark tunnel, maneuvering the crisp orange beam of her flashlight until she found the outline of Mulder's shoulders a few feet ahead. She could hear her partner's low voice over the rumble of the underground ventilation system, and she hurried her pace, closing the distance. Detective Barrett came into view, her huge form hovering just ahead of Mulder in the darkness. Mulder was pointing at the heavy revolver that hung from Barrett's right paw.

"He's not in control," Mulder was arguing. "Certainly, there are more humane ways to bring him in."

"He's a murderer," Barrett hissed back, "and I'm not going to put myself or my officers at risk. If you feel comfortable armed with a chunk of plastic and a battery, that's your prerogative."

Scully glanced down at the stun gun in her gloved left hand. She and Mulder had procured the nonlethal weapons at the FBI East Side armory on the way to the subway terminal. The device was about the size of a paperback book, no more than three pounds. The textured plastic handle felt warm through the latex enveloping Scully's fingers.

"The Taser is just as effective as a bullet," Mulder said. "It can disable a three-hundred-pound man without causing any permanent damage."

"I know what the manual says," Barrett shot back. "But have you ever aimed one of those toys at a junkie in a PCP rage? Roughly equivalent to poking a rattlesnake with a paper clip."

Scully cleared her throat. In her mind, the discussion was moot. The other three police officers were at least twenty yards ahead by now, and all were armed with high-powered service revolvers. Barrett had sent the officers ahead because two of them had worked for the Transit Police before and knew the tunnel layout. "Hopefully, there won't be any need for lethal force. Detective Barrett, how far does this tunnel go before we reach the next platform?"

"About half a mile," Barrett responded, heading forward again. "But there are numerous junctions leading off the main line. Construction adjuncts, equipment areas, voltage rooms; plenty of places for Stanton to hide. I've got teams guarding all the exits—but if we don't find him now, we'll have to call in the dogs and the search squads."

Scully took a deep breath, nearly choking on the dank, heavy air. She could imagine the fear and confusion Stanton was feeling as he ran through the darkness—his brain misinterpreting every signal from his nervous system, his psychotic paranoia sending him farther away from the people who were trying to help.

A few minutes passed in determined silence as they worked their way deeper into the tunnel. The ground was uneven around the tracks, covered in packed dirt and gravel. The walls were curved and roughly tiled, huge chunks of stone jutting out from a thick infrastructure of cement and steel.

Up ahead, Scully made out a sharp left turn. Beneath an orange emergency lantern stood one of the three police officers. The cop waved them forward, and Scully quickened her gait. She followed the turn up a slow incline and found herself at a junction between two tunnels. The subway track continued to the left, into the better-lit shaft. The other shaft angled into pure darkness, the walls and floor carved out of what looked to be jagged limestone.

"It's the new line," the officer explained. He was mildly overweight, and sweat ran in rivulets down the sides of his red face. "Still under construction. Leary spotted him 'bout thirty yards ahead. He and Kenyon went in after 'im."

Scully pointed her flashlight into the pitch-black shaft. The hungry air swallowed the orange beam after only a few yards. She glanced at Mulder and Barrett. The under-construction tunnel was a dangerous place to chase the carrier of a rare, fatal disease. She contemplated asking Barrett to call for backup—when a thunderous crack echoed off the limestone walls.

Scully's stomach lurched as she recognized the echoing report of a police-issue nine millimeter. She saw Mulder dart forward, and quickly rushed to follow. She could hear Barrett and the overweight officer a few steps behind her, but she forced them out of her thoughts, concentrating on the dark floor beneath her feet. Her flashlight beam bounced over slabs of stone and chunks of rail, and she tried to keep her feet as light as possible. She saw Mulder cut sharply to the right and found herself stumbling up a narrow incline. She guessed it was some sort of construction access—perhaps leading all the way to the surface. If so, there would be a team of officers waiting at the top. If they had heard the gunshot, they would already be streaming inside—

Scully nearly collided with Mulder's back as he reared up, his flashlight diving toward the floor. Scully added her own orange beam and saw the officer curled up against the stone wall. She recognized the man's bright red hair and quickly dropped to one knee. She saw a thin pool of blood seeping out from just above Leary's right ear. She reached forward, feeling for the man's pulse.

"He's alive," she whispered, applying gentle but constant pressure to the bleeding head wound. "Looks like he got hit with something, probably a metal pipe or a heavy rock. Maybe a skull fracture."

"Gun's still in his hand," Mulder responded, also dropping to his knees. "The barrel's warm. Three bullets missing from the chamber."

There were heavy footsteps from behind, and Scully quickly looked over her shoulder. She watched Barrett lumber the last few steps, followed by the overweight officer.

"Christ," Barrett said, looking at the downed man. Then she glanced up the narrow, black incline that seemed to continue on forever. "Where the hell is Kenyon?"

Scully turned her attention back to the man in front of her, trying to get a better look at his wound. "I need a medical kit right away. And we've got to get paramedics down here immediately."

"There's a kit back at the junction," the portly cop said. Barrett nodded at him, and he raced back in the direction they had come from. Meanwhile, Mulder had taken a few more steps up the dark incline. He glanced back at Scully, and she nodded.

Mulder started forward, his stun gun out ahead of him. Barrett quickly moved past Scully and the downed officer. Her intention was obvious. Mulder gestured toward the revolver in her gloved right hand. "Just remember, one of your officers is somewhere up ahead."

Barrett nodded. Scully called after them, as they faded into the darkness, "I'll follow when the paramedics get here—and I'll make sure he doesn't double back and get away. That's if he hasn't already reached the surface."

"He's not going to reach the surface," Barrett responded.

"Why is that?" Scully asked.

"Because it's a dead end. They capped this construction access off with three tons of cement two weeks ago." Barrett's voice trailed off as she and Mulder moved out of range.

Mulder's chest burned as the adrenaline pumped through his body. His eyes were wide-open, chasing the orange beam from his flashlight as he navigated across the uneven tunnel floor. He could hear Barrett's heavy gasps from a few feet behind his right shoulder; every few seconds a curse echoed into his ears as she struggled to keep up.

A dozen yards into the tunnel, the air began to taste vaguely metallic, and a thick, mildewy scent rose off the limestone walls. The tunnel seemed to be narrowing as they neared the surface, the curved walls closing in like the inner curls of an angry fist. Mulder slowed his pace, motioning for Barrett to keep quiet. They were close to the dead end—and that meant Perry Stanton and the other officer had to be nearby.

The tunnel took a sharp right, and suddenly Mulder found himself in the entrance to a small, rectangular corridor. Mulder moved the flashlight along the walls and saw wires and steel cables running in parallel twists across the limestone. Every few feet he made out little dark alcoves dug directly into the walls.

"Generator room," Barrett whispered as she joined him in the entrance to the corridor. "They powered the excavation equipment from generators housed in those empty alcoves. The cement wall should be right on the other side of this corridor."

Mulder pointed his flashlight toward the nearest generator alcove. The space looked to be about ten feet deep, and at least three feet in diameter. Easily enough room for a diminutive professor. *Or an officer's body.*

Mulder raised his stun gun and slowly advanced into the corridor. His neck tingled as he swung the flashlight back and forth, trying to illuminate as much area as possible. Despite his efforts, he was surrounded by black air. After a few feet, he realized the danger he was in; Stanton could hit him from either side, and he'd never see him coming. He was about to turn back toward Barrett—when his right foot touched something soft.

He quickly aimed the flashlight toward the ground. He saw wisps of blue, marred by spots of seeping red. Then the orange beam touched the shiny curves of a police badge.

He was about to call for Barrett when there was a sudden motion from his right. He turned just as the shape hit him, right below the shoulder. His stun gun went off, sparks flying through the darkness as the twin metal contacts glanced off a limestone wall.

Mulder's shoulder hit the ground, and the air was knocked out of him. His hands opened, and the flashlight and stun gun clattered away. The flashlight beam twirled through the blackness, and he caught sight of Perry Stanton's face rearing up above him, a look of anguish in his blue eyes. Then he saw Stanton's hands, clenched into wiry fists, rising above his head. Stanton leaped toward him, and Mulder shouted, raising his arms, wondering why the hell he always seemed to lose his weapon at the worst time—when, suddenly, there was a high-pitched buzzing. Stanton froze midstep, his eyes widening, his mouth curling open. Convulsions rocked his body, his muscles twisting into strange knots beneath his skin. He arched backward, his knees giving out. He collapsed to the ground a few feet away, his arms and legs twitching. Then he went still.

Mulder crawled to his knees as Scully entered the corridor, the stun gun hanging loosely from her right hand. Barrett rushed out from behind her, her revolver uselessly pointed at Stanton's prone body. "I couldn't get a clear shot. Christ, he came at you so fast."

Scully hurried to Mulder's side. She was out of breath, sweat dripping into her eyes. "Are you okay? Leary regained consciousness shortly after we separated. I decided he could wait for the paramedics on his own."

"Good timing, Scully. And even better aim."

Scully smiled. "Actually, I didn't aim. I just fired. You got lucky and saved yourself a nasty hangover."

Mulder gestured toward the cop lying in the middle of the corridor. "Officer Kenyon wasn't so lucky."

Scully followed her flashlight to the man and checked his pulse. Then she pushed his shoulder, turning him onto his side. She looked up, and Mulder saw the stricken look on her face. He glanced at the officer—and realized the man's head was facing the wrong direction. Stanton had twisted his neck 180 degrees, snapping his spinal column.

Barrett saw the dead officer and noisily reholstered her gun. "The damn animal. I don't care how sick he is—I'm gonna make sure he spends the rest of his life in a cell."

Mulder didn't respond to Barrett's angry comment. No matter how tragic the situation—he didn't believe Stanton was responsible. He thought about the anguished look in the professor's eyes—and the strange convulsions that had racked his body. It had almost seemed as if Stanton's muscles had been fighting his skin—struggling to tear through.

Mulder rose slowly and found his flashlight along the nearby wall. Then he trained the light on the downed professor. Stanton was lying on his back, his arms and legs twisted unnaturally at his sides. His eyes were wide open, his lips curled back. Mulder took a tentative step forward. *Something wasn't right.*

"Scully," he said, focusing the flashlight on Stanton's still chest, "I don't think he's breathing."

Scully stepped away from the dead officer. "He's just stunned, Mulder. The voltage running through the Taser contacts wasn't anywhere near enough to kill him."

Just the same, she moved to the little man's side and dropped to her knees. She carefully leaned forward, holding her ear above his mouth. Then her eyebrows rose, and she quickly touched the side of his neck with a gloved finger.

She drew her hand away, staring. Sudden alarm swept across her features. She tilted Stanton's head back, searching his mouth and throat for obstructions. Then she moved both hands over his chest and started vigorous CPR. Mulder dropped next to her, leaning over to give mouth-to-mouth. Scully stopped him with her hand. "Mulder, the lethargica."

Mulder shrugged her hand away. Even if she was right— and Stanton was infected with the blood-borne strain of encephalitis, Mulder knew the odds were enormously in his favor. Saliva, on its own, was not a likely carrier. And he couldn't get the vision of Emily Kysdale out of his mind. *Despite what he had done—this was a young woman's father.*

He pressed his mouth over Stanton's open lips and exhaled, inflating the man's chest. Scully continued the cardiac compressions, while Barrett stood watching. The minutes passed in silence, Mulder and Scully working together to bring the man back.

Finally, Scully stopped, leaning back from the body. Her red hair was damp with effort. "He's gone, Mulder. I don't understand. He didn't have a heart condition. He was strong enough to kill an officer. How could a stun gun have done this to him?"

Mulder didn't have an answer. As voices drifted into the corridor from out in the tunnel, a strange thought struck him. Leary had fired a total of three shots at Stanton—and hadn't slowed him down. Scully had hit him once with the electric stun gun, and he had died. Similarly, the John Doe had quite possibly fallen out of a moving van at seventy miles per hour, and had not received a scratch. Then two interns had shocked him with a defibrillator—*and he had died on the stretcher*.

"Scully," he started—but then stopped himself as a team of paramedics rushed a portable stretcher into the corridor. They were followed by a handful of uniformed officers. Barrett started shouting orders, and the paramedics rushed to the dead officer's side. Then they saw Stanton, and shouted for a second stretcher.

Mulder and Scully stepped out of the way as more paramedics moved into the corridor and lifted Stanton onto another stretcher. Scully watched with determined eyes. "I'm going to get to the bottom of this, Mulder. I'm going to perform the autopsy myself—and find out what really killed him."

Mulder felt the same level of determination move through him. Stanton was dead, but the case was far from over. Mulder was still convinced—Perry Stanton may have killed a nurse and a police officer, but he was not a murderer. He was a victim.

Mulder had seen it in his anguished eyes.

11

The digitized view screen flickered, then changed to a dull green color. Scully leaned back in the leather office chair, her arms stretched out in front of her. A radiology tech in a white lab coat hovered over her shoulder, his warm breath nipping at her earlobe. "Just another few seconds."

Scully tapped the edge of the keyboard beneath the screen, anticipation rising through her tense muscles. She pictured Stanton's body engulfed by the enormous, cylindrical MRI machine two rooms away. Mulder had remained with the body while she had accompanied the tech to the viewing room. They would regroup at the pathology lab downstairs, where they would be joined by Barrett and the investigator from the CDC.

"You want print copies as well, correct?" the tech asked, interrupting her thoughts. Scully nodded, and the tech hit a sequence of keys on a color laser printer next to the viewing screen. The young man was short and had thick, plastic-rimmed glasses. He was obviously enjoying her company—and the opportunity to show off his expertise with the MRI machine.

The MRI scan was not normal autopsy procedure, but

Scully had decided to take every extra measure possible to understand what had happened to Perry Stanton. In truth, she couldn't help feeling a tinge of guilt at Stanton's sudden death. She knew it was not really her fault—but she *had* fired the stun gun. At the very least, she needed to know why his body had so fatally overreacted.

"Here we go," the tech coughed, pointing at the screen. The printer began to hum just as the screen flickered again, and suddenly the dull green display was replaced by a shifting sea of gray. The gray conformed roughly to the shape of a human skull, representing a vertical cross section taken through the direct center of Perry Stanton's brain.

It took Scully less than a second to realize that all of her previous assumptions had to be reevaluated. Even without the autopsy, she knew for a fact that Stanton had not died from anything related to the encephalitis virus. "This can't be right."

The tech glanced at the screen, then turned to the printer and pulled out a stack of pages. The pages showed the same image, multiplied four times at slightly different angles. "This is the sequence you ordered. The machine's been in use all morning—and nobody's had a complaint."

Scully took the pictures from him, looking them over. She had never seen anything like it before. There was no edema, none of the cerebral swelling she would have expected from encephalitis lethargica—but Stanton's brain was anything but normal. She reached forward with a finger and traced a large, dark gray spot near the center of the picture. It was the hypothalamus, the gland that regulated the nervous system—but it was enormous, nearly three times as large as normal. Surrounding the engorged gland were half a dozen strange polyp-type growths, arranged in a rough semicircle. In all her time spent in pathology labs, she had never seen such a manifestation.

She rose quickly from the leather chair, the pictures tucked under her right arm. She wanted to get to that autopsy room as soon as possible. She watched as the tech hit a few computer keys, sending the viewing screen back to its original green. "We'll keep the pictures on file for as long as you'd like. Just ask for me if you need a second look."

The young man winked from behind his thick glasses, but Scully was already moving out into the radiology wing. Her thoughts were three floors away, in a basement lab filled with plastic organ trays and steel fluid gutters.

Scully never made it to the autopsy room. She had taken three steps out of the elevator when she heard Mulder's angry voice echoing through the cinder-block pathology ward.

She found her partner blockaded in the long central hall-way that ran down the center of the ward by three red-faced men wearing white lab coats. All of the coats had name tags, with tiny red seals that Scully recognized from her previous dealings with the CDC. Mulder's focus was the tallest man, a mid-fifties African American with thick eyelids and speckled gray hair. The man had his arms crossed against his chest, a disdainful look in his eyes. His name tag identified him as Dr. Basil Georgian, a senior infectious disease investigator. Scully caught the tail end of Mulder's heated interchange as she arrived at his side.

"This isn't merely an infectious disease scare," Mulder was near-shouting. "It's an FBI investigation. You don't have automatic priority or jurisdiction."

Georgian shook his head. "That's where you're wrong. We've got two reported cases of encephalitis lethargica. That's all the jurisdiction we need. Your murderer is dead, Agent Mulder. He's not going to go anywhere. Our virus is still very much alive—at least in one coma victim. We've got to make sure that's where it stays contained."

Mulder turned to Scully. "These guys seem to think they're going to run off with our body."

Scully looked at Georgian. Georgian shrugged. "Our superiors in Atlanta have already spoken to your superiors in Washington. Everyone agrees that it's more appropriate for us to handle the autopsy in our biocontainment lab in Hoboken— where the microbe can be properly studied, handled, and contained. We'll send you the reports when we're finished. Lethargica doesn't come around often, and we intend to figure out what it's doing in New York."

Without another word, Georgian spun on his heels and headed down the hallway, flanked by his two associates. Scully could see Stanton's stretcher being wheeled through a pair of double doors another ten yards beyond them—most likely to an underground garage, where an ambulance was waiting. Mulder started after them—but she stopped him with an outstretched hand. "They aren't going to change their minds. And they do have priority. From an official standpoint, our investigation is finished. Our perp is in custody—so to speak."

Mulder sighed, shaking his head. *"They'll send us their report?* That's ridiculous. This is our case."

"But the infectious disease makes it their concern. Mulder, I don't think we have much choice."

"So we just let it go?"

Scully didn't like the idea any more than he did. But they had to let the CDC scientists do their job. In the meantime— Scully still had the MRI scans. She pulled them out from under her arm and showed one of the views to Mulder. "While we're waiting for their autopsy report, we still have a lead to work with. This is one of the strangest MRIs I've ever seen. You see these polyps surrounding the hypothalamus?"

Mulder squinted, following her finger. To an untrained observer, the idiosyncrasy was fairly obtuse—but to Scully it was like a massive neon sign. "Given Stanton's sudden onset of psychosis, my guess is these polyps might have something to do with excess dopamine production. That would involve the hypothalamus—and explain the violence and disorientation."

"Dopamine," Mulder repeated. "That's a neurotransmitter, right? A chemical used by the nervous system to transmit information?"

Scully nodded. She wouldn't know for sure until she saw the CDC autopsy report, but it seemed a viable possibility. Still, it wasn't an explanation. "I'd like to run these pictures through the hospital's Medline system, see if anything like this has been reported before."

Mulder was still looking longingly in the direction of Stanton's body. "Scully, how many times have we worked with the CDC before?"

Scully raised an eyebrow. "A half dozen. Maybe more. Why?"

Mulder shrugged. "First the John Doe. Now Perry Stanton. It seems that people are going to great lengths to keep us from getting our hands on anyone involved in that skin transplant."

Scully resisted the urge to roll her eyes. "Mulder, I called the CDC about the lethargica—not the other way around."

Mulder gestured toward the MRI scans. "Does that look like lethargica?"

Scully paused. "The truth is, I have no idea what this is. That's why we need to find out if it's ever happened before."

Ten minutes later, Scully and Mulder huddled together in the corner of a cramped administrative office located one floor above the pathology ward. They had borrowed the office from a human-resources manager, bypassing any questions or possible red tape with a flick of their federal IDs. The office was sparse, containing little more than a desk, a few chairs, and an IBM workstation. In other words, it was a no-frills window into cyberspace.

The computer whirred as the inboard modem connected the two agents to the nationwide medical data base located in Washington, DC. Scully was closest to the screen, and her face glowed a techno blue as she maneuvered a plastic track ball through a half dozen menus loaded with options and navigational commands. Mulder had already placed one of the MRI pictures into the scanner next to the oversize processor, and in a few minutes they would begin to search the hundred million stored files for any possible match.

"This search should cover any MRIs, CAT scans, or skull X rays with similar manifestations," Scully said. "The Medline system is linked to every hospital in the country, and many throughout the world. If there's an associated syndrome, we'll surely find something—"

She paused, as the screen began to change. Suddenly, her eyes widened. Mulder read the notice at the top of the file that had suddenly appeared. "One match. New York Hospital, 1984."

Scully immediately realized the significance of the notice. As she skimmed the first paragraph of the file, her shock grew. The MRI scan had matched a pair of CAT scans taken on two inmates of Rikers Island in New York, shortly before their deaths. Both inmates had been part of some sort of volunteer experimental study performed in the early eighties. Even more stunning, according to the file, the study was conducted under the auspices of a fledgling biotech company located just outside Manhattan. Scully immediately recognized the company's name.

"Fibrol International," Mulder stated, his voice characteristically calm. "The same company that manufactures the red powder I found at the accident scene."

Scully didn't know what to say. She scrolled further down the file and found the two CAT scans that had heralded the match. In both images, she saw the same unmistakable pattern of polyps surrounding an enlarged hypothalamus. At the bottom of the file she found a link to an attached file. She hit the link, and the CAT scans were replaced by a single page of official-looking text.

"It's a prosecutorial assessment," she said, reading the heading. "There was a criminal investigation into the man behind the experimentation—Fibrol's founder and CEO, Emile Paladin. But it looks as though it never came to trial. According to this, the experiment had been conducted with full permission from the inmates. There's no explanation of the cause of death—just that it was accidental."

"Look at this," Mulder said, tapping a paragraph lower down in the assessment. There was a brief description of the nature of the experiment. "Skin transplantation, Scully. The experiment had to do with a radical new method of skin transplantation."

Scully rubbed her scalp with her fingers. It was hard to believe. Perry Stanton's brain had been ravaged by the same polyps that had killed the two inmates. But Stanton had not been the subject of an experimental transplantation.

"The red powder," Mulder continued. "It's the link—and Fibrol is the common denominator. We've got to find this Emile Paladin."

"This happened fifteen years ago," Scully responded. "And Perry Stanton wasn't part of any radical experiment."

"Not directly. But the John Doe might have been. And Stanton's wearing his skin."

Scully shook her head. What Mulder was implying was extremely unlikely. What sort of mechanism could transfer such a fatal cerebral reaction—through nothing more than a slab of harvested skin? It didn't make medical sense.

Still, she didn't know what to make of the connection to Fibrol. They needed to find out more about the experiment that had killed the two prisoners. And Mulder was right, they needed to track down Emile Paladin.

Maybe he could tell them how a skin transplant could ravage a man's brain from the inside—and what any of this had to do with the encephalitis lethargica that had felled the two med students.

Maybe Emile Paladin had some idea what had really happened to Perry Stanton.

12

The huge crimson atrium spilled out in front of the electronic revolving door like blood from a gunshot wound. Mulder paused to catch his breath as he and Scully stepped from inside the moving triangle of smoked glass. Twenty yards ahead stood an enormous black-glass desk, staffed by three men in similar dark blue suits. Behind the desk, the walls curved upward in magnificent swells of stone to the paneled black ceiling lined with more than a dozen miniature spotlights, a synthetic night sky gazing down upon a mock vermilion desert carved out of imported marble.

The interior of the Fibrol complex was nothing like the nondescript, blank-walled three-storied boxes he and Scully had seen from the highway. Even when they had passed through the twin security checkpoints on the way into the parking lot, Mulder had not realized the extent of the building's architectural deception. From the outside, Fibrol's main offices seemed no different from the hundreds of other corporate headquarters lodged in the grassy foothills that surrounded New York City. But the interior decor told a story more in line with the S&P reports the agents had scoured after leaving New York

Hospital. Fibrol had grown wealthy during the biotech boom of the late eighties, burgeoning into one of the nation's largest suppliers of burn-transplantation materials. Along with their most recent product—the antibacterial Dust—Fibrol held over three hundred patents on products in use at major hospitals and research centers. The company operated a half dozen burn clinics in the Northeast, and satellite offices in Los Angeles, Seattle, London, Tokyo, Paris, and Rome.

Mulder's shoes clicked against the polished marble as he and Scully bisected the huge atrium. He noticed a long glass case running along the wall to his right, containing strange-looking metal and plastic tools; each tool had a plaque explaining its use and date of development, and by the third scalpel-like object, Mulder realized the case was a visual history of the transplantation art. He looked more closely as he reached the last section of the case. He passed what appeared to be microscalpels and needles, lying next to a specialized microscope. To the right of the microscope, he recognized a laser device similar to the machine Dr. Bernstein had used to remove the tattoo. Then he came to the red powder, spread out in three equal piles above a metallic plaque.

He paused, tapping Scully's arm. The plaque was dated thirteen months ago, and contained a single caption in gilded script:

Antibacterial Compound 1279
EFFECTIVE IN REDUCING CONSEQUENTIAL SEPTICITY
AFTER RADICAL TRANSPLANTATION

Mulder was about to ask for a medical definition of "consequential septicity" when a high voice impaled his right ear. "Agents Mulder and Scully? I trust you had no problem following my directions?"

Mulder looked up from the glass case. One of the blue-suited men had risen from behind the black desk. Just a kid, really—he looked no older than twenty-three, with short blond hair and an acne-covered face. His thin limbs were swimming in his suit. Scully nodded in his direction. "Are you the man we spoke to on the phone?"

The kid smiled, coming around the edge of the desk. "Dick Baxter. I set up your appointment with Dr. Kyle, our director of research. He's waiting in his office. I'll take you right to him."

Mulder and Scully shook Baxter's hand. Enthusiasm leaked out of the kid's every pore.

"Dr. Kyle?" Mulder asked. He remembered seeing Julian Kyle's name in the S&P files. Kyle was responsible for a number of Fibrol's patents, spanning back to the company's inception. Still, Mulder had hoped their FBI status would get them access to someone higher up than a director of research.

Then again, Mulder didn't yet know enough about Fibrol's leadership to complain. He and Scully had been hoping to find Emile Paladin still at the helm of the company—but to their surprise, they had discovered that Fibrol's founder and CEO had died in an accident overseas shortly after the experiment involving the Rikers Island prisoners. Since then, the company had gone through two acting CEOs, and at present no CEO was in place. Perhaps Julian Kyle was as close to the company's true leadership as Mulder and Scully were going to get.

"You asked to speak to the person in charge of our East Coast operations, didn't you?" Baxter continued. "Julian Kyle heads up all new projects at Fibrol. His finger is on the pulse of everything that goes on around here."

Mulder and Scully followed the young man as he strolled past the desk to an opaque glass door embedded in the marble wall. Baxter paused, pressing his hand against a plastic circular plate next to the door. There was a short metallic whir, and the door slid open, revealing a long corridor with matching crimson walls.

"Pretty high-tech," Scully commented.

"Infrared imaging," Baxter said, smiling proudly. "It's a lot more comfortable than a retinal scanner, and certainly more accurate than a thumb pad. Of course, it's much more expensive than either technology."

Mulder glanced back toward the spectacular front atrium. "Doesn't look like Fibrol is too concerned with expense."

Baxter laughed. "Not lately. We've got a number of major new developments coming down the pipeline. Already, our foreign division has tripled in revenues—just in the past two years. The new board of directors has decided to update our look, to reflect this new level of success. They've redesigned much of the complex; you should see the new labs in the basement—we're talking major high-tech."

Mulder raised his eyebrows, glancing at Scully as they followed the young man through the security door and into the long corridor. "You seem pretty excited about the changes. Is that why they have you working the door?"

Baxter laughed, pulling at the lapels of his blue suit. "Actually, I'm a Ph.D. student at NYU. I'm working here through the summer—but I hope to be hired full-time after I graduate. Maybe start as a junior scientist and claw my way up in the research department. Beats the hell out of academia, and you get to really see your work transformed into something useful."

Mulder kept his eyes moving as they sliced through the inner corridors of the complex. The place was built like a maze, and Mulder was reminded of the interior floor plan of the Pentagon. They passed many unmarked offices, each with opaque glass security doors. None of the doors had knobs. Instead, each was fitted with the same plastic handplate. A very efficient security system, probably routed through a computer center somewhere in the complex. Mulder also noticed closed-circuit television cameras at ten-foot intervals along the hallway ceiling. The cameras were painted the same crimson as the walls. He touched Scully's arm, pointing. "Fibrol seems to take its security fairly seriously. Cameras, infrared access panels, and the twin security checks on the way into the fenced parking lot."

Baxter overheard his comment and nodded vigorously. "Oh, yes. We're very concerned with keeping our work private. You'd be surprised at the sort of thing that goes on in the biotech industry. Theft, sabotage, corporate spying, Internet hacking—just last month we had an incident with the janitorial staff. A cleaning lady on the third floor was caught stealing the shredded paper from a central wastebasket."

"Shredded paper?" Scully asked.

Baxter had a serious look on his face. "A hacker employed by a rival biotech company could have extracted password information from the stolen garbage. Once inside our computer banks, there's no telling what sort of damage they could have done."

Mulder stifled a smile. It seemed he did not have a monopoly on paranoia. Then again, perhaps Baxter was right. Mulder knew that the biotech industry relied on its secrets to survive. Patents could only protect inventions that were already complete—every step along the way was a fierce race. And judging from the lavish front atrium with its expensive marble walls, the payoff could be impressive.

Baxter stopped in front of another glass door, again placing his palm against an infrared panel. After two clicks the door slid open, and Baxter gestured for the two agents to step inside.

"Dr. Kyle will answer all your questions from here on out. I hope you enjoy your visit."

Mulder could see the sincerity in Baxter's eyes. The kid was nearly floating on the balls of his feet, not an ounce of cynicism in his slender body. As long as he kept his attitude, he'd probably go far in the corporate-industrial world. *Great brochure material.*

Mulder and Scully thanked him, and together they stepped into Julian Kyle's office.

"Damn it! Just stay where you are. I'll get them back on in a second."

Mulder stood frozen next to Scully in complete darkness, his skin tingling as his pupils tried to dilate. The lights had gone off the second the door had slid shut behind them. He had caught a brief glance of a stocky man in a white lab coat moving toward them across a large, well-appointed office—then everything had gone black. A second later, there had been a loud crash, followed by the sound of breaking glass.

"It's this new environmentally sensitive system," the frustrated voice continued from a corner of the room. "It's all Bill Gates's fault. He had to go and build that intelligent house, and suddenly every new designer wants to copy his technology. The system is supposed to shut the lights when you *leave* the room—not when someone else enters. Hold on, here we go."

There was a metallic cough, and suddenly a panel of fluorescent lights flickered to life. The office was about thirty feet across, square, with two wide picture windows overlooking the parking lot and the same crimson walls that lined the building's corridors. There was a glass desk at one end of the airy room, covered with fancy computer equipment and neat little stacks of CD-ROMs. In front of the desk crouched a black leather love seat with high armrests. Directly to the left of the love seat, a display case's chrome frame lay surrounded by a pile of broken glass. Half-buried in the glass was a shiny plastic rectangle painted in colors running from pink to beige.

"Shit. If it's broken, I'm going to charge it to the board. This whole reconstruction was their idea. I thought we were doing fine with white walls, doorknobs, and light switches."

Julian Kyle swept out of the far corner of the room, his white coat flapping behind him. He was built like a fire hydrant, with solid shoulders, stumpy legs, and a cube-shaped head. His silver hair was cropped close to the planes of his skull, and his face was remarkably chiseled and unwrinkled for a man of his age. Sixty-five, Mulder guessed, but it was difficult to be sure. There was a vigorous spring in the doctor's step as he rushed to the destroyed display case and carefully reached for the large plastic object.

"Can we help?" Scully asked, as both agents moved forward. Kyle shook his head, carefully lifting the object and shaking away the broken glass. Mulder saw that it was some sort of model, made up of different-colored horizontal layers, each a few inches in height.

"An award from the International Burn Victim's Society," Kyle explained, reverently checking the model for scratches. "It's a three-dimensional cross section of an undamaged segment of human skin. See, it's even got the melanocyte layer—done in bronze leaf."

Mulder looked more closely at the model as Kyle placed it gently on an empty corner of his glass desk. The cross section was divided into three parts, showing the epidermis at the top, then the thick, beige dermis, and finally the white layer of subcutaneous fat. Tiny blood vessels and twisting branches of nerves curled through the middle section, winding delicately around tubular sweat glands and dark, towering follicles of hair. Mulder was struck by the intricacy of the skin's structure. He knew skin was an organ—the body's largest—but he had never considered what that meant. To Mulder, skin was just *there*. It could be rough or soft, porcelain like Scully's or stained and creased like the Cancer Man's.

Kyle noticed Mulder's focus as he moved to the other side of his desk. "Most people suffer from a misconception when it comes to skin. They assume it's something static; like a leather coat wrapped around your body to keep your skeleton warm. But nothing could be further from the truth. The skin is an amazing organ. It's in a constant state of motion; basal cells migrating upward to replace the dying epidermal cells, nerves reacting to inputs from the outside, blood vessels feeding muscles and fat, sweat glands struggling to regulate the body's temperature as the cells twist and stretch to accommodate movement. Not to mention the constant healing and recovery process, or the battle to stay moist and elastic."

Mulder lowered himself next to Scully onto the leather two-seater as Kyle took a seat behind the desk, holding his hands out in front of him, palms inward. He wriggled his fingers as if typing on an invisible keyboard. "We never notice our skin until there's something wrong with it. A cut, a rash—or a burn. Then we realize how important it really is. How much we'd be willing to pay to get it back to normal."

Mulder nodded, thinking of the building's front atrium. "Enough to import most of the marble in Italy."

Kyle laughed. Then his smile turned down at the corners, as he waved his hands at the walls on either side. "And have this entire complex dyed crimson. It had to be the worst decision this new board's ever made. Yes, we specialize in burn-transplant materials—but do we need the constant, fiery reminder on every wall in this damn complex? Still, they tell me that it impresses our foreign visitors, the corporate honchos from Tokyo, Seoul, and now Beijing."

"Sounds like business is good," Scully commented.

"Literally," Kyle beamed. "Our new product line is helping thousands of people survive transplants that would have seemed pointless just a few years ago. We've got new salve bandages, a whole new stock of microscalpels, an innovative new dry-chemical wrap—just to mention a few of our recent breakthroughs."

Mulder listened to the laundry list in silence. Julian Kyle seemed as enthusiastic about Fibrol as the kid at the front desk was—only Kyle's fervor had an edge of self-importance to it. It was as if he was telling them that Fibrol had accomplished these things directly because of his efforts.

"Actually," Scully said, as Kyle's monologue finally drew to a close, "it's your company's past that interests us at the moment. Specifically, an episode in 1984 involving two prisoners at Rikers Island."

Kyle raised his gray eyebrows. The motion pulled at the taut skin around his jaw, revealing a perfectly centered cleft. His face had an almost military bearing—and Mulder guessed he would have been just as comfortable in fatigues and an army helmet as he was in the white lab coat. "Forgive my surprise, Agent Scully. It's been a long time since anyone has asked about that. It's something we've put way behind us— ever since Emile's death."

The air in the small office had changed, as if the molecules themselves had somehow tightened along with Kyle's mood. Mulder tried to read the man's expression, searching for any sense of guilt or signs of hidden knowledge. But the man's surprise seemed sincere.

"It was an unfortunate incident," Kyle continued. "And I'm afraid I don't have much to tell you. Emile Paladin was a very private, controlling man. The experiment was entirely under his control, conducted in his own private clinic a hundred miles upstate. It had something to do with a new transplant procedure—but beyond that, I don't know any of the details."

Mulder saw the frustrated lines appear on Scully's forehead. She had expected a simple answer and instead, they had run into another wall. Kyle spread his hands out against the desk, continuing in a casual voice. "After the criminal charges were dropped, Paladin announced the experimental procedure an unsalvageable failure and refocused the company toward the development of assistance products, rather than transplant techniques. Barely six months later, he died—but Fibrol continued to grow in the new direction."

Mulder shifted against the leather couch. Kyle had told them exactly what they already knew from the S&P reports. The blame had been shifted to Fibrol's founder, and since his death the company had moved in a different direction.

Scully cleared her throat, getting straight to the point. "Dr. Kyle, we have reason to believe that an individual died this morning from complications similar to those that killed the two prisoners. Do you have any idea how that might be possible?"

Kyle stared at her in shock. "Not at all. As I said, Paladin was the only one who knew anything about the experiment, and Paladin died almost fifteen years ago. I can't imagine how anything so recent could be connected."

Scully cocked her head. "We read that Paladin died in some sort of accident overseas?"

Kyle nodded. "A hiking accident in Thailand. It was his second home, ever since the Vietnam War. He had been stationed in a MASH unit, and after the incident he had wanted to take some time off in a serene, comfortable place. He had a home outside a little fishing village called Alkut, two hundred miles east of Bangkok. He died while climbing in the mountains around his home."

"And after his death," Scully interrupted. "Who inherited control of the company? Did he leave behind any family?"

"A brother. Andrew Paladin. But although Andrew is the major stockholder, he doesn't have any involvement with the company. You see, Andrew's what you'd call a recluse. He served in the Vietnam War about the same time as his brother, and in the early seventies an injury landed him in Emile's MASH unit in Alkut. After the war he settled in Thailand, and he hasn't left the country since."

"Is there some way we can get in touch with him?" Scully asked. "To see if he has any more information on Paladin's experiment?"

Kyle shrugged. "Not that I know of. He employed a lawyer in Bangkok around the time of his brother's death, but we haven't heard from him in more than ten years. From what I understand, nobody is even sure of his current address. But I'd doubt he'd be useful, even if you found him. As I said, Paladin was extremely independent. He kept his work private."

Kyle crossed his arms against his chest. To him, the interview was ending. But Mulder wasn't near finished. He leaned close to the desk, abruptly changing tack. "Dr. Kyle, tell us about Antibacterial Compound 1279."

For the first time in the short interview, Kyle's calm seemed to break. It was barely perceptible—a tightening of the skin around his eyes—and it vanished as quickly as it had appeared. But Mulder was acutely attuned to the signs of human discomfort—and he knew when someone suddenly found himself unprepared.

"The Dust?" Kyle responded. "I'm amazed you've even

heard of it. We only received the patent last year. It's going to be one of our major market leaders within the next decade. Why are you interested in our antibacterial powder? It's a very recent development—it had nothing at all to do with Emile Paladin's work."

Mulder glanced at Scully. He had not mentioned any connection to Paladin's experiment—Kyle had made the jump himself. Scully followed Mulder's lead, her voice stiff but nonconfrontational. "Dr. Kyle, yesterday morning we found a sample of your powder in a breakdown lane on the FDR Drive."

Kyle wrinkled the skin above his eyes. Then he rubbed a hand against his jaw. "That's certainly strange. None of the New York hospitals are using the Dust yet. Still, I guess it could have come from a shipment between a couple of our clinics. Our largest burn center is twenty miles north of here, and we have a research laboratory down in Hoboken, New Jersey. It's something I can easily check out."

Scully nodded—but Mulder wasn't about to leave it at that. "We'd also like to consider another possibility. Could the Dust have been left behind by a recent transplant patient?"

Kyle stared at him in silence. Then he laughed curtly. "That's extremely unlikely. In fact, I'd say it's damn near impossible. The Dust is used only on radical transplant patients. These are not patients who get up and walk around. They can't even survive transport in ambulances. There's no way such a patient would be found out of a hospital. Not even for a moment."

Mulder was surprised by Kyle's adamant tone. Even if it was unlikely—was it really impossible that a burn clinic might have decided to transport a patient, despite the risks? "Well, perhaps you could show us some data on the powder, to help us understand. Maybe a list of the types of patients you've used it on—"

"I'm sorry," Kyle interrupted, rising from his chair. He was still smiling, but his eyes were now miles away. "But I really need to speak to the board before I can get to any of our records. I don't mean to be difficult—but this is a very competitive time for our company. I need to go through the proper channels before I release any proprietary information."

Kyle hadn't mentioned a search warrant, but it was obvious to Mulder that it would take a warrant to get the information he'd requested. The question was—was Kyle just being a good, loyal employee? Or was there something else going on?

Scully got up from the love seat first, and Mulder followed as Kyle hit an intercom buzzer on his desk, then strolled toward the couch. Mulder was much taller than the doctor—but still, Kyle cut an impressive, intimidating figure. As Kyle showed the two agents to the door, Mulder finally asked the question that had been on his mind since the beginning of the interview. "Dr. Kyle—I hope you don't mind my asking—but did you serve in the military?"

Scully glanced at Mulder, surprised by the question. But Kyle simply smiled. "For twelve years. I joined up in the mid-fifties. I was promoted to major during Vietnam. It's where I met Emile Paladin. I served under him in Alkut. It's where I was first introduced to the art of transplantation. I saw firsthand how important the skin could be—and how easily, and painfully, it could be damaged."

There was a near fanatic's determination in Kyle's eyes. Mulder had no doubt that Kyle would do anything necessary to protect Fibrol from danger—real or perceived.

"I'm sorry I couldn't be more helpful," Kyle continued, as he put his palm against the plate next to the door. "Mr. Baxter will show you back to your car. I'll be in touch if I find any more information for you."

The door hissed open, and Mulder and Scully were once again face to face with Dick Baxter. They followed the smiling young man back through the network of crimson hallways.

It wasn't until they were back in the privacy of their rental Chevrolet that Mulder finally told Scully what he was thinking. "Kyle knows something. About the red powder—and about Paladin's experiment. We need to keep digging."

Scully was momentarily silent, her hands on the dashboard in front of her. Finally, she shrugged. "It won't be easy. Emile Paladin died nearly fifteen years ago. According to Kyle, he took the secrets of his experiment with him."

Mulder wasn't going to accept anything Kyle had said at face value. Paladin might have died years ago—but his experiment was more than history. It was somehow involved in the Stanton case. "And what about the red powder? And the link to the John Doe?"

"I thought Kyle was pretty convincing. It could have fallen out of a shipment of medical supplies. The link with the John Doe is still unproven."

Mulder turned the ignition, and the car kicked to life. "Fibrol's involved; the MRI pictures don't lie. Stanton was another victim of Emile Paladin's transplantation experiment. And if Kyle can't tell us how that's possible—then we've got to find someone who can."

He could see that Scully was thinking along the same lines. As they were waved through the first security checkpoint at the edge of the parking lot, she put words to his thoughts. "Andrew Paladin. The recluse brother. He might have been the last person to speak to Emile Paladin before he died."

Mulder nodded, glancing at the boxlike complex shrinking

rapidly in the Chevy's rearview mirror. They could spend weeks, even months, trying to crack through Fibrol's nondescript facade; but Mulder had a strong feeling that the answers they were looking for lay all the way on the other side of the world.

13

 Left alone in his windowless office, Julian Kyle placed both hands flat on the cold surface of his glass desk, staring intently at the two imprints in the leather couch across from him. He wondered how many millions of plate-shaped epidermal cells rested in the microscopic canyons in the leather, how many millions of infinitesimal, cellular reminders of the FBI agents floated in the invisible drafts of air. He thought about Agent Mulder's dark, intelligent eyes, and Scully's determined, penetrating voice. He thought about the questions they had asked—and their reactions to his answers.

Kyle considered himself good at reading people—but the two agents were a mystery. Their texture was all wrong. They did not seem like the carbon-copy intelligence officers Kyle had dealt with many times in his career. They were smart, and they would not give up easily.

Kyle thought for a long moment, then reached beneath his desk and hit a small button located just above his knees. A few seconds later the door to his office slid open.

He watched as the tall young man with slicked-back sable hair slid into the room and tossed himself onto the couch, his long legs hooked nonchalantly over one of the armrests. The man's narrow eyes flickered playfully toward the shattered display case beside the desk, a smirk settling on his lips. "Having a bad day, Uncle Julian?"

Kyle grimaced as the man's heavy Thai accent trickled into his ears. He hated the artificial familiarity. He had watched the young man grow up—but thankfully, there was no physical relationship between them. Kyle considered himself a religious, moral man. The man was something altogether different. Warped. Perverted. Dangerous. *All of his father's sins—without any of his father's virtues.*

"We have a problem, Quo Tien," Kyle responded, keeping the conversation as short as possible. "The situation has not yet been contained."

The young man raised an eyebrow. Then he stretched his arms above his head. Kyle could see the sinewy muscles stretching beneath Quo Tien's caramel skin. An involuntary shudder moved through Kyle's shoulders. He had served in Vietnam, had known many dangerous men; but the Amerasian man truly terrified him. He knew the pleasure Quo Tien took in his work, the sheer, almost sexual enthusiasm that accompanied his acts of silent violence. For years, he had witnessed the limitless exploitation of the child's perverse appetite.

He hated the fact that he, too, had taken part in that exploitation. And that conditions might force him to use the young man once again. "These two FBI agents aren't going to be easily dissuaded. They can't be allowed to get any closer."

"You worry too much," Quo Tien interrupted, running a hand through his dark hair. "They don't even have a body to work with. As long as we remain a step ahead of them, they'll have nothing but guesses."

Kyle rubbed his square jaw. Quo Tien was right—but Kyle didn't like to take chances. Especially so close to the final phase of the experiment. "At this stage, even guesses can be danger-ous."

The Amerasian laced his fingers together, then shrugged. "As always, I eagerly await your orders."

Kyle searched the young man's eyes for some deeper mean-ing—but saw nothing but limitless black pits. He took a deep breath, slowly reaching for his phone. "It's not *my* orders you follow, Quo Tien. Don't you ever forget that. For both our sakes."

14

 Scully watched the creases appear above Assistant Director Skinner's eyeglasses as he drummed his fingers against the open file on his desk. As usual, Scully felt stiff and uncomfortable in Skinner's wood-paneled office on the third floor of the FBI head-quarters in Washington. Mulder looked much more relaxed on the shiny leather couch to her right, but she knew it was a well-practiced facade. Her own turbulent alliance with their supervisor did not compare to the chaotic, sometimes violent relationship between Mulder and the bald, spectacled ex-Marine who governed both their careers.

Well over six feet tall, Skinner had a professional athlete's body, chiseled features, and stone gray eyes. A perpetual frown was carved above his prominent jaw, and the packed muscles in his neck and shoulders struggled against the material of his dignified, dark suit. Power emanated from every inch of his body, and Scully had no doubt that Skinner could easily snap Mulder over one knee. At the same time, the man's brutish physique belied an intense and brilliant deductive mind; there wasn't much that went on in Washington Skinner didn't know about. That knowledge—and Skinner's ambiguous association with both the established military and the shadowy men behind the scenes—made him a natural target for Mulder's paranoia. Likewise, Mulder's unorthodox methods and non-conformist beliefs constantly antagonized Skinner, sometimes pushing him past the point of control. Scully prayed the afternoon meeting would be brief.

Skinner closed the file and crossed his arms against his chest. He shifted his gaze toward the window, letting the hazy sunlight play across the curves of his glasses. Behind him, Skinner's office was spartan, another reflection of the AD's personality. Aside from the wood paneling and the pristine leather furniture, the only distinguishing possessions were a colorful U.S. wall map, and a framed photo of Janet Reno by the door. The map was covered in plastic pushpins, each representing an open federal case. Scully could not help but notice the large white pin jutting out of Manhattan.

"Red powder picked off of a highway and a few MRI scans," Skinner finally commented, still gazing out the window. "It's not much to go on. Especially when you consider the expense, and the red tape involved."

Scully nodded. "We wouldn't be here if there was any other way, sir. It's a unique situation. Perry Stanton's condition—a condition that caused him to commit murder—needs to be explained. At the moment, Agent Mulder and I believe that Fibrol is a dead end; even with a search warrant, it's doubtful we'll find any evidence of Emile Paladin's work, or any connection to the current MRIs. We believe that the only possible source of new information is in Thailand."

Skinner turned back from the window. "Andrew Paladin. The deceased subject's brother. You say he lives in the vicinity of a town called Alkut."

"It's a tiny fishing village on the southeastern coast," Scully continued. She had researched Alkut by airphone during the

THE X-FILES

short shuttle flight from New York. "The population is around five thousand, mostly fishermen and their families. No tourist industry as of yet, because the town is still inaccessible by train or airplane. There's no local police force to speak of, and not much of a municipal structure. There's no way to reach Andrew Paladin through the local authorities."

Skinner nodded. "What about one of our foreign agencies? State Department, CIA, perhaps even the DEA? They've got people all over Southeast Asia."

Mulder coughed, crossing his legs. He avoided looking Skinner directly in the eyes. "Our investigation is still in a fetal stage, sir. Andrew Paladin is not the final step—just the necessary next step. It's not simply a matter of having him answer a few questions."

Skinner raised his eyebrows. He leaned back in his high-backed chair. "Agent Scully? Do you agree with Agent Mulder? Is Thailand the necessary next step?"

Scully took a deep breath. She did not relish the idea of traveling halfway around the world. But she knew there was little choice; Stanton's MRIs were impossible to explain—and as long as his death was a mystery, the case was still open. The only real clue they had was the connection to Fibrol and Emile Paladin's fifteen-year-old experiment. In New York, that translated to a corporate dead end; Julian Kyle could hide behind his board of directors for months, and the investigation would get nowhere. That had left them with two options: leave the case standing—or follow the only real avenue left open.

Scully met Skinner's gaze. She knew his decision would be based on her answer. "If we want to question Andrew Paladin about his brother's activities, we're going to have to do it in person. That's if we can find him at all."

Skinner paused, watching her expression. Finally, he nodded.

*   *   *

Six hours later, Scully's fingers dug into a thick faux-leather seat cushion as the 747 wide-body lurched upward, ambushed by turbulent swirls of dense black air. There was a sudden moment of weightlessness; then the plane rolled sickeningly to the right. Scully glanced toward the oval window next to her—but it was like staring into a pool of oil, shades of sable broken only by the distant flash of lightning.

"It's moments like these that make me glad I'm a believer," Mulder commented from the seat to Scully's right, nervously stretching his arms out in front of him. "I think I've discovered twelve new religions in the last five minutes alone."

"I'm still hanging on to the laws of aerodynamics and the statistics of air travel," Scully responded. "But if it gets any worse, I'll be getting my rosary beads out of the overhead compartment. This is pretty damn intense."

"Southeast Asia in July, Scully. The fun's just getting started. In a couple of weeks this will look like a calm spring evening."

Scully turned away from the window and tried to concentrate on the laptop computer resting precariously on her knees. The screen had changed from green to gray as the internal modem struggled to extract information from the static-ridden airphone link Scully had established before the storm set in. She tapped her fingers against the keyboard, trying to shake life into her fatigued muscles. It had been a long, tedious flight. Even in the relative comfort of Thai Airline's business class, twenty-two hours felt like an eternity.

But as she had told Assistant Director Skinner, there had been no other choice. They needed information, and the only true source was in Thailand.

"Andrew Paladin," Scully said out loud, as her laptop suddenly cleared. The picture took up half of the screen, and Mulder leaned closer to get a better look. Tall, muscular, with wide shoulders and a blond crew cut. Wearing a green infantry uniform, arms stiffly at his side. It was obviously an army recruitment photo, and Andrew Paladin had the dead look of a career foot soldier in his narrow blue eyes.

"He looks a lot heavier than his brother," Mulder commented. "Wider in the shoulders, maybe a few inches shorter."

Scully nodded. They had already looked through a dozen photos of Emile Paladin, most taken around the time of the Fibrol scandal involving the prisoners. Emile Paladin had been a handsome man, long and thin, with intelligent eyes and an amiable smile. He had photographed well—and often. Especially in the years just before his death. But Andrew Paladin was a different story. "This is all I can find, Mulder. I've been through every data bank I can think of, and all I'm getting is an army recruitment photo and a paragraph of statistics. Born in upstate New York like his brother, served two years in South Vietnam before getting wounded in action. He was twenty-two years old at the time, and a pretty good soldier. Decorated twice for heroism, consistently good reports from his commanding officers. But after his injury, the reports end. He was sent to his brother's MASH unit in Alkut—and pretty much disappeared from record."

Mulder caught the side of the laptop as the airplane jerked hard to the left. "What about his wounds? Anything in his file about where he was hit—or how badly?"

Scully shook her head. She had skimmed Andrew Paladin's brief military file while Mulder had watched the third in-flight movie, *something about a family of talking cats.* "Well, his injuries were bad enough to take him out of the war. He received a medical discharge three months after arriving in Alkut. But there are no specifics in his file. It's odd, Mulder; the army is usually pretty good about this sort of thing. There should be some sort of medical chart, something the VA hospital system could refer to in case of future problems."

"Well," Mulder said, thinking out loud, "Emile Paladin was in charge of his brother's medical care, right? If he had wanted to keep the details off the record, he wouldn't have had much trouble."

Scully caught her breath as the lights in the cabin flickered, then resumed. The storm seemed to be getting worse, huge raindrops crackling against the Plexiglas double window. "Why would he want to keep his brother's medical state a secret?"

Mulder paused, as if debating bringing something out in the open. As usual, he decided not to edit his thoughts. "Emile Paladin might have had something to hide. He might still have something to hide."

Scully stared at him. "Mulder, Emile Paladin died fifteen years ago."

"Right on the tail of a scandal that could have landed him in jail—or threatened the company he had built."

Scully paused. "So you think the timing of his death is a bit convenient."

"And the circumstances, Scully. He died in an accident overseas. His recluse brother inherited controlling interest in his company—but remained completely invisible, without even an address or a phone number on record. A brother whose history seems to have ended more than twenty-five years ago—again, in mysterious circumstances."

Scully shook her head. "I agree that there are a lot of loose ends. But to suggest that Emile Paladin faked his death—for what reason, Mulder? And how does Andrew Paladin fit in?"

Mulder shrugged. "Perhaps Emile Paladin wanted to continue his research in secret. Perhaps his brother is helping him keep his work private. And perhaps, somehow, Emile Paladin let something leak out—something that caused Perry Stanton's rampage and death. Something that forced a cover-up that led to the murder of two medical students."

Scully leaned back in her seat, her thoughts as turbulent as the air outside. Mulder's paranoia had caused him to jump beyond the evidence—to conclusions he could not back up with facts. There was no reason to believe that Emile Paladin was still alive. Nor was there any way to connect the polyps inside Perry Stanton's skull with the deaths of the two medical students—much less classify their deaths as murder. But at the same time, Scully knew better than to discard Mulder's theory out of hand. His intuition—as insane as it often seemed—was unparalleled. "We're not here to chase a dead man, Mulder. We're here to find Andrew Paladin."

Mulder was about to respond when the 747 suddenly dipped forward, the cabin lights blinking three times. A heavily accented voice explained that the airplane was beginning its descent toward Bangkok International Airport. Mulder waited for the captain to turn his attention back to the storm before clearing his throat. "You're right. Andrew Paladin is where we have to start. But I don't think this investigation is going to end with a few answers from a recluse brother."

Scully let the thought sit in the air between them, as the airplane slipped downward through the frantic black air.

Six rows back, Quo Tien's long fingers crawled spiderlike down the window by his shoulder, chasing the teardrops of rain on the other side. He could just barely see the cluttered lights of Bangkok breaking through the cloud cover as the 747 sank toward the waiting runway. The sprawling metropolis evoked conflicting emotions inside of him; he thought about the years he had spent in the city's nocturnal alleys, practicing his art, keeping himself toned and in tune—waiting for the next call to service. For seven years, Bangkok had fed his existence—but only Alkut had ever been his home.

Tien was a half-breed, the son of an American soldier and a

Thai prostitute; in his culture, that made him polluted, untouchable. Still, he had never cursed the nature of his birth. The distance between himself and the children he had grown up with had nothing to do with the muted color of his skin. It had always been a matter of appetite. *A matter of hunger*.

He thought about the two agents seated a few yards away from him, and his stomach churned, a heat dancing up through his body. A smile spilled across his thin face, and he closed his eyes, caressed by the rhythm of the storm.

15

Twelve hours later, the rain was coming down in wide gray sheets as Mulder navigated a rented four-wheel-drive Jeep down a road rapidly changing from dirt to mud. Scully had a U.S. Army surplus map open on her lap, and she was struggling to match the surroundings with twenty-year-old military notations. Mulder could see that she was both tired and frustrated; every time the Jeep hit one of the crater-sized potholes that seemed to spring up out of nowhere, Scully let out a curse, strands of wet hair flopping into her eyes. In truth, Mulder sympathized with her worsening disposition. Hunched forward over the jerking steering wheel, sweat running down his back and chest, his fingers aching from the pitted road and the Jeep's overtaxed, circa 1960's manual transmission—he felt anything but fresh.

So far, Thailand was not the tropical paradise he had imagined. The beauty of the country had gotten lost somewhere in the midst of the rain, the oppressive heat, the choking humidity—and the increasingly primitive conditions. Mulder had already stripped down to his thin cotton shirt and trousers—and still his skin felt prickly where the material stuck to him, each breath catching in his throat as he strove to adapt to the nearly gelatinous air.

Ahead, the road seemed almost a living thing, serpentine twists of dark mud slithering between the lush green trees. The sky had long ago vanished behind a canopy of rain clouds, and the Jeep's fog lights danced like ghosts as Mulder fought to keep the vehicle from pitching into the encroaching forest on either side.

Physical conditions aside, it had been an exhausting twelve hours since he and Scully had landed in Bangkok. After deplaning, they had been met at the terminal by their military liaison, an army corporal in dress uniform with a permanent sneer embedded in his chiseled face. Timothy Van Epps was a career soldier with little time or regard for FBI agents so far from their jurisdiction—and it was obvious he had been given the assignment at the last minute, without his approval. After taking the agents to a small, lifeless office behind the airport customs desk, he had rushed them through a brief discussion of the present state of U.S. relations with the Thai monarchy, and had handed them a sheet of printed directions to Alkut. Along with the directions came a map of the tiny fishing village and the surrounding geography—and a disclaimer: "Things may be a hell of a lot different in real life than they appear on that piece of toilet paper. We haven't had much use for that area since Vietnam—so most of those notations are twenty-five years old at best. If you want, you can fax me an updated version when you're done with your little trip."

Mulder doubted the U.S. Army needed FBI agents to update its information—especially in a region of Southeast Asia where it had once deployed extensive military resources. It was much more likely that Van Epps had been ordered—or had taken it upon himself—to be less than helpful. Not because of some sort of overarching conspiracy—although Scully would have assumed that was where Mulder's line of thought was heading—but simply because it was in the military's nature. The military often saw the FBI as an errant little sibling—to be tolerated, but certainly not encouraged. Especially when the little brother wanted to join in the fun overseas.

After giving them the map and information, Van Epps had escorted them to a government sedan with diplomatic plates and transported them from the airport to Hua Lamphong, Bangkok's main train station. The trip had been mind-numbing after the tedious flight. The Thai capital redefined the notion of an urban jungle: narrow, tightly packed streets jammed with compact cars, open-air buses, bicycles, and moped rickshaws—and everywhere you looked, people, so many millions of people. Thai men dressed in white business shirts and women in silk dresses, children in dark school uniforms and monks in bright orange robes: a never-ending sea of people, bouncing through the sidewalks like balls in a pachinko machine. Rising up above the sidewalks, the buildings themselves were something out of a schizophrenic's dream. Glass-and-steel offices towered over ancient, golden-roofed temples, while apartment complexes sprang up on every corner, each a mixture of a half dozen different architectural styles: jutting spires, cubic balconies, curved white corners, levels constructed of wood, plaster, stone, and steel. The buildings seemed locked in a battle between old and new, and the only constant was growth—perpetual, throbbing, unstoppable.

Mulder and Scully never had a chance to digest the eclectic images; Van Epps squired them to the crowded train station, a fairly modern complex lodged near the center of the city. He had pointed them toward the right set of iron rails, then waved them on their way. Mulder had not minded the hands-off treatment; he did not trust men like Van Epps, nor did he enjoy having the military watching over his shoulder. He and Scully were now free to conduct their investigation on their own terms and timetable.

Soon the swollen city of Bangkok had given way to a lush green countryside of dense forests and unending rice fields, as the train had briefly wound its way into the interior of the country on its journey toward the southeastern coast. Mulder had spent much of the trip conversing—in a mixture of English and inadequate French—with a Thai farmer on his way back home after a three-week trip to the great capital. When Mulder had told the rugged-looking ma.. their destination, he had reacted strangely, backing away while grabbing at something near the collar of his shirt. Mulder had seen it was an amulet of some kind—a common Thai accoutrement. The Thai were one of the most superstitious and spiritual people on Earth, and most Thai men wore at least one Buddhist charm. Still, Mulder wondered why the mere mention of Alkut had caused such a reaction.

When Mulder had pressed the farmer on the issue, the man mumbled something about *mai dee phis*—literally, "bad spirits," as Mulder's English-Thai dictionary informed him. For the rest of the trip, he had stared out the window, avoiding conversation.

The train had taken the two agents as far as Rayong, a gulf town surrounded by white-sand beaches and sprawling European-style resorts. A fishing village famous for its *nam plaa*—"fish sauce," the most popular condiment in Thailand—Rayong bristled with coffee shops and souvenir markets catering to the large number of tourists visiting the nearby newly finished resorts.

Mulder and Scully had rented the Jeep just outside the town limits and begun the long drive away from the tourist centers, trekking deeper into the untouched southern regions of the country. The roads had quickly gone from asphalt to dirt, the scenery from controlled, sandy beauty spotted by palm trees and waterfront hotels to uninhabited tracts of dense forest and rocky cliffs. The closer they got to Alkut, the worse the conditions; in some instances, it seemed as if they had driven right off the edge of civilization.

"The town shouldn't be much farther," Scully commented as she unfolded a corner of the map and gestured at a break in the trees just beyond Mulder's shoulder. "I think the Gulf of Thailand is directly down that slope. And that outcropping to the right—that leads straight up into the mountains. See Dum Kao—'the Black Hills.' A twelve-thousand-foot ascension to its highest peak, dropping off right into the border with Kampuchea. According to the map, the See Dum range encompasses an area of nearly two hundred square miles. Mostly unlivable and uncharted—rife with mud slides, avalanches, predators, and disease-carrying insects."

"Recluse heaven," Mulder said. "Hide out in a cave somewhere, eat a few indigenous animals for supper, have your recluse buddies over on the weekends to watch the mud slides—"

"Mulder!"

The Jeep tipped perilously forward as the dirt road suddenly disappeared in a descending tangle of thick vegetation and loose rocks. Mulder yanked the steering wheel hard to the right, fighting to keep the headlights facing forward as the Jeep tumbled down the steep embankment. Tree branches lashed at the side windows as rocks the size of basketballs shot up around the churning tires. There was a brief second of dead silence as the Jeep lurched over some sort of rotted trunk—then the tires crashed down against packed dirt.

Mulder slammed his foot against the brake. The Jeep fishtailed to the left, then skidded to a complete stop. Eyes wild, Mulder looked up—and saw that they were parked at the edge of a cobblestone road, facing a long, flat valley bordered on three sides by the rising forest. The Gulf of Thailand was no more than three hundred yards to the left, separated from the road by huge granite boulders and gnarled trees that looked like a cross between a palm and a birch. Mulder was momentarily stunned by the sight; the clear blue water stretched on forever beneath the sky, flat and glistening like a plane of opaque glass. Mulder could make out a long wooden dock fifty yards away, surrounded by brightly colored Chinese-style junks and smaller, motorized fishing boats. The rain did not seem to deter the fishermen—tiny shapes garbed in dark green, hooded smocks moved on the boat's decks and along the dock. Mulder watched for a full minute as four fishermen struggled with a tangled net hanging off the back of one of the junks. Then he turned his attention back to the road ahead as he carefully restarted the Jeep's engine.

"I think we've found Alkut," Scully commented, breathing hard. She lifted her hands off the dashboard and pushed her hair out of her eyes. Mulder followed her gaze, letting the Jeep idle as he surveyed the scenery.

The cobblestone road ran parallel to the Gulf, leading toward the center of the quiet fishing village. Beginning twenty yards ahead, low wooden buildings were spaced every few hundred feet along both sides of the road, with shuttered windows and colorful vinyl overhangs covered in huge Thai letters. Most of the buildings seemed to be commercial shops, but Mulder recognized a few traditional Thai houses, with thatched roofs and slanted outer walls. Most of the buildings stood on short wooden stilts, and Mulder had a feeling the town spent many weeks of the rainy season under a few feet of water.

Farther down the road, the commercial buildings and traditional houses seemed to cling closer together, spreading backward from the main road in dense pockets, some rising as high as two or three stories. People of various ages, shapes, and sizes moved between the buildings, and Mulder counted at least a dozen other cars in the vicinity—most even older and more dilapidated than the mud-spattered rented Jeep. The cars shared the road with brightly colored wooden rickshaws, attached to rusty bicycles with wide umbrellas sticking up from their handlebars. Like the fishermen out by the dock, nobody seemed to notice the rain. The rickshaws careened between the cars, the drivers shouting at one another in singsongy Thai syllables. A small group of children ran along the edge of the road ten feet ahead, a pair of barking dogs following behind. To their right, two old women haggled loudly over a line of dried fish spread across a huge blanket beneath one of the vinyl overhangs.

"It's certainly quaint," Scully said, as the Jeep rolled toward the center of town. "And quite different from Bangkok. It's hard to believe they're both part of the same country."

Mulder nodded. "It's a nation in transition. Bangkok is a microcosm of the whole—a totally modern, commercialized city with a preindustrial feel. Alkut, on the other hand, seems lodged much further in the country's past. Less than five thousand residents, probably no tourist industry to speak of. Just fishermen and their families. And maybe a couple of Westerners left over from the war."

As he spoke, his gaze settled on an elderly man standing by the edge of the road, a wide, toothless smile on his lips. The man wore three necklaces around his thin, bare chest, each supporting a tiny rectangular block of jade. *Amulets, like the one worn by the farmer on the train*, Mulder reminded himself: The country had more spirits per capita than anywhere else in the world. Men wore as many as a dozen amulets to guard against everything from disease to fishing accidents. Still, something about the old man unnerved Mulder. Not merely his relative indifference at seeing two *farangs* rolling into town—but something deeper, something in his smile and his dark eyes. It was almost as though he had been expecting the two agents.

Mulder shook his head, telling himself it was just the rain, the unending sheets of gray screwing with his perspective. The old man was simply friendly—like most Thais. The next few villagers they passed offered up the same genuine smile, and Mulder's suspicions trickled away. As the Jeep moved deeper into Alkut, he glanced at the map in Scully's hands. "See anything that resembles a hotel?"

Scully shrugged. "I'm sure we'll find something near the center of town. Nothing fancy—but we just need a place to dump our stuff. Then we can start tracking down Andrew Paladin."

Mulder tossed a quick glance at the forest that rose up above the town, leading into the foothills of the See Dum mountain range. He thought about the two hundred square miles of uncharted land surrounding Alkut. He wondered which was easier, tracking a recluse in all that expanse of wilderness—or trailing a man who had supposedly died fifteen years ago. He had a feeling that both searches would lead to the same goal—the truth behind what had happened to Perry Stanton.

"This looks like the spot," Scully said, huddled next to Mulder beneath the skimpy overhang of a tired-looking palm tree. "According to the army's records, this clinic was built over the original location of Emile Paladin's MASH unit."

Mulder kicked water out of his right shoe, then pushed back a wet palm leaf to get a better look at the building before them. The clinic was low and rectangular, stretching along the muddy road for about twenty yards. The walls were made of aging yellow cinder blocks, and the roof was sloped and encircled by a patchwork of iron rain gutters, overflowing at the corners into huge wooden barrels lodged in the thick mud. There were a half dozen crude windows cut into the cinder-block facade, covered in thick sheets of transparent plastic. Above the nondescript main entrance was a carved, grinning Buddha sunk directly into the wall, beneath two rows of Thai lettering. The Buddha was plated in gold, seated with crossed legs, palms facing upward in what Mulder recognized as the southern, meditative style. According to the white-haired old man who ran the small hotel where Mulder and Scully had deposited their things, Buddhist monks had been running the clinic for nearly ten years.

"Mulder, check out the building across the street. Isn't that a church?"

Mulder turned to look at the small two-story structure that faced the clinic. The building was painted white, with a single conic steeple rising almost twenty feet above the slanted roof. The top of the steeple housed a small bell tower, but the bell was missing, along with a fair-sized chunk of plaster where the steeple met the church's slanted roof. The place looked as though it had been shut down a long time ago, and the front doors were covered in the same transparent plastic as the clinic's windows. "It doesn't look as if they're doing a very brisk business."

"Thailand is the only country in Southeast Asia never to have been a European colony," Scully commented. "Christianity never gained a foothold here."

Mulder turned away from the church and gestured toward an object just in front of the clinic. It was a small wooden dollhouse set on top of a cylindrical post. The miniature house was three feet long and half as high, and had obviously been constructed with great care. The walls were painted in bright colors, and the roof was tiled in strips of what looked to be pure gold. The tiny windows had polished glass panes, and even the doorknobs had been molded out of brass. Someone had recently placed mounds of fresh garlands around the base of the house, and two long sticks of incense leaked smoke past the tiny glass windows. "Christianity never had a chance. The indigenous religion is too strong."

Mulder started forward toward the little house and the entrance to the clinic. His shoulders involuntarily arched forward against the warm rain. "It's a spirit house, Scully. They're a common sight in any town in Thailand—even in Bangkok, the most sophisticated city in the country. They serve as the homes of the resident *phis*—spirits—of the particular building nearby."

Scully raised her eyebrows as they passed close to the spirit house. She leaned over the beautiful pressed flowers that peeked from the tiny windows. "You seem to know a lot about the Thai religion, Mulder."

Mulder smiled as they reached the door to the clinic. "I have an enormous respect for the Thai—always have. Their spirituality is extremely individualistic. In fact, the word *Thai* means 'free.' Their beliefs aren't a matter of doctrine—but of day-to-day observation. If they choose to placate a certain spirit, it's because they've witnessed the results of having that spirit become angry. Not because someone has told them it's the right thing to do."

Scully glanced at Mulder. He knew that she was trying to gauge whether or not he was serious. His face gave her no clues as he reached for the door to the clinic. "There's something to be said for a culture that's remained independent—without even a single civil war—for over eight hundred years."

The door came open, and Mulder felt cool air touch his wet cheeks. He ushered Scully out of the rain and shut the door behind them. They were standing at the edge of a wide rectangular hall with plaster walls and a cement floor. The place was well lit by a pair of fluorescent tubes hanging from the high tiled ceiling, and a crisp, antiseptic scent filled the air. More than a dozen litters were set up along the two sidewalls, complete with IV racks, medical carts, and the odd EKG machine. The litters were modern, with chrome frames, steel wheels, and thick hospital bedding. At least half the litters were occupied.

Buddhist monks in orange robes moved among the patients, followed by nurses in white Red Cross uniforms. Mulder noticed that the monks were wearing latex gloves and many had stethoscopes around their necks. All things considered, the place was sparser than a Western clinic, but seemed modern and efficient. Compared to the rest of the sleepy fishing village, the clinic was almost cosmopolitan.

Scully touched Mulder's shoulder, pointing toward one of the litters. Two monks hovered over the chrome rail, watching as a tall, blond Caucasian woman leaned close to the patient's chest. Mulder noticed that her jacket was different from the ones worn by the Red Cross nurses, longer in the back with an open front. Beneath the jacket, the woman was wearing light blue surgical scrubs.

"Looks like she's in charge," Scully said. "That's an MD's jacket. And the way she's wearing her stethoscope—she's trained in the U.S. At least through her internship."

As Mulder and Scully approached the litter, the woman stepped back, letting the two monks have a better look at what she had just done. Mulder's eyes shifted to the patient. The man was mid-forties, conscious, with his shirt tied down around his waist. A thin line of fresh sutures ran from his upper abdomen to just below his collarbone. Mulder could see the approval in Scully's eyes; the woman had done a good job closing the wound.

"We'll put him on antibiotics for three weeks," the woman said to the monks. "He should be as good as new. Unless he gets in the way of another swordfish hook."

The monks nodded vigorously, and the woman turned, noticing the two agents for the first time. "You two look like you're from out of town. I'm Dr. Lianna Fielding. Is there something I can help you with?"

Mulder slid his ID out of his pants pocket, watching Fielding's expression as she studied the FBI seal. She was tall— almost Mulder's height, with sharp features and narrow blue eyes. "I'm Fox Mulder, this is my partner, Dana Scully. We're U.S. federal agents, and we were hoping you could spare a moment of your time. Are you a full-time resident of Alkut, Dr. Fielding?"

Fielding pulled off her latex gloves and tossed them toward a plastic waste bin. "Actually, I'm attached to the local division of the Red Cross. I make a tour of all of the towns and villages in the area, teaching and assisting as much as I can. U.S. federal agents? You're rather far from home, aren't you?"

Scully had stepped next to the litter and was surveying the stitches. The two monks were next to her, conversing in quiet Thai. Mulder noticed that Scully was being careful to keep a respectable distance between herself and the monks, as Buddhist law dictated. "From your cross-stitching, Dr. Fielding, my guess is you trained in the States. Is that right?"

"Chicago. Are you a doctor?"

Scully nodded. "Forensic pathology. But I'm not here in that capacity."

"We're investigating a case that goes back fifteen years," Mulder interrupted. "We're interested in finding two men connected to the MASH unit that used to be located on this spot. Emile and Andrew Paladin—"

Fielding coughed, then glanced at the two monks, who had

both looked up at the mention of the names. "If you're federal agents, I'm sure you must know that Emile Paladin died a long time ago."

Mulder's instincts kicked in as he watched the two monks whispering to one another. Something about Emile Paladin's name had struck a nerve—fifteen years after the fact. Lianna Fielding noticed the change in Mulder's eyes and made an attempt at explanation. "Emile Paladin is a part of this town's history, Agent Mulder. His MASH unit was many of the towns-people's first real contact with the outside world. And as you probably know, the Thai have an extremely—creative—way of thinking. Things that are different inspire stories, legends— and fear. And from what I understand, Emile Paladin was indeed different."

Mulder felt his muscles tense. "How do you mean?"

Fielding started to answer when a commotion broke out near the doorway to the clinic. Mulder turned and saw an old man being half-carried toward a litter by two younger men in fishing gear. The old man was moaning in obvious, excru-ciating pain, clutching wildly at his leg. Without a word, Fielding quickly grabbed a fresh pair of gloves from a nearby cart and rushed past the two agents. She shouted something in Thai to one of the young men, and received a high-pitched response.

Fielding reached the litter a few steps ahead of Scully. Mulder saw that the old man's pants had been torn away below the knee. His right leg had turned a strange purple color and was speckled with circular blisters. Fielding spoke quietly to the man, trying to calm him, as a monk handed her a vial of clear liquid. She poured the liquid over the purple area, and Mulder caught the distinct scent of vinegar.

"Jellyfish," Scully commented, watching Fielding work. "Maybe a man-of-war. Incredibly painful, sometimes even fatally so. The vinegar fixes the nematocysts—stinging cells—onto the skin, to prevent further encroachment."

Fielding began applying a dry powder over the wound. "Meat tenderizer," Scully explained. "It makes the nematocysts stick together, and neutralizes the acid venom."

Fielding reached for a scalpel from a small tray held by one of the monks. She carefully began to scrape the top layer of skin off of the old man's leg. The man's pain seemed to lessen as she shaved away the nematocysts. Still, he seemed dazed, nearly catatonic. Mulder's thoughts drifted back to Perry Stanton as he watched Fielding work with the scalpel. He remembered the wild look in Stanton's eyes as he leapt at him in the subway tunnel. Stanton had been completely out of his mind, in agony—not so different from the old man on the litter. *Both were trapped in the torment of their own skin.*

Finally, Fielding set the scalpel back on the tray and began to rinse the wound. As the patient settled back against the stretcher, Fielding turned toward Mulder. "As I was about to say, I'm not really the person you should be talking to. I'm not a native of this town—and I have no personal knowledge of either of the Paladins. But there is someone who might be able to help you. Allan Trowbridge, one of the clinic's founders."

Scully had her notepad out of her pocket and was shaking rainwater out of the binding. "Did Trowbridge know Emile Paladin?"

"Allan served as an orderly with the MASH unit during the war. He decided to settle in Alkut after the war ended. He helped set up this clinic—and was responsible for getting the Red Cross to send much of the equipment. He's very well respected in the community."

"Is he here at the clinic?" Mulder asked, his interest growing.

"Today is his day off. You can probably find him at home—I'll give you directions. A friendly warning, though; from what

I've heard about Emile Paladin and his MASH unit—you aren't going to be making many friends, bringing up that past. Some things are better left alone."

Mulder raised his eyebrows. The cryptic statement was just the sort of thing to make him want to dig deeper.

16

Mulder's face caught fire from the inside, followed by a shrill ringing deep in his ears. He quickly reached for his drink, but his eyes were watering so much he couldn't find the glass. He opened his mouth to beg for help, but all he could manage was a fierce choking sound, somewhat akin to a chain saw cutting through bone.

His attempts at communication were met by a gale of laughter from the other side of the low wooden table. Allan Trowbridge slammed his beefy palms together, a huge smile on his lips. "Like I said, *som-dtam* is an acquired taste. Even the Thais treat the northern dish with respect."

Mulder finally found his glass of *bia*—Thai beer—letting the harsh bubbles chase the fire away. He rubbed the tears out of his eyes and looked at Scully, who was seated cross-legged on the wood-paneled floor next to him, her chopsticks hovering above the oversize dish. "Dive right in, Scully. Don't let me suffer alone."

Scully paused for a moment, then shrugged and lifted one of the noodlelike strips to her lips. The moment she closed her mouth, her eyes sprang open and red cauliflowers appeared on

157

her cheeks. She coughed, grabbing Mulder's glass right out of his hand. Mulder turned back toward Trowbridge, who was thoroughly enjoying the show.

"You know," Mulder joked, "assaulting FBI agents is a federal crime. What did you say was in this concoction?"

Before Trowbridge could answer, his wife sidled up next to him, bowing softly as she took her seat at the low pine table. Her appearance was a striking contrast to her husband's. Trowbridge was a huge man, over six feet tall and at least 220 pounds. His barrel chest swelled against the table with each breath, and his bright red beard seemed to spring out over his square jaw like moss on a boulder. Rina Trowbridge, on the other hand, was a tiny woman—barely five feet tall, with thin, delicate features. Her jet-black hair was tied back behind her head in a complex system of buns, and she was wearing an elegant, jade green silk smock, buttoned at the throat.

"First," Rina said, her English draped in the velvet tones of her Thai accent, "we start with raw papaya. Then we add lime juice, a handful of chilies, dried shrimp, and tiny salted land crabs. The finished product is pounded in a pestle, and served as is. I apologize for the lack of warning—my husband is a sadist."

Mulder laughed. In truth, Allan Trowbridge seemed to be a genuinely amiable man. Despite Dr. Fielding's warnings, Trowbridge had not seemed upset by Mulder and Scully's arrival—or their front line of questions about Emile Paladin and the MASH unit. Instead of displaying any anger, he had immediately demanded that the two agents join him for lunch. His wife had happily added two settings to the table.

Mulder's gaze swept across the small living area as he gingerly scooped a small ball of *khao niew*—sticky rice—into his serving bowl. The narrow, wood-walled room had a warm and friendly feel to it, from the loosely woven hangings to the plush, faded crimson oriental carpet that covered most of the floor. There was a tall rattan bookshelf by the door, filled with medical manuals and Thai-to-English dictionaries. In the far corner, there was a small Buddhist shrine, complete with a four-foot-high golden Buddha seated cross-legged, palms up, on a marble pedestal. The Buddha was surrounded by unlit incense and dried garlands, and there were two sets of cloth slippers beneath the pedestal. No doubt, Trowbridge had picked up some of his wife's culture—and perhaps that accounted for his easygoing attitude. Along with their spirituality and superstitions, the Thai were also known for their relaxed way of life.

"You've come a long way to ask questions about ancient history," Trowbridge said as he picked at the last remnants of his meal—finally turning the conversation back to Mulder and Scully's entrance. "Emile and Andrew Paladin are a part of this village's past—but certainly not part of its present. I haven't spoken either of those names in a long, long time. And I don't know anything about Andrew Paladin's whereabouts. I've heard rumors that he lives up in the mountains—but I haven't seen him since the war. So I'm not sure how I can help you."

"But you did serve under Emile Paladin in the MASH unit?" Scully asked, still sipping Mulder's beer. "Dr. Fielding led us to believe that Paladin and his unit were not something Alkut was very fond of remembering."

Trowbridge nodded, his smile weakening slightly. "Well, it was a time of war. And Emile Paladin was an intimidating, obsessive man. He ran the MASH unit as if it was his private fiefdom. And to the villagers, who weren't used to the effects of modern warfare—sometimes the place seemed like a hell on Earth. And I guess that made Emile Paladin into some sort of devil."

Mulder paused, as he saw a tiny, inadvertent shiver move

through Trowbridge's shoulders. It was the first crack in the man's amiable facade, and it made Mulder wonder—was there something hidden behind that smile? "What exactly do you mean?"

Trowbridge spread his hands against the table, his eyes shifting downward for a brief second. "Our MASH unit specialized in napalm injuries, Agent Mulder. They sent us the absolute worst of the worst—men with burns over fifty percent of their body. A steady stream of horribly scorched soldiers, most without faces. Without hair. Without skin. Men who should have died on the battlefield but had somehow survived—burned to the last inch of their humanity."

Trowbridge's voice wavered, and Mulder watched as his wife rose from the table and crossed to the golden Buddha in the far corner. She leaned forward and took a match from beneath the garlands. Carefully, she lit one of the sticks of incense.

"Emile Paladin was their doctor," Trowbridge continued, his smile now gone but his expression still light. "And they were his obsession. He spent his days and nights surrounded by those tortured souls. He hardly spoke to anyone."

Scully leaned forward, the beautiful cuisine suddenly forgotten. "Were you aware of what he was working on?"

Trowbridge glanced at his wife, who was lighting a second stick of incense. The enormous man took a deep breath, his face slightly paled. "Skin. He was searching for the perfect synthetic skin. Something that could trick the body's defenses, that would be accepted by the immune system, that could repair the damage from the napalm. It was his quest, the only thing that mattered to him. He would spend weeks locked in his research laboratory, working on his skin. By the end, the only one he allowed inside with him was his son."

Mulder turned toward Trowbridge, wondering if he had

misheard. *Emile Paladin had a son?* Julian Kyle had not mentioned anything about a son. Nor had there been anything in the military or FBI files on Emile Paladin about progeny. Mulder shifted his head and saw that Scully was staring at Trowbridge with the same intensity.

"Paladin had a child?" she asked.

Trowbridge looked toward his wife again, who instantly met his gaze. The fear was plainly written across her face. She didn't want her husband to say anything more. But Trowbridge shook his head, turning back to the agents. It seemed that he wanted to tell the story—as if he had been waiting a long time to let it out. "The boy's name was Quo Tien. He was born to a prostitute who lived near the MASH unit. She died during childbirth, and Paladin took the child as his own. He raised the boy among his burned, tortured patients. As you can guess, the boy did not turn out well."

Mulder wasn't sure what that meant. He waited for Trowbridge to continue, but instead the big man leaned back from the table, his face sagging. He shook his head, as if chasing the memories away. "As I said, that's all ancient history. The war ended, the MASH unit closed up shop. Emile Paladin was forced to continue his research elsewhere. He and his son moved out of Alkut. And a few years later—as you know—he died."

End of story, Trowbridge seemed to want to add. But something in his eyes told Mulder the story was actually far from over. Mulder aimed his chopsticks at another ball of sticky rice. "A hiking accident. That's what we were told."

"And that's what's on the death certificate," Trowbridge said, speaking quietly. "He fell into a deep ravine while hiking in the mountains. During the war, he had often taken trips up See Dum Kao. He was an avid student of Thai mythology, and there are many ancient ruins in those mountains. But the terrain can be quite treacherous—and according to the story, Paladin broke his neck in a canyon near the range's peak. His body was greatly damaged by the fall—and picked clean by local wildlife."

Rina Trowbridge was bent in ritual prostration before the Buddhist shrine. She suddenly cleared her throat, drawing the attention away from her husband. When she turned away from the Buddha, her face was strangely stiff, her eyes smoldering. "My husband has not told you the entire story. My husband is afraid. We are both afraid."

Mulder was shocked by the sudden admission. The tension was as palpable as the strong scent of incense. Trowbridge whispered something in Thai to his wife. She lowered her eyes. Mulder felt Scully's hand on his arm—but he couldn't let things lie. His senses told him they were on the edge of something vitally important. "Mr. Trowbridge, if you're in some kind of danger—"

"It's nothing," Trowbridge loudly interrupted, not meeting Mulder's eyes. "An old wives' tale, a foolish myth, a farmer's superstition. Rumors—"

"They're not rumors," Rina Trowbridge declared, stepping toward the table. "*Gin-Korng-Pew* is not a rumor."

Mulder searched his memory for the words, but found nothing that matched. He could hear Scully moving uncomfortably next to him; she could tell they were about to delve into Mulder territory, and she wasn't happy about it. They were supposed to be searching for Andrew Paladin. But from the looks on Rina's and Allan Trowbridge's faces—Mulder knew, this was too important to pass over.

"It's a local legend," Trowbridge finally explained, though something in his face told Mulder that he was not as skeptical as his words, "dating back many centuries. *Gin-Korng-Pew* means, literally, the Skin Eater. It's the name of a mythical creature that supposedly lives in a cave at the base of the See Dum range."

"The Skin Eater?" Scully repeated.

"I know how foolish it sounds," Trowbridge responded, facing her. "But as the story goes, around three hundred years ago, bodies began to crop up around the town—minus their skin. Usually vagrants, sometimes farm animals, sometimes missing children—and always the corpses were found in the same state, completely skinned. A local cult grew up around the mysterious deaths—and a small temple was even erected, out near the edge of town. Sacrifices were made, and about a century ago the corpses stopped appearing. According to the myth, Gin-Korng-Pew was sated; the creature went into an indefinite hibernation in his cave."

Rina lowered herself to her husband's side. "But his hibernation was interrupted. Twenty-five years ago—around the same time the MASH unit opened its doors—the skinned bodies began appearing again. First farm animals. Then a pair of brothers, lost on a hunting expedition. Then more and more villagers—poor souls who had wandered too far from home. Every week, it seemed, there was another skinned corpse found near the town. It got so bad, people were afraid to leave their houses. And of course, everyone knew it was because of the MASH unit."

Mulder did not need to see Scully's expression to know what she was thinking. But he was not so quick to dismiss the woman's story. In his experience, old wives' tales usually had a basis in facts. It just took a certain sort of vision to see those facts. "And why was that, Mrs. Trowbridge?"

"Emile Paladin had awakened the Skin Eater. Either through his hikes in the mountains—or because of the thousands of horribly tormented soldiers he brought to Alkut. He had awakened Gin-Korng-Pew after so many years. And the creature was hungry."

"And now?" Scully asked, trying to keep the skepticism out of her voice. "Are there still skinless corpses appearing around town?"

Rina Trowbridge shook her head. "Emile Paladin was their last victim. After his death, the creature returned to his hibernation."

Scully touched Mulder's shoulder as she rose to her feet. Mulder could tell—she had heard enough. "Thank you both for lunch, and for your time. I'm sorry we can't stay any longer, but we need to continue our search for Andrew Paladin."

Trowbridge nodded. "I'm sorry I can't help you there. You might try speaking to David Kuo—he's the only lawyer in town, and he probably had some connection to the Paladins at the time of Emile's death. His office is connected to the town hall. The small circular building a block past the clinic."

Mulder shook Trowbridge's hand and bowed to his wife, thanking her for the meal. He waited until he and Scully had reached the door before letting his thoughts form a question. "You mentioned a temple built to placate Gin-Korng-Pew. Does it still exist?"

Trowbridge seemed surprised by Mulder's interest. Maybe he had assumed that an FBI agent couldn't possibly put stock in such a story. He didn't realize that Mulder could have told him a hundred stories that were equally as bizarre—and all based on fact.

"At the very edge of town," Trowbridge answered. "A stone building with a domed roof. It is run by a cadre of monks in dark red robes—the cult of Gin-Korng-Pew. They keep the temple in order in case, well—"

"In case of his reawakening," Rina Trowbridge finished, her face serious. Mulder felt a chill that had nothing to do with the rain spattering down outside. No matter what Scully thought, he could not discount the story he had just heard.

Skin

Skinless corpses. A scientist whose life had been dedicated to the search for the perfect synthetic skin. And a few thousand miles away, a man who had murdered—and died—because of something that had been done to his skin.

These were the elements of an X-File.

17

 Quo Tien watched from across the street until the two agents turned the corner, heading toward the center of town. Then he quietly approached the traditional wooden house. His long, thin body was draped in a flowing black smock, and his slicked-back hair glistened in the perpetual rain. There was a heavy burlap bag hanging from the belt around his waist, and a dark rucksack slung over his left shoulder.

When he arrived at the front steps leading up to the house, he reached into an inner pocket in his smock and withdrew a shiny steel straight razor with a molded plastic handle. The blade was three and a quarter inches long, the handle specially designed to conform to Tien's fingers. A surge of hunger swept through him as he climbed the low steps, his free hand forming a gentle fist. He knocked twice on the painted wood.

The anticipation was intense, as he listened to the heavy footsteps on the other side of the door. He kept his hands at his sides, the straight razor hidden beneath his oversized sleeve. He could feel the rain running in twisting rivulets down his exposed neck, and the anticipation multiplied, turning virulent. Patience. Patience. *Patience.*

A few seconds later, the door swung inward. There was a brief pause—then recognition snapped across Allan Trowbridge's face. His eyes went wide, his mouth jerked open and closed. He looked like a marionette with tangled strings. Tien smiled. "Hello, Allan. Mind if I come inside?"

Trowbridge's cheeks turned chalky white. His thick shoulders shook with fear. "Please. I didn't tell them anything. I swear—"

"My father taught me never to swear, Allan. It's a straight shot to hell."

Suddenly, Quo Tien's right arm whipped forward. The razor sliced through the soft skin beneath Trowbridge's jaw, digging back almost to his spine. The huge man's head lolled to the side, and a fountain of bright blood spattered against the open door.

Tien caught Trowbridge by the waist as the man's body teetered forward. A second later he had dragged Trowbridge through the entrance of his home, gently shutting the door with the heel of his foot. He laid Trowbridge's body on the floor, kneeling so close he could hear the blood gurgling out of the gash in the man's throat. As he watched the man die, an incredible heat moved through his groin. He moaned softly, his eyes rolling back in his head.

Then the wonderful feeling grew, as a softly accented voice rang out from an inner room in the house. "Allan? Is everything all right?"

Tien leaned back, rubbing the back of his hand against his lips. He unslung his rucksack and placed it lightly on the floor next to the body. Then he retrieved his straight razor and slipped it back beneath his sleeve.

"Everything is just fine," he whispered. "It's just an old friend stopping by to say hello."

He rose to his feet and slid quietly across the front entrance.

He could hear the small woman approaching from around the corner, and he waited with his back against the wall, measuring the distance by the sound of her feet. When she was just a few feet away, he leapt forward, his body uncoiling like a striking snake.

Rina Trowbridge saw him and froze. Her pretty features contorted as she saw the razor flash out from beneath his sleeve. She tried to run—but he was too fast. His free hand caught her by the hair, and she was yanked backward. The razor arced toward her throat. There was a spray of blood— and her small body slumped back against his chest. He leaned close, so that his bloody lips were inches from her ear.

"Hello," he whispered, as he twisted the razor free.

18

"Hello? Is anyone home?"

Mulder stood in the arched entrance to the stone temple, staring down a long, dark corridor with smooth, rounded walls and a packed-mud floor. Although it was still midafternoon, shadows played across his shoulders, dribbling down against the tops of his waterlogged shoes. He glanced upward toward the canopy of tree branches that stretched, like living tentacles, over the domed roof of the building. It seemed as though the trees were clutching at the temple, malevolent green fingers trying to drag the brutalized stone back into the encroaching wilderness. Mulder smiled inwardly at his own dark thoughts.

It had not been difficult to locate the temple at the far edge of the village. After he had dropped Scully off at the town hall—a meandering wooden construct of offices and meeting rooms—he had simply followed the main cobblestone road to its conclusion, then taken a hard right toward the forest. Fifty yards from the road, he had caught sight of the charcoal-colored building jutting out from beneath the tree cover.

At first glance, the temple looked as if it had been carved from a single, mammoth boulder; the temple was shaped like the top half of an egg, with smooth outer walls that curved upward nearly twenty feet to the domed roof. The roof was tiled with alternating strips of gold and silver, and the walls were decorated with Thai script, white and black letters curling across almost every inch of the smooth structure. Just above the entrance was another statue of the Buddha, this one chiseled out of shiny green jade. Set against the massive temple, the Buddha looked helpless and forlorn, and Mulder wondered if the idol had been an afterthought. The Buddha did not seem to fit with the architecture of the temple, which seemed more archaic, a product of a totemic-styled cult rather than a religion based on philosophical enlightenment. Compared to the rest of Alkut, the egg-shaped temple had been built on an artificially impressive—and emotionally driven—scale: more evidence that there was real gravity behind the legend of the Skin Eater, at least in the minds of the villagers. *They had not skimped in their efforts to placate the beast.*

Mulder took a tiny step forward, listening to his own voice echoing back at him from the darkness. He had been surprised to find the heavy wooden door to the temple hanging partially open, and he had waited a full minute before allowing his curiosity to tempt him forward. He knew it was bad form to trespass on a religious shrine—but he couldn't wait forever. In half an hour, he was meeting Scully outside the town hall to discuss her progress with the lawyer—and Mulder had three centuries of myths to decipher in that short time. Even if David Kuo could help them track down Andrew Paladin—Mulder was sure that the legend of the Skin Eater was somehow involved.

His mind made up, he continued forward down the dark corridor. The air was dense and cool, a stark contrast to the sweltering atmosphere outside. The walls on either side were smooth stone, polished to the point of reflection. There were wooden torches that smelled vaguely of kerosene mounted every few feet along the walls, none of them lit—and Mulder chided himself for not carrying matches. Then again, he didn't know if it was proper etiquette to trespass into a temple waving a burning torch. Instead, he watched as his reflection dimmed, each step moving him farther from the gray light of the outside world.

A few yards before total darkness, Mulder came to a second door, covered in some sort of frayed cloth. Mulder felt around the face of the material, but couldn't find anything resembling a doorknob. The cloth felt strangely warm, and Mulder wondered if there was something burning on the other side of the door. He pressed both palms flat against the thin material and gave a gentle shove.

The door swung inward. A sudden wave of heat splashed against Mulder's face. The strong scent of burning oil hit his nostrils, and he stifled a cough. He blinked rapidly, his eyes watering from the strong smell. As his pupils adjusted to the flickering firelight, Mulder saw that he was standing at the mouth of a circular inner chamber, with a polished stone floor and high, roughly hewn rock walls. There was an ancient-looking clay altar in the center of the chamber ten yards ahead of him, a waist-high pedestal construction with a wide rectangular base. Bright flames leaped high into the air above the clay, barely contained by a red-hot steel bowl filled with flammable, pitch-black liquid. Just beyond the steel bowl, seeming to shiver in the intense heat of the flames, stood an enormous statue made of some sort of shiny black stone. The statue was like nothing Mulder had ever seen before.

"Gin-Korng-Pew," Mulder whispered, as his eyes rode up the face of the stone beast. The black statue had a long, ridged snout like an emaciated wolf. The lips were curled back to reveal multiple rows of razor-sharp fangs. Two five-foot-long, curved tusks jutted out from the stone creature's bottom jaw, crisscrossing together just below its flared nostrils. The beast's eyes were enormous, with bright red spirals instead of pupils. Hundreds of spaghetti-strand tentacles sprang out of its head, each tipped by a single curved claw. It was a nightmare turned to stone—and it set off something primal inside Mulder, something he couldn't begin to explain. Though he knew it was a statue, he had the sudden urge to run. At the same time, his muscles felt paralyzed, he couldn't turn away.

"Every culture has its monsters," a voice suddenly echoed in his ears. "But they are all cut from the same soul."

Mulder whirled toward the voice. He saw that the far wall of the chamber was lined with dark alcoves, dug directly into the rough stone. Each alcove was at least five feet tall, and it was impossible to gauge how deeply they were dug into the temple. As Mulder watched, a stooped figure stepped out of the center alcove. The figure was wearing a bright red monk's robe, tied around his bare shoulder. His bald head glistened in the light from the fire. He looked at Mulder—and Mulder realized that he recognized the monk's face.

It was the old man who had watched him and Scully drive into town. The man with the multiple amulets who had stood at the edge of the road, smiling as if he had expected them all along.

Mulder stared at the man, stunned. The old monk noticed his expression and laughed. "Are you more afraid of the statue, or of me?"

Mulder swallowed, trying to regain his composure. Scully would say it was a coincidence, of course. The old man was a member of the Skin Eater cult. He had been standing by the side of the road when they had driven into Alkut. No mystery, no magic.

But the one thing Mulder *didn't* believe in was coincidence. He cleared his throat. "You speak English."

The monk nodded. "I spent three years at the university in Bangkok. As you can imagine, I was a theology major. My name is Ganon."

Mulder gestured toward the statue behind the flaming altar. "And is this the Skin Eater?"

Ganon paused, his gaze still pinned to Mulder's face. "Nobody alive has ever seen Gin-Korng-Pew. This statue is based on an ancient drawing found in a cave not far from this temple. Perhaps it is the creature. Perhaps it is a fairy tale, chiseled out of polished stone."

Ganon made a brief motion with his hand, and a teenage boy in a similar red robe stepped out of one of the other alcoves. Mulder wondered whether there was a roomful of monks behind the wall, waiting for Ganon's cues. He shifted his eyes back to the old monk. "But you don't believe it's a fairy tale. You believe the monster is real."

Ganon shrugged, a coy smile on his lips. He snapped the fingers of his right hand, and the teenager quickly crossed the room to where Mulder was standing. The boy was extremely thin, almost emaciated, with an oblong, shaved head and sunken eyes. Without a word, the boy pulled a small glass vial out of his robe. The vial was filled with some sort of clear liquid, with tiny leaves floating inside.

"It is unimportant what I believe," Ganon said. "I am a lowly servant of this temple. My role is to keep that altar lit. And to offer my protection to those who seek it."

He nodded, and the emaciated boy opened the vial and poured a few droplets of the clear liquid into his palm. He approached Mulder and reached for Mulder's cheek. Mulder involuntarily drew back.

"Malku will not hurt you. The balm is a spirit repellent. It is designed to protect the skin. All who journey into the mountains surrounding Alkut must wear the balm—or risk a horrible fate."

Mulder raised his eyebrows as he let the boy rub the liquid into his cheeks. It had a strong scent, bitter like almonds, with a tinge of something sulfurous. "And you think I'm going to journey into the mountains?"

Ganon shrugged. "Again, it is unimportant what I believe."

Mulder narrowed his eyes, trying to read the expression on the old man's face. Meanwhile, the teenager stepped back, then placed the vial in Mulder's hand. "Take. Makes skin taste bad. Take."

Mulder watched as the boy turned and shuffled back toward his alcove. "Is that what the creature does—eat the skin? As its name implies?"

"As the story goes," Ganon answered, moving gracefully toward the altar, "skin is the source of its immortality. Gin-Korng-Pew feeds on the skin of the unlucky—to replenish itself. When it is asleep, it does not need to feed. Only when it is disturbed does it feel the hunger."

Mulder watched as Ganon reached the altar. He wasn't sure yet how the information fit into the case—but he knew it was significant. *Skin is the source of its immortality.* The words echoed through Mulder's thoughts. Somehow, the Skin Eater was connected to Emile Paladin—and through him, to Perry Stanton. Mulder had to fill in the links.

"So the MASH unit woke the creature and sent it on a hungry rampage," Mulder said, "Somehow, Emile Paladin upset the beast, and the town suffered because of him. Now the creature is once again in hibernation. Somewhere in the mountains."

Ganon did not respond. Instead, he reached beneath the altar and pulled out a long metal staff with a tiny cup on one end. He carefully dipped the end of the staff into the flammable liquid in the metal fire bowl and gently stirred in a circular motion. The flames rose higher, daggers of orange twisting like living ropes around the tusks of the monstrous statue.

"Somewhere in See Dum Kao," Ganon repeated, staring at the flames. "A vast cave called *Thum Phi*—the spirit cavern."

Mulder had a sudden, strange feeling that Ganon was hinting that he knew where Thum Phi was located; the old monk knew where the mythical beast lived.

Mulder looked at the glass vial in his hand. Then his gaze shifted to the statue of the Skin Eater. Maybe Ganon was just telling him what he had already guessed—that the answers he was looking for were in those mountains.

Waiting for him.

Thirty minutes later, Mulder found Scully sitting on the partially enclosed front steps leading up to the town hall, leafing through a manila folder. The steps bisected a small flower garden, row after row of colorful buds creeping up between high blades of bright green grass. The air was thick with the scent of foreign pollen, and Mulder's throat itched as he dropped down next to his partner. He ran both hands through his sopping-wet hair, glancing back at the entrance to the town hall behind them. Above the high double doors he saw two floors of shuttered windows, and near the thatched roof an iron rain gutter like the one he had seen ringing the top of the clinic.

Mulder had barely noticed the perpetual gray sheets on his quick walk back from the temple. His thoughts were still consumed by Ganon and the Skin Eater; when he closed his eyes to blink, he could see the creature's face, the wolfish snout, the crisscrossed tusks, the razor-clawed tentacles.

Scully finally looked up from the manila folder, noticing the expression on his face. "You look as if you just met the bogeyman."

Mulder smiled. "I think maybe I did. How was your visit with David Kuo? Anything interesting?"

Scully sighed. "He doesn't know anything about Andrew's whereabouts. He was Emile Paladin's lawyer—but only in name. He had very little contact with the man since the war, and almost zero contact with his brother."

"So what's in the folder?"

Scully patted it with her fingers. "Kuo retrieved this for me from the town hall records. It's the ME's file from Emile Paladin's autopsy. And before you start telling me about your bogeyman—Emile Paladin died from a broken neck. The pathologist estimated a fall of at least fifty feet."

Mulder's expression didn't change. He reached down past the edge of the steps and yanked a yellow flower out of the garden. The petals were almost as long as his fingers. "And what about his skin? Or lack thereof?"

"Again, no great mystery. His body was mutilated by three different types of predators—all readily identifiable by the teeth marks. Two types of wolf and a mountain lion."

Mulder nodded, yanking one of the petals free. He hadn't expected an autopsy report full of tusks and clawed tentacles. *It was never that simple.* "Sounds like Paladin made quite a picnic."

"The damage was so bad, the positive ID was made from a dental match. Two teeth, to be exact—a left front incisor and a right canine. But there was no doubt. It was Paladin. According to the report, Andrew claimed the body, and it was cremated a few days after the autopsy."

Cremated. Mulder leaned back against the steps, stretching his neck side to side. Scully rolled her eyes. "Mulder, the body was cremated *after* the autopsy, not before. There's no mystery here. Emile Paladin died in a hiking accident."

Mulder didn't respond. Scully exhaled, frustrated. "It's a myth, Mulder. A fairy tale. And it has nothing to do with our case. Perry Stanton didn't have his skin eaten by some beast. Neither did Emile Paladin."

Mulder nodded, tossing the yellow flower back into the garden. He still couldn't shake the idea that the Skin Eater was involved. He remembered what Ganon had told him—that the Skin Eater's source of power was its supply of skin. It coincided closely with his own theory about the source of Stanton's invulnerability, and his incredible athletic feats. And the timing of the Skin Eater's hunger—the link to the MASH unit and to Emile Paladin's presence in Alkut—was impossible to ignore. "I just don't think we can discount anything out of hand."

"Mulder," Scully started, but she was interrupted by a frightened shout from down the street. Mulder looked up to see a pair of orange-robed monks running toward them, their faces masks of terror. Mulder noted that both monks were wearing latex gloves. He realized he had seen them before. They were the two monks from the clinic.

"Quickly!" the larger of the two shouted. "Please! Terrible thing! Terrible thing!"

He waved his arms wildly, pointing down the cobblestone street. The second monk was babbling in Thai, and Mulder saw that there were tears in the corners of his eyes. Mulder rose quickly, following Scully down the steps. The monks nodded vigorously, then turned and rushed down the street. Mulder and Scully had to jog to keep up. The cobblestones were tricky to navigate, but there was no sidewalk, and the mud on either side of the street would have been even worse. Mulder kept his head down, ignoring the buildings that flashed by on either side, as he and Scully struggled to stay close to the sprinting monks.

"This sounds pretty serious," Scully shouted, as she leapt over a puddle of murky rainwater in front of a small, open-air shop selling bowls filled with fishtails. "How did they know where to find us?"

Mulder shrugged, narrowly avoiding a rusted bicycle lying

at the side of the road a few feet past the fishtail shop. He thought about Ganon and the man's knowing eyes. But he decided it was probably nothing so mysterious. "It's a small town. And we're pretty hard to miss."

The monks turned an abrupt corner, winding out of the center of town. Residential homes sprang up on stilts to the left and right, triangular thatched roofs spitting rainwater toward the street in controlled, noisy waterfalls. With a start, Mulder realized the direction they were heading. "Scully, don't the Trowbridges live down the next street?"

Scully looked at him. Both agents hurried their pace, catching up to the monks. As they approached the Trowbridges' home, Mulder saw that a small crowd of people had gathered on the front lawn. Mostly women and young children, dressed in loose smocks and homemade sandals. The women were whispering to one another in worried voices, and Mulder made out the distinct sound of weeping. He swallowed, a dull feeling in his stomach. Then he saw Ganon at the edge of the crowd, and their eyes met. Ganon nodded, his mouth moving, the words disappearing in the gray rain. Mulder didn't need to hear them to know their sound.

"Gin-Korng-Pew."

19

Scully squared her shoulders as she and Mulder worked their way through the crowd. Her face and body quickly took on the controlled veneer of a career federal agent as her left hand slipped to her shoulder holster, checking to see that the snap was undone. She could tell by the grim faces in the crowd that something horrible had happened, and she prayed that the thoughts streaking from her own imagination were way off base. Then she caught sight of the open door, stained in bright red blood—and her heart sank. There was no longer any doubt; they had arrived at a crime scene.

The two monks disappeared into the stilted house, but Scully stopped next to Mulder in the doorway. She surveyed the pattern of blood, how it spread upward along the inside of the wooden door. She then turned her gaze downward, to the crimson, riverlike trail leading into the house.

"Carotid artery," she said, half to herself. The blood on the door was well above eye level, which meant the victim had been standing. From the angle and arc of the spatter, Scully knew it could not have been a bullet wound. It had been something sharp, like a knife or a razor blade.

"The kill was made here," she continued, slowly strolling forward. She followed the trail of blood, walking as lightly as possible. The blood had soaked into the fading oriental carpet, darkening the crimson material like spilled red wine. She tried to forget that just hours ago, she and Mulder had eaten lunch a few yards away. She needed to be objective, to remain clinically detached—

Mulder grabbed her shoulder, stopping her in the narrow hallway that led to the living area. His eyes were wide, and he was pointing toward the edge of the open main room. Scully saw Dr. Fielding hunched near the end of the trail of blood. Fielding was on her knees on the carpet, her face hidden in her hands. The two bodies were on the floor in front of her.

"My God," Scully whispered. She could hear her heart pounding as she plodded forward. Mulder kept his hand on her shoulder. They had both seen horrors before. Dozens of brutal crime scenes, corpses in states too miserable to describe. Still, the sight of the two bodies was difficult to take. Despite all of her training, despite everything she had seen—Scully wanted to turn away.

"Skinned," Fielding said, lifting her head out of her hands. "Every inch removed, along with a fair amount of muscle and interior tissue. I sent for you as soon as I got here. The police are on their way from Rayong; there aren't any full-time officers here in Alkut. I figured you were the next best thing."

"Christ," Mulder said, standing over the corpses. The entire living room seemed covered in blood. The oriental carpet beneath the bodies was saturated with it. There were bits of muscle and organs sticking to the legs of the low pine table where Mulder and Scully had eaten lunch. "It's them, right? Allan and Rina Trowbridge?"

Scully dropped to one knee, next to the larger corpse. It was like looking at an animal on a butcher's block—but the animal was human, and the butchering had been crude and brutal. She tried to re-create the event, using the cues of her profession. She imagined that the first incision had been made directly under the jaw. The face had been peeled back, the ears sliced off, the entire scalp removed in one piece. Then the attention had shifted to the trunk. An incision had most likely been made down the center line, the skin pared open to reveal the rib cage and the organs beneath. Multiple slashes had been necessary to skin the pelvic region, the legs, down to the feet.

Scully shifted her eyes to the second body. Rina Trowbridge had not taken nearly as long. Scully could see strands of Rina's silky dark hair stuck to the bloodied mass that had once been her face. Then she saw one of Rina's eyeballs hanging from a strand of optic nerve, and her jaw clenched. She needed to concentrate. This was a crime scene. *This was a crime.*

She turned her attention back to the larger corpse's pelvic area, and below. "Dr. Fielding, do you have an extra pair of gloves?"

Fielding nodded, fishing through the pockets of her coat. Scully took the gloves from her and slid them over her fingers. She reached forward, gently running her index finger over a piece of exposed tibia. There was a sharp groove right above the knee. She found similar grooves higher up, near the pelvic bone. Then she found a series of slightly less pronounced scratches around the hip joint. She paused, thinking.

"The place looks pretty trashed," Mulder commented, from somewhere behind her. He was carefully picking his way through the small house, searching for clues. Soon, the Thai police would arrive—probably along with government investigators from Bangkok. Scully knew that the FBI would not be welcomed in the investigation, certainly not of a crime of this nature—and not in a town with Alkut's history. Though the town was off the beaten trail, the nation of Thailand was a tourist's paradise. Heinous double murders—even in the sticks—did not make for good tourism.

So Mulder was using the time they had to conduct a quick survey of the crime scene. Likewise, Scully could not count on getting the results of an autopsy. She had to find answers right here, right now. "Dr. Fielding, do you see these grooves and these scratches?"

Fielding leaned closer. She had been momentarily over-whelmed by the sight of the bodies; she had known the Trowbridges, had spoken very highly of Allan. But in her heart she was a doctor. "The grooves look as if they were made by some sort of blade. A few inches long. But I've never seen scratches like those before."

Scully nodded. The grooves were easy. Any forensic patholo-gist could have identified the blade. "The grooves were made by a straight razor. Very controlled, practiced strokes."

"And the scratches?"

Scully paused a moment longer. "I can't be sure. But I think the killer used a dermatome to skin these bodies."

"A dermatome?" Mulder asked. He had paused in front of the Buddhist shrine in the far corner. The shrine seemed the only thing in the room that hadn't been overturned. His sur-prised expression swam across the curved surface of the gold Buddha. "Isn't that the tool that skin harvesters use? Like a supersharp cheese slicer?"

Scully nodded. The dermatome had been set to an incredi-bly brutal depth—all the way through the subcutaneous layer of fat, almost to the bone. "Whoever did this was extremely skilled. He's had some level of medical training. And he's done this many times before."

"He?" Mulder asked.

"Possibly a she. But it certainly wasn't an it, despite what the crowd outside might think. These incisions follow a controlled, determined pattern. It isn't easy to skin a body. It takes practice and a fair amount of strength. More than that, it takes preparation. Someplace to put the skin, some way to carry it away from the scene."

"But why?" Fielding asked, her voice weak. "Why the Trowbridges—and why like this?"

Scully didn't answer the first part of Fielding's question. She had a sickening feeling that the Trowbridges were killed because of her and Mulder's investigation. Either because of something the Trowbridges had said—or because of something they had withheld. The second part of Fielding's question seemed even more obvious.

"To feed the legend," Mulder answered for her. He was leaning forward over the Buddhist shrine, both palms gently touching the gold statue's belly. It looked as though something about the idol was bothering him. "It's an easy cover for a double murder—and it turns Alkut against our investigative efforts. Two foreigners stirring up trouble—waking the beast once again, sending it on a deadly rampage. We're going to be on our own from here on out."

Fielding rose, taking a deep breath. "I'll go and speak to some of the neighbors. Perhaps someone saw something. In any case, there's nothing more I can do here. It's so bloody tragic. I keep remembering their wedding—how they looked into each other's eyes. Both of them were foreign to this place—she a transplant from the north, he from America. But they had found each other. That was all that mattered."

Fielding sighed heavily, rubbing at her eyes with the backs of her hands. Then she shrugged and quietly exited the house, leaving Scully and Mulder alone with the bodies.

Scully pushed Fielding's sentimental thoughts out of her head. It didn't help to see these bodies as people. With practiced clinical detachment, she ran her gloved fingers through the pool of blood covering most of the floor, trying to estimate the exact time of death from the consistency of the fluid. Without skin or forensic tools, she had nothing else to go by.

"We left them about three hours ago," she said out loud. "Whoever did this must have been waiting just outside. Probably watched us leave."

"Maybe he's out there now," Mulder commented. "Still watching us to see what we do next. Or maybe he thinks he's done what he came here to do—cut off our line of information."

Scully rose, slowly. She crossed to Mulder's side, watching curiously as he continued to rub the golden Buddha. The statue was three feet high, and looked as if it weighed more than fifty pounds. The gold was well polished, though there were dark hints where the smoke from years of burning incense had stained the soft metal. The Buddha's wide expression was peaceful and strangely content—despite the flecks of fresh blood sprinkled across its globular cheeks. "Mulder, I'm just glad you're not out there with them. I was expecting you to argue with my conclusions."

"Monsters don't search people's houses after they kill them," Mulder said, suddenly straining against the statue. "And they aren't superstitious enough to leave a Buddhist shrine untouched."

There was a loud metallic click, and the front of the statue came loose from its pedestal. Scully was shocked to see that the Buddha was attached to the back of its base by two oversized metal hinges. She stared at Mulder as he pushed the statue back, revealing a deep, rectangular hiding place.

"Mulder—how did you know?"

"Actually," Mulder responded, as he reached into the opening, "the lunch menu gave it away, even before Fielding's comments a few minutes ago. *Som-dtam* and *khao niew* are northern delicacies. That led me to believe that Rina Trowbridge was a transplant from the northern regions of the country—which Fielding just verified. But this Buddha has his arms crossed at the waist, palms up. That's usually a southern representation of the master. It didn't make sense to me—until I saw the shrine untouched by our killer."

He pulled a thick envelope from the pedestal, then stepped back from the shrine. "A southern Thai wouldn't think to desecrate a shrine like this. That made it the perfect hiding place."

Scully was impressed. Mulder's eye for detail was truly amazing. She watched eagerly while he opened the envelope and peered inside.

"Photographs," he said, evenly. "About a dozen, divided into two sets. And a few printed pages."

He reached inside and removed the photographs. The two sets were bundled separately with rubber bands. Mulder crossed to the low lunch table and spread the two sets out against the wood.

The first set that caught Scully's eye were almost as horrible as the two bodies on the floor. They were pictures of burned patients, lying naked on military-style hospital stretchers. Each picture had a date in the corner—and according to the notations, all were taken between the years of 1970 and 1973. "Full-thickness napalm burns," she commented. "At least seventy percent of their bodies. These patients were all terminal—if not postmortem."

She shifted her eyes to the second set of photos. These were of naked men as well, lying on similar hospital stretchers. But none of these men were burned. All seemed in perfect health. The second set of photos had dates as well—but all the dates were the same: June 7, 1975.

Scully tried to make sense of what she was looking at. "The stretchers look as though they could be MASH unit standard issue, circa Vietnam."

She paused, noticing that Mulder was frozen in place, staring at two of the photos. One was of a burn victim, the other of one of the unmarred men. He had placed the two photos next to one another on the table.

"Mulder?"

"Scully, look."

Scully leaned close, and realized that the burn victim's face was partially recognizable. When she shifted her gaze to the unmarred man—she realized they were photos of the same man. She reread the dates in the corners, then shook her head. "These dates must be incorrect. Burns like that don't heal. Even if he did somehow recover—he would have been covered in transplant scars."

Mulder didn't seem to be listening. He was carefully arranging the two sets of photos, burn victims next to their unmarred counterparts. An eye here, an ear there—he was using whatever clues he could find to pair them up. Some of the pairs seemed incontrovertible, others more like guesswork. But in every case, the effect was the same. A horribly burned body dated between 1970 and 1973, and a healthy body dated 1975.

When Mulder was finished, he looked at Scully. She shook her head. "I know what you're thinking. But it's impossible. Synthetic skin for limited transplantation, maybe. But nothing like this. Medicine isn't magic. This isn't medicine—this is raising the dead. These dates are wrong, Mulder."

Mulder tapped his fingers against the table. He didn't believe her—but he didn't have any proof to the contrary. Instead of responding, he turned back to the folder and removed the rest of its contents: two printed pages of paper.

The first page contained some sort of list. A row of names, numbers, and medical conditions, all divided into columns. Scully quickly recognized that the list was a hospital admission register. The figures were army serial numbers. And the conditions were all strikingly similar. Burns of various degrees, either from napalm or other chemical-based weapons. None of the patients had burns over less than fifty percent of his body. Most were charred beyond the seventy percent range—again, all were terminal.

"A hundred and thirty," Mulder said after a few moments, "all horribly burned, like the men in those pictures—"

Mulder stopped, his brow furrowed. He pointed at one of the names. Scully read it aloud. "Andrew Paladin. Napalm burns, full torso, sixty-eight percent of his face and legs."

"Another mistake?" Mulder asked. "Like the dates on those pictures?"

"It must be," Scully commented, nonplussed. "Or someone's created a long trail of lies. Andrew Paladin could not have survived his brother with burns like that. And if, somehow, he had survived—he'd be confined to a burn clinic, in permanent ICU. Not living as a recluse up in the mountains."

"Unless those pictures are real," Mulder said, as he turned to the second sheet of paper from the folder. "Unless Paladin's search for his perfect synthetic skin was successful."

"Mulder—"

"Take a look at this," Mulder interrupted, not letting Scully stop him mid-fantasy. "It's a map. It looks similar to the map of the MASH unit we got from Van Epps. But this one's got a basement level."

Scully took the sheet of paper from him. Indeed, it was a map of the Alkut MASH unit. A second level was superimposed beneath the roughly drawn complex, showing a series of tunnels and underground chambers. The chambers were marked by numbers and letters—but there was no key, no explanation of what they meant. Still, it was significant. The official map of the MASH unit did not indicate the existence of an underground floor.

"It might still be there," Mulder said, his eyes bright. "The tunnels might still be down there, beneath the clinic. Maybe there's more evidence of Paladin's research."

Scully watched as Mulder gathered up the photos and list of wounded soldiers and shoved them back into the envelope. He folded the map in half and slid it into his pocket. It was obvious what he intended to do. He was going to head back to the clinic and see for himself.

"It's been twenty years," Scully said. "Even if the tunnels still exist, there won't be anything down there."

"It's worth a look." Mulder paused, gesturing toward the two mutilated bodies on the floor. "They died for a reason, Scully. They were hiding something—and I think we found it."

Scully envied his conviction, despite how baseless it seemed. "What did we find, Mulder?"

"Evidence of Paladin's success. And, perhaps, of his continued success. If the men on that list came into Alkut with seventy and eighty percent napalm burns—and came out like the healthy men in those pictures, then Paladin really did achieve a miracle. But that miracle might have had a price. Perry Stanton might have paid that price—along with everyone who got in his way. Indirectly, Allan and Rina Trowbridge might have also paid that price."

There were so many holes in Mulder's theory, it was barely a theory at all. *At least he hadn't mentioned anything about a mythical, skin-eating beast.* "Why would anyone keep something like this a secret? Why kill innocent people to cover up a miracle?"

"I don't know. But we won't find out standing around here."

Scully paused, thinking. Mulder had a point. They had leads to follow—even if the leads seemed insane. She made up her mind and took the envelope with the photos and hospital admission list out of his hands. "All right. As long as we're here, we'll follow this wherever it leads. You search for those tunnels. I'm going to find out what I can about the names on this list. If these men were casualties of the Vietnam War, I should be able to find files on them. If they died in Alkut, then there's a good chance Andrew Paladin died alongside them—and we just wasted a whole lot of federal money tracking down two dead brothers."

Mulder was already heading toward the door. Scully waited a few seconds before following him, her eyes drifting to the two mutilated bodies. Wordlessly, she crossed herself, then squeezed her hand tight around the tiny silver cross she wore around her neck.

The truth was, they *were* chasing a monster. The violent actions of Perry Stanton—the case that had brought them to Thailand in the first place—seemed to pale in comparison to the tragedy on the floor in front of her.

Like Mulder, Scully wanted to catch the monster. But she did not share Mulder's bravado. Staring at the two skinned bodies, she was gripped by a single, sobering thought.

If they got too close to the truth—the monster would be chasing *them*.

20

Mulder's shoulders ached as he strained against the heavy steel equipment shelf, rocking it carefully back into place against the cinder-block wall. The tiny storage room was cramped and claustrophobic, a cluttered swamp of Red Cross surplus, outdated radiology machines, linens, and folded military cots. The walls were lined with off-white plaster, the ceiling covered in similarly colored tiles. A small fluorescent tube lodged in one corner of the ceiling gave the room a sickly yellow, hepatic glow.

The storage room was the fifth and last interior space Mulder had found within the clinic, and he had no idea where to go next. He had kicked every wall, stamped on every inch of floor—and he had not found anything resembling an entrance to an underground level.

He stepped back from the steel shelf, breathing hard. He was becoming more frustrated by the second. The investigation was at a critical point; the double murder had significantly raised the stakes. The Thai police had arrived from Rayong shortly after Mulder and Scully had shifted the Buddha back into place, and had confiscated both bodies for their own investigative efforts. Mulder had a sinking feeling that he and

Scully did not have much time before the Thai authorities co-opted their case. As Scully had inferred, an FBI investigation of a vicious double murder did not make good copy for Thai tourism brochures.

Mulder hastily reached into his pocket and retrieved the folded map. He studied it for the hundredth time, trying to find some sort of physical logic. Since there were no notations of scale or direction, it was impossible to match the tunnels to the geography of the clinic. The MASH unit had consisted of more than a dozen freestanding structures. The triage room and the recovery ward were by far the largest of the buildings, followed by the command office and the barracks. The tunnels seemed to originate beneath the command office, with a second entrance just beyond the edge of the camp.

Mulder leaned back against the door to the small storage room, his eyes shifting to the sheer cement floor. He knew that the tunnels were down there—but he also knew it would take excavation equipment to get through that floor. If an entrance still existed, it wasn't inside the clinic.

He shoved the map back into his pocket and headed out of the storage room. There were three monks clustered around Fielding at the far end of the main room, speaking in hushed tones. The monks looked up as he moved past, and Fielding offered a weak smile. The entire town was shocked by the murder—and rumors about the reawakening of the Skin Eater were rapidly spreading from household to household. Mulder could feel the tension in the air, the sense that something ancient and terrifying had returned.

Shivering, Mulder cast a final look at the interior of the building, then stepped out through the front door. The rain had finally slowed to a light drizzle, and he could see breaks in the clouds above the high wooden steeple of the dilapidated church across the street. Mulder paused as the clinic door swung shut behind him, his eyes resting on the miniature spirit house just a few feet away. Someone had placed fresh flowers along the base, and there were more than a dozen sticks of incense jutting from the little windows. Even the post had been decorated, twists of garlands mingling with colorful silk tassels and strings of beads.

Mulder felt his muscles sagging as he thought about Trowbridge and his wife. Fielding had informed him when the police had carted the bodies off, and he had considered going after them—offering his support to the Thai investigation. But he knew it was pointless. It would be near impossible to explain the connection to Perry Stanton. And any reference to the Skin Eater or Paladin's miraculous research would be considered an offense. The Skin Eater was a village myth, a matter of belief—not of forensic science. As for Paladin's research— Mulder had nothing but a series of photographs as proof.

Still, he had to live with the guilt of the Trowbridges' deaths. They had been murdered because of their connection to the FBI investigation. In a way, Mulder and Scully *had* awakened the Skin Eater.

Mulder started forward, intending to head back to the hotel, where Scully was using her laptop computer to research the list of burned soldiers. But as he stepped past the spirit house he paused, bothered by something across the street.

There was a young man standing in the doorway to the Church. He was tall and thin, with slicked-back hair and caramel skin, wearing a long dark smock with baggy sleeves. He was leaning nonchalantly against the half-open church door, a serene smile on his thin face. As Mulder watched, the young man turned and slipped inside the church. The door clicked shut behind him.

Mulder felt his stomach tighten. There was something about the young man that bothered him. He wasn't sure—but he thought he recognized that caramel face. He had seen a similar man on line at customs in the airport in Bangkok. He couldn't be sure—but the young man might have been on the same flight from New York.

Mulder realized immediately what that might mean. Then another thought hit him, and he quickly retrieved the folded map from his pocket. He ran his eyes over the map, focusing on the distance between the major structures. He looked at the church, the way it was perched close to the road that separated it from the clinic, the way it seemed to have been built on a slight angle to accommodate the small plot of land beneath. He came to a sudden realization.

The area where the church was built could have also been part of the MASH unit.

He jammed the map back into his pocket and rushed into the street. His heart was racing, and his hand automatically went to his gun. He unbuttoned his holster and let his fingers rest on the grooved handle of his Smith & Wesson. If he was right about the young man's arrival in Thailand coinciding with his own—then there was a good chance he was heading toward a trap. But he couldn't risk losing a potential suspect in the Trowbridges' double murder. And a possible link to Emile Paladin's research.

He reached the door to the church, pressing his body against the nearby wall. There was a pile of transparent plastic a few feet away, and he remembered seeing the door covered when he and Scully had first arrived. He had assumed the church was closed down, out of use. It was a good cover for a research laboratory, especially in a place like Alkut. The Buddhist villagers had no use for a Catholic church, with their spirit houses and their Buddhist shrines.

Mulder took a deep breath, letting his heart rate slow. He wished there was some way he could contact Scully—but he knew his cell phone was useless, since Alkut was out of his cell's satellite window.

He placed his free hand against the door and gave it a quick shove. The door swung inward, clanging against the inside wall. The sound reverberated through the air, indicating a wide, open space. Mulder drew his automatic, clicking back the safety.

He crouched low and maneuvered around the doorframe. The air was thick and musty, tinged with the distinct scent of rotting wood. Mulder was standing at the back of a long rectangular hall with a twenty-foot arched ceiling and wood-paneled walls. The walls were partially covered by a green-hued mural of the Last Supper, but many of the panels were missing, gaping holes in the place of holy guests.

Mulder quietly slid along the back of the hall, his eyes adjusting to the strange lighting. Huge stained-glass windows on either side cast rainbows across the wooden pews, revealing dark gashes where the benches had been randomly torn out from the floor. Near the front of the room, Mulder saw a tangle of wood that used to be the support beams of a stage. Rising up from somewhere near the center of the tangle was a row of rusted organ pipes, dented and twisted by age and the warm, moist air.

The hall seemed deserted; Mulder moved forward carefully, trying to keep track of the floor in front of his feet. As with the clinic, the floor was made of cement, though it looked as though there had once been carpeting; tufts of moldy green padding speckled the aisle between the pews.

Mulder had nearly reached the destroyed stage when his gaze settled on a pair of thick, forest green curtains hanging down along the back wall. Between the curtains was a door, attached at a disturbed angle by a single warped hinge. There was easily enough room between the door and the frame for someone to slip through.

Mulder hurried his pace, his gun trained on the dark opening. He could hear the blood rushing through his ears, and his knees burned from the controlled crouch. He reached the curtains and kneeled next to the broken door. The room on the other side looked small, dimly lit by a single, painted window. It seemed deserted as well, and Mulder slid inside, shoulder first.

It was some sort of priest's chambers. There was a low table in the center, and an overturned chair by the wall. A pair of crucifixes hung at eye level above the chair. Beneath the crucifixes stood a small shelf of sacramental items: a few cheap-looking goblets, a pair of candles, an empty wine bottle. Next to the shelf hung an enormous, faded tapestry, taking up almost half of the back wall. Mulder could make out the outline of three separate miracles imprinted on the tapestry, but the details had long since eroded.

Mulder slid toward the tapestry, his feet making as little sound as possible. The bottom of the tapestry was swinging, as if brushed by a gentle wind. Mulder grabbed a handful of the thick material and lifted.

He found himself peering into a dark, descending stairwell. The steps looked worn and scuffed, and Mulder could see they had once been covered in the same green carpeting as the front hall. He smiled, then narrowed his eyes. Caution demanded that he head back to the inn and get Scully—perhaps even contact Van Epps for some armed military backup. He had no idea what he was going to find in those tunnels.

But the longer he waited, the less chance he would find answers. The young man could easily slip away. Mulder shook away his reservations, bent low, and carefully slid beneath the tapestry. He slowly worked his way down the stairs, one hand gliding along the cold stone wall.

The stairs ended about twenty-five feet below the church, at the mouth of a long tunnel. The tunnel had porcelain-tiled walls, with steel support beams rising out of the cement floor at regular intervals. It looked roughly as Mulder had imagined; more modern and clean than the subway tunnels where he and Scully had found Perry Stanton, but certainly not the sort of thing you'd find in any urban mall in the U.S.

To Mulder's surprise, the tunnel was well lit by fluorescent light strips set every few yards into the curved ceiling. The lights meant two things; there was some sort of power source beneath the church. And the underground tunnels had not been abandoned twenty years ago with the rest of the MASH unit.

Mulder headed forward, calling on his training to keep his progress near silent. The air had a brisk, cavernous feel, and Mulder wondered if there was a ventilation system in place. He thought he could detect the soft hum of a fan in the distance, but he couldn't be sure.

Ten yards beyond the stairwell, the tunnel branched out in two directions. Mulder paused at the fork, his back hard against one of the steel struts rising up along the wall. To the left, the tunnel seemed to go on forever, winding like a snake beneath Alkut. To the right, the curved walls opened up into some sort of chamber.

Mulder shifted his gun to his other hand and retrieved his map one more time. He tried to place himself near one of the major chambers—but he couldn't be sure where he had entered the underground compound. His best guess was that he was a few feet from a large, oval room labeled C23. Judging from the distance he had just traveled, C23 appeared to be about fifty feet across.

Mulder decided it was worth investigating, and exchanged the map for the automatic. He held the gun with both hands, index finger beneath the trigger. Then he swung around the corner and through the entrance to the chamber.

He had accurately judged the dimensions of the room. The ceiling was higher than in the tunnels, curved like the inside of a tennis ball. As in the tunnels, the walls were covered in porcelain tiles, but the tiles had gone from light green to a much deeper, oceanic blue. The floor was still cement, and there were two steel posts in the center of the chamber supporting the high ceiling. At the back of the chamber was the opening to what looked to be another tunnel.

Mulder's eyes widened as he saw row after row of hospital stretchers taking up most of the sheer cement floor. Each stretcher was partially concealed by a light blue, circular plastic curtain. Next to the stretchers stood chrome IV racks trailing long yellow rubber IV wires.

The walls on either side of the chamber were lined with high-tech medical equipment—much fancier and certainly more expensive than anything he had seen in Fielding's clinic. He saw what looked to be an ultrasound station, a pair of EEG machines, and at least a dozen crash carts trailing defibrillator wires. Next to the crash carts stood an electron microscope, next to that a computer cabinet supporting a row of state-of-the-art monitors. The monitors' screens all emitted a blank blue light.

Across from the monitors stood a high glass shelf full of chemical vials and test-tube racks. Next to the shelf was a freestanding machine Mulder recognized as an autoclave, a steam sterilizing unit with a clear glass front and a digital control panel. The autoclave was about the size of a small closet, and the control panel was lit; the machine seemed to be in use. Between the sterilizer, the computers, and the various machines, this chamber was drawing a lot of power.

Mulder moved forward, counting the partially curtained stretchers. His eyebrows rose as he reached 130, closely packed together in groups of ten and twenty. *Altogether, the same num-*

ber of stretchers as patients on the Trowbridges' list. Mulder reached the center of the chamber, his thoughts swirling. Was it possible that a group of horribly burned soldiers had been kept here, alive, for more than twenty-five years? Was it possible that Emile Paladin had truly discovered a miracle—

Mulder froze, as sudden footsteps echoed through the chamber. He spun toward the sound—and saw the thin young man standing at the entrance to the chamber. Now that there was less distance between them, he noticed that the man was of mixed origin. His eyes were narrow and dark, his face sharply angled. He was a good two inches taller than Mulder, and his lithe muscles looked like twisted ropes beneath his skin.

The young man's hands were hidden beneath the wide sleeves of his smock. Mulder made sure his gun was clearly visible. "I'm Agent Mulder of the American FBI. I'm going to approach, slowly. Don't make any sudden motions."

The young man smiled. There was a loud shuffling from somewhere behind Mulder's right shoulder. Mulder jerked his body to the side—and saw three men enter the chamber from the opposite entrance. All three were tall, and looked to be in their early twenties. They had matching crew cuts and seemed to be in excellent physical shape. They moved easily into the room, spreading out as they closed toward Mulder. The largest of the three strolled directly toward him, and Mulder noticed that he had something in his right hand: a syringe filled with clear liquid.

Mulder aimed his gun at the man's chest. "Stay where you are."

The man continued forward. Mulder realized there was something off about his face. The man's eyes seemed strangely overdilated. He was looking right at Mulder—but he seemed somewhere else entirely, locked in some sort of daze.

"Not another step," Mulder warned, flipping the safety off his automatic. "I said stop!"

The two wingmen were within fifteen feet, now closing toward him. The man with the syringe was barely ten feet away. Mulder aimed directly at his chest. The man paused—but not because of the gun. He was looking at the syringe. He tapped it against his arm, knocking away an air bubble. *This was going to get ugly.*

Suddenly, all three men dived forward. Mulder fired twice, the gun kicking into the air. The lead man jerked back on his feet, then regained his momentum and continued toward Mulder. Before Mulder could fire again, incredibly strong arms grabbed his wrists, twisting his hands behind his back. The Smith & Wesson clattered to the floor.

He kicked out, trying desperately to twist free. The man with the syringe leaned over him, and he caught a glimpse of something that sent his terrified mind spinning. The man had a circular red rash on the back of his neck.

Mulder felt a sharp prick just above his collarbone. The three men suddenly released him, stepping back. Mulder's knees buckled, and he fell, trying limply to catch himself on the curtain around a nearby stretcher. The curtain snapped free, and he hit the ground. He heard laughter behind him, and he used all his strength to turn his head. The Amerasian was watching him, smiling. The smile seemed to extend at the corners, twisting and turning like a rope made of blood. Mulder tried to crawl away, but he couldn't get the commands to his muscles. His body had changed to liquid. Green clouds swept across his vision, and he felt the cold floor against his cheek. A second later, everything turned black.

Quo Tien shouted a blunt command, and the three drones started back toward the other side of the room. Tien watched their fluid progress, intrigued by their perfect muscle control, the lack of stagger in their walk. He remembered how it was in the beginning. The plodding, slow movements, the limited limb control. The progress was indeed impressive. But it was only partially complete. The drones represented only the first stage of the experiment. In a few hours, the final stage would begin. Twenty-five years of research funneled into a single operation—an operation that was going to make Tien immensely rich. And now there was nothing to stand in the way.

Tien turned his attention back to the FBI agent lying on the floor. A shiver moved through him as he flicked the straight razor out from beneath his sleeve. He could imagine the man's blood flowing just beneath his skin. He wanted to taste that blood, to feel it spread over his hands and lips.

He slid forward. The FBI agent was lying on his side, legs curled in a fetal position. His dark hair was spiked with sweat, and his face was drawn, his eyes moving rapidly beneath his eyelids. Tien dropped to his knees inches away. He ran a finger down the man's bare arm, feeling the slick sweat and the tense muscles beneath. He carefully lifted the razor—

"Tien. Put it down."

Tien looked up, anger flickering across his face. He watched as Julian Kyle strolled into the chamber. Julian was wearing a white lab coat over surgical scrubs. His hands were covered with latex gloves, and there was a heavy cooler under his right arm.

"Uncle Julian," Tien spit. "You're ruining my moment."

"He's an agent with the FBI," Kyle said, sternly. "It isn't as simple as that."

"It can be," Tien responded, glancing at the razor's blade. "This is Thailand, not the U.S."

"It doesn't matter. They'll send agents. The military will get involved. We can't risk the interruptions—not so close to the final experiment. And there's a better way."

Skin

Kyle raised the plastic cooler. Tien sighed, leaning back from the FBI agent's body. He knew the real reason for Kyle's reticence. Julian Kyle was weak. But there was logic in his words. "I guess it's not for either of us to decide."

Tien rose, sliding the straight razor back into his sleeve. In truth, both FBI agents had determined their own fate the minute they had entered Alkut.

"And the woman?" Kyle asked, setting the cooler down on one of the stretchers. "She's being dealt with as well?"

Tien nodded. "I sent a drone. He should be arriving at her room any moment."

"And one drone will be enough?"

Tien laughed. The drones were primitive compared to what was coming—but certainly, a single drone could handle the female agent. Kyle nodded, realizing it was true. It was just a matter of time before Dana Scully's body was laid out next to her partner's.

21

 Scully watched from fifteen feet away as the small green lizard crawled across the perforated metal screen. The lizard had bulging black eyes, dark red spots, and a curved, tapered tail; probably some sort of Asian gecko, she mused, the remnants of some species of dinosaur too primitive to realize it was supposed to be extinct. At the moment, the gecko was doing its best to right evolution's mistake. Inches beneath the metal screen, a pair of propeller-shaped fan blades whirled by, pushing dense waves of humid air across the cramped hotel bedroom. As the gecko crawled across the circular mesh covering, its tail dangled precariously close to the blades. Any second, the fan would consume the little creature, spreading its bits and pieces across the room.

Jackson Pollock gone reptilian: In Scully's opinion, it certainly wouldn't hurt the hotel's spartan sense of decor. The squat, antique fan sat atop a teak bed table, next to a pair of twin-sized, water-stained mattresses. There was a loosely woven throw rug on the floor, and a warped wooden dresser by the closet door. A chest-high, rusting metal lamp stood a few feet from the desk where Scully sat, a single bulb flickering behind a goatskin shade as a tangle of exposed wires near the bottom of the base struggled noisily with the current coming out of the wall socket.

The desk itself was barely larger than the bed table, the chair designed for small Thai bodies. A perfect fit for Scully's concise frame, but Mulder would have had a hell of a time getting his long legs beneath the drawers.

Still, there was room in the closet for their bags, a phone jack, and an adaptable socket to plug in Scully's laptop computer. It was all she needed to link up with the FBI computer banks in Washington.

Scully rolled her shoulders back against the tight chair, shifting her attention from the doomed little dinosaur to the open laptop on the desk in front of her. The cursor blinked at her impatience, while the processor struggled to download her request to the data banks ten thousand miles away. She had laboriously plugged in the list of names—minus Andrew Paladin. Soon the computer would tell her if the men had indeed served in the Vietnam War. She had also asked for army registration photos, current addresses, and medical records; she knew how Mulder's mind worked, and she needed to be thorough. She intended to disprove the notion that these men had somehow survived horrific napalm burns.

Scully simply could not believe that Emile Paladin had invented some sort of miraculous synthetic skin—and had killed to keep its existence a secret. If Perry Stanton had died as the result of an experiment gone bad, it was a recent experiment, perhaps some re-creation of the procedure that had killed the Rikers Island prisoners. It was implausible to think that Stanton's death was somehow related to a twenty-four-year-old secret cure.

A series of beeps emanated from the laptop, and Scully sat up in her chair. The list of names began to spill across the screen, followed by concise FBI terminology. Scully furrowed her brow as she quickly interpreted the data. At first glance, the data confirmed her suspicions. The men were listed as casualties of the Vietnam War. But Scully noticed a strange discrepancy. The men were all registered as having been killed in action between 1970 and 1973; none was listed as having been transported to any army MASH unit, let alone the unit in Alkut.

Scully tapped her lips with her fingers. It didn't make any sense. She and Mulder had found a list registering dead men as admissions to the Alkut MASH. Either the list was a complete fabrication, or someone had falsified death records and admitted the men unofficially. Of course, the first case seemed more likely. The list was nothing more than a piece of paper—even if it had been found in the house of a viciously murdered couple.

Scully paused as the laptop screen changed color. Thumbnail pictures materialized along the horizontal—and by midscreen, she realized things were not as simple as they seemed. The photos had been lifted directly from army registration files, and at least three were clearly recognizable. They were the same photos she and Mulder had taken from the Trowbridges' envelope.

The photos weren't proof that the men had been admitted to the MASH unit—but they certainly implied a connection to Alkut. Scully leaned close to the screen, scanning the photos as they appeared, searching for more matches—

A sudden sound caught her attention, and she looked up from the screen. The sound had come from the other side of the bedroom door. A click of metal against metal, as if someone had tried turning the knob to see if it was locked.

"Hello?" Scully called, but there was no answer. "Mulder, is that you?"

Silence. Scully rose from the chair, her heart pounding. Her gun was in its holster, sitting on the bed table behind the propeller fan. She cleared her throat. "If someone's out there, please identify yourself!"

The doorknob exploded inward, a rain of wood splinters and mangled steel spiraling into the room. Scully jerked back, stunned, her hips slamming into the desk. A man was standing in the open doorway. Tall, well built, with a crew cut and high, chiseled features. He was wearing a loose white shirt and military green slacks. His eyes seemed strange, his pupils overdilated. The muscles in his cheeks and jaw were slack, and Scully immediately thought of drugs—something depressive, perhaps a tranquilizer or an antipsychotic.

The man stepped into the room. Scully's eyes drifted downward, and she watched as he drew something out of the right pocket of his slacks. A hypodermic, with a three-inch-long syringe. Scully's pulse rocketed as she pressed back against the desk.

"Stay where you are," she said in her strongest voice. "I'm a U.S. federal agent."

The man didn't seem to hear her. He took another step forward, his dull eyes trained on her face. Despite his numb expression, his movements were gracefully fluid. Scully thought about her gun fifteen feet away—and realized he would reach her before she was halfway there. She had no way of knowing what was in the syringe, but she had to assume it was something lethal. She needed to disarm the man before going for her gun. She searched the room rapidly—and her gaze settled on the chest-high lamp a few feet past the edge of the desk. It looked heavy enough to cause damage, and close enough to reach. The exposed wires near the bottom of the base were menacing, but if she was careful, she could avoid electrocuting herself.

The man moved closer. He raised the syringe, shaking it

until a droplet of liquid dangled pendulously from the point. Scully kept her eyes on the needle as she slid along the desk toward the lamp. She could hear her heart in her chest, and she took deep breaths, chasing the panic away.

As the man took another step forward, Scully suddenly leapt to the side, grabbing the lamp halfway up its metal base. Without pause, she swung the makeshift weapon in a sweeping arc, aiming for the hypodermic. The goatskin shade toppled away, revealing a naked bulb and more exposed wires. There was a flash of light as the bulb hit the syringe dead on. Then a rainbow of bright sparks burst into the air as the steel needle touched the light socket.

Scully dropped the lamp and dived for the bed table. She was halfway there when she realized the man wasn't chasing her. She turned and watched him convulse backward, the still-sparking lamp lying in front of him, smoke rising from the hypodermic in his hand. The man's knees suddenly went limp, and his body collapsed to the floor.

Scully stared, surprised. The syringe had only touched the light socket for a few seconds; the electric shock should have been strong enough to stun the man—but not enough to cause him serious harm. Scully grabbed her gun from the bed table and stepped cautiously toward him, the barrel aimed at his head. His arms were twisted unnaturally behind his back, his eyes wide-open. His head was partially to one side, and Scully noticed a red rash on the back of his neck. Her cheeks flushed as she remembered that both Perry Stanton and the John Doe had had similar rashes.

She stopped a few feet from the collapsed man and lowered herself to one knee. Keeping the gun a careful distance away, she reached forward and checked his pulse.

Nothing. Scully grabbed the man's shoulder and rolled him over onto his back. His chest was still, his eyes shifting back in their sockets. Scully made a quick decision and slipped her gun into the back of her waistband. She began CPR, pressing as hard as she could against the man's muscular chest.

A few minutes into the CPR she realized it was pointless. The man was dead. As had happened with Perry Stanton, this man had been killed by a relatively small jolt of electricity. Although it was possible for a lamp to draw enough power to cause a cardiac arrest—it was definitely unlikely.

Scully shifted her gaze to the rash on the nape of the dead man's neck. She saw that it consisted of thousands of tiny red dots, arranged in a circular pattern. Like Perry Stanton's and the John Doe's rashes. And all three men had died after receiving electric shocks. Scully wondered—what would this man's autopsy show? She needed to get the body to an operating room. She hoped Fielding would let her use the clinic—

She froze, her gaze shifting to the syringe still clamped in the man's right hand. The clinic. Mulder was there, searching for the underground tunnels. If they had come for Scully, then they must have gone after Mulder as well.

A second later, Scully was on her feet and heading for the door.

22

 Mulder tried to scream, but the beast was too fast. Its enormous black body hurtled toward him through the milky gray air. The monster landed on his chest, its heavy body crushing him back against the stretcher. The wolfish snout was inches from his face, and he stared in terror at the fiery red spirals that were the creature's eyes. The curved, crisscrossing tusks scraped together like kissing scimitars, while a stream of fetid yellow saliva dribbled against his cheeks.

Suddenly, the halo of clawed tentacles on top of the beast's head lashed forward. Mulder felt his skin being flayed away in burning white strips. Again and again the tentacles slashed at him, ruining his face, his neck, his chest. He writhed back and forth, trying to dodge the claws, but the beast was unrelenting. The Skin Eater had been disturbed—and he was hungry. He would tear at Mulder until every ounce of Mulder's skin had been removed. His tentacles and his tusks and his spiral eyes, slashing, gouging, gorging! Mulder convulsed upward with every ounce of strength, refusing to give in, refusing to let the beast have him so easily. He wasn't ready to die . . .

Mulder's eyes came open. His vision swirled, a wave of

nausea working upward through his throat. He gagged, trying to lift himself to a sitting position—but his arms were pinned at his sides. He blinked rapidly, letting the yellowish light clear away the fog. He was staring at a curved stone ceiling, lined by fluorescent light strips. He shifted his head to the side and saw that he was surrounded by a blue plastic curtain. He realized immediately where he was. *The underground chamber.*

His head fell back against the stretcher. He blinked rapidly, fighting away the nausea. He did not know how long he had been unconscious, but from the lack of pain in his muscles, he guessed it was not more than a few hours. There was a black Velcro belt running around his chest and down beneath the stretcher, holding his arms in place. There was a similar restraint around his ankles. He could move his hands a few inches and wiggle his toes—but other than that, he was completely immobilized.

His thoughts shifted back to the violent attack. The three men had overpowered him without much effort. He had fired two shots—could he have missed at point-blank range? Unlikely, but not impossible. And the circular red rash he had seen on the back of his attacker's neck? Was it the same rash that had been reported on both Perry Stanton and the John Doe? And how was it connected to the dazed, overdilated look in the man's eyes?

Mulder took a deep breath, calming himself. He didn't want to use up his energy building theories. He remembered the smiling young Amerasian man. There had been violence behind that smile—a sort of violence that Mulder well recognized. The same edge he had seen in dozens of serial killers throughout his career. *Controlled psychosis.* The Amerasian was a killer. Perhaps he was the young man Trowbridge had spoken about, Emile Paladin's son. Perhaps he had been responsible for the brutal double murder. Perhaps he was stalking Scully right now . . .

Mulder clenched his teeth and slammed his body back against the stretcher. He was helpless, impotent. He couldn't protect his partner. He couldn't even protect himself.

Or could he? He had a strange, sudden thought. He twisted his body a few inches beneath the Velcro strap and felt something hard and cylindrical in his right pocket—just within reach. Slowly, carefully, his fingers crawled toward the object.

With effort, he managed to get the vial free from his pants. Using his index finger and thumb, he went to work on the cap. It finally came free, and a bitter scent wafted up toward his nose. He remembered what the emaciated teenage monk had said when he had given him the balm: "Makes the skin taste bad." He thought about the monster in his dream, picturing the crisscrossing tusks. He shivered, gripping the vial tightly in his hand. Then he flicked his wrist upward toward his body.

He felt the transparent liquid splashing across his chest. A few drops touched his chin and neck, a few more landed on his shoulder and cheeks. The bitter, sulfuric scent burned at his nostrils. He knew Scully would have thought he was insane. He was in an underground research lab—not a monster's cave. But he couldn't shake the feeling that, somehow, the Skin Eater was involved. Either way, he wanted his skin to taste as bad as possible—

He froze, as footsteps reverberated through the stretcher beneath him. Someone was approaching the curtain from the other side. Mulder quickly pushed the empty vial beneath his leg, hiding it from view.

The curtain whipped back, and Mulder squinted at the apparition standing a few feet away. Over six feet tall, long-limbed, with narrow shoulders. The man was wearing light blue scrubs, latex gloves, and a white surgical mask. His hair was completely covered by a surgical cap. The only features Mulder could make out were the man's eyes. A flickering, almost transparent blue—like the base of a flame. Mulder swallowed, trying to appear calm. But those eyes were almost as unnerving as never-ending spirals. Mulder wondered—*could this be Emile Paladin?*

The man turned and said something in a quiet voice. There were other people in the room, just out of view. Gloved hands held out a thin plastic tray. The blue-eyed man took two objects from the tray and turned back to Mulder.

Mulder's gaze dropped to the man's hands. In the right, he held a steel device shaped like an oversize stapler. Mulder remembered a conversation from days ago, when he and Scully had questioned Perry Stanton's plastic surgeon. Something about a stapler used in skin-transplantation procedures. *Christ.* Mulder's eyes shifted to the man's other hand. He saw a long pair of steel tweezers, delicately gripped around a four-inch strip of something thin and yellow. The material looked organic and wet, as if it had just been removed from some sort of preserving solution. *Washed and ready for transplantation.*

"Wait," Mulder whispered. He tried to regain his composure. "You're making a big mistake. They'll send people looking for me."

The blue-eyed man shook the tweezers, and tiny droplets of liquid splattered toward the floor. "Put him under. Now."

Suddenly, strong hands clamped a rubber gas mask over Mulder's mouth and nose. He stared wildly at the square face leaning over him from the head of the stretcher. The second man was also wearing a surgical mask, but Mulder recognized the cubic shape of his head. *Julian Kyle. Here, in Thailand.* Mulder held his breath, struggling violently against the old scientist's grip. But the ex–military man was too strong.

"Take a deep breath," Kyle whispered into his ear. "You won't feel any pain."

Mulder arched his back against the Velcro strap. His lungs

spasmed, but still he held on. Kyle pressed the mask tighter against his face. "It has to be this way."

Mulder saw spots in the corner of his vision, and suddenly he couldn't fight any longer. He gasped, filling his lungs. A sweet taste touched the back of his tongue, and his eyelids fluttered shut. He heard the material of his slacks tearing, and he felt something touching his left calf. Something cold and wet. *My god, my god, my god!* But he was helpless, fading fast. As he flirted with consciousness, a faraway voice swirled in his ear.

"He won't cause us any more problems."

"And his partner?" came the response. There was a brief pause. When the first voice answered, it had a tinny, almost musical quality.

"Something went wrong. It was a mistake to send a first-stage drone on an unobserved mission. We need to send Tien—"

"Julian, we don't have time."

"But his partner—"

"Forget her," the first voice snapped. "We need to head back to the main lab and proceed with the final stage. The satellite link will allow us only a small window for our demonstration."

The voices disintegrated as Mulder's limp body settled back against the stretcher. Reality faded away to the rhythmic click click click of an oversize steel stapler.

23

Scully sat on the wet front steps of the clinic, staring in frustration at the blueprint open on her lap. It had been more than two hours since she had left the hotel, and still she had found no trace of Mulder. She had scoured every inch of the clinic, had questioned Fielding and her staff; Mulder had left the clinic the same way he had come—through the front door. He had found no underground tunnels, no hint of the basement floor.

But Scully knew better than to discount Mulder's ability to find what didn't seem to exist. After searching the clinic, she had headed straight to the records library in the town hall. While at the town hall, she had considered reporting the body in her hotel room—but had decided she didn't have time. She had to make sure Mulder was all right.

She ran her fingers across the center of the blueprint, tracing a shadowy line that she assumed represented Alkut's main road. She had found the blueprint in a booklet printed by the national Thai power company—an idea that had come to her while looking at the electrocuted man in her bedroom. Someone had dug power lines beneath the town's streets, which meant there had to be a better map of the town—and perhaps its underground—than the one provided by the U.S. military.

But after twenty minutes of trying to decipher the strange Thai notations and geographic cues that covered most of the power-company blueprint, Scully was no longer sure that the map was going to provide much help. The town's buildings were represented by little more than numbered dots, connected by dark lines that could have been anything from dirt paths to paved highways. The only structures represented clearly on the blueprint were the power lines; the entire map was covered in spiderwebs of bright red ink, connected by larger blue trunks. The blue trunks seemed to be focused near the larger town buildings, such as the clinic and the town hall. Scully guessed they were the feeder lines, connected directly to the hydraulic power plant located a half mile beyond the north edge of town.

Scully flicked an oversize mosquito off the blueprint as her fingers reached the junction between the main road and the street where the clinic was located. The mosquito angrily buzzed off, leaving behind one of its front legs. Beneath the leg ran one of the blue trunks leading toward the clinic. Scully followed it with her eyes, her mind wandering to Mulder. *Damn it, where the hell are you?* In a few minutes she was going to have to put in a call to Washington, then another to Van Epps. On orders from Washington, the military would turn the town upside down searching for a missing FBI agent—and in the process, scare off any chance they had of solving the mysteries of the Stanton case.

Scully heard a buzzing in her right ear, and felt the injured mosquito land on her exposed neck. Even missing a leg, it would not give up. Like the lizard on the fan, it was a creature too simple to face reality. She was about to slap it away when her eyes involuntarily focused on a spot on the blueprint.

She saw that three of the blue trunks converged within a few centimeters of each other, somewhere close to the clinic.

She leaned over the map, trying to decipher the exact location. She barely even noticed the sharp pinch as the mosquito dug its nose into her skin. Her head was spinning as she traced the few centimeters of map between the clinic and the three blue trunks. She suddenly looked up.

She stared at the decrepit building across the street. Then she moved her eyes from the steeple to the door—to the heap of plastic sheeting next to the front entrance. She remembered how the sheeting had covered the door. She had assumed that the church was abandoned.

She turned back to the blueprint, oblivious of the bloated, sated mosquito that lifted off from her neck and flew past her face. The blueprint didn't make any sense—unless she and Mulder had both been looking in the wrong place. The thought was like a gunshot, sending Scully to her feet.

If she had read the blueprint right, there were three power lines feeding electricity to the abandoned church across the street.

24

Mulder's throat constricted, and he lurched forward, gasping for air. His skull throbbed, and he violently shook his head back and forth, desperate to silence the horrid ringing in his ears. Then his eyes came open—and memory crashed into him with a burst of fluorescent light.

He was lying on the same stretcher in the same underground chamber, but the Velcro straps were gone. The curtain was pulled back, and there was no sign of the blue-eyed man or Julian Kyle. As far as Mulder could tell, he was alone in the chamber. He noticed with a start that his clothes were gone; he was wearing a white hospital smock, and there was a thin rubber wire sticking out of his right arm. Eyes wide, he followed the rubber wire to a bottle of yellowish liquid hanging from the IV rack above his shoulder.

Without thought, he grabbed the wire and yanked it out of his arm. Thin drops of blood dribbled down his wrist, and he quickly applied pressure, cursing at the sharp pain. As he stared at the yellow liquid dripping from the detached IV wire, his entire body started to tremble. A strange, crawling feeling was moving up his left leg. It felt like a thousand worms twitching through his skin.

He clenched his teeth and yanked the smock up. A dozen oversize staples were sticking out from his calf, winding down toward his Achilles tendon. To his surprise, the yellow strip below the staples had shriveled into a hard mass, barely touching the skin beneath. Mulder quickly grabbed the withered slab and yanked as hard as he could. It tore free, dragging half the staples with it. Blood ran freely down his calf, but he barely noticed. He was staring at the failed transplant, relief billowing through him. As he pressed the slab between his fingers, it disintegrated to a fine dust. Mulder exhaled, watching the dust flow through his fingers to the floor.

"I've heard of a patient rejecting a skin transplant," he mused, "but never a transplant rejecting a patient."

He carefully tore a strip of material from the bottom of his smock and wrapped it tightly around his calf. The bleeding slowed, and although he could still feel the few remaining staples, he barely felt any pain. He thought about the balm he had splashed on himself, and how the transplanted skin had reacted. In his mind, connections were forming. But he still needed more information to convince himself that his theories were true.

He shifted his legs off the stretcher, ignoring the dull pounding in his skull. No worse than a bad hangover, he told himself—*a cup of coffee and you'll be as good as new*. His feet touched the cold cement floor, and a new shiver moved up through his shoulders. He felt exposed in the thin hospital smock, and he half expected the blue-eyed man to return with another slab of skin. This time, he would not have the balm to protect him. The transplant would stick—and then? He had a feeling he knew exactly what would happen. But he needed proof.

He rose, slowly, and staggered through the open curtain that surrounded his stretcher. The other stretchers that filled the chamber were still empty, and he noticed again that each had a single IV rack nearby, supporting similar bottles of yellowish liquid. As he moved past the stretchers, he scratched the tiny wound in his forearm, wondering how long he had been unconscious—and how much of the unknown substance was coursing through his veins.

He reached the far wall of the chamber and paused, his eyes shifting across the medical machinery. He was a few feet away from the electron microscope, and his gaze settled on the row of computer monitors nearby. As before, the monitors were all switched on, the screens glowing blue. Mulder noticed that the processors beneath the monitors were connected by a series of wires to the electron microscope. It was a situation he could not resist.

He ran his fingers along the boxlike microscope housing and found a pair of switches. He flicked both of them to the on position, and watched as the computer screens changed color. A second later, tiny, plate-shaped objects bounced across a background of swirling red. Mulder recognized the objects from the broken model in Julian Kyle's office. Epidermal cells; but there was something unnatural about the way they were moving—an almost violent cadence spurred by some unknown desire. The skin cells seemed—for lack of a better word—hungry.

Mulder chided himself. His body and mind had suffered extreme abuse in the past few hours, and he was letting his thoughts get carried away. He drifted past the computer screens—and noticed a small steel file cabinet by the last monitor. The cabinet was barely waist high, and he hadn't noticed it before. A thrill moved through him as he dropped to one knee. *File cabinets were an FBI agent's pornography.*

Mulder began rifling through the drawers. Within a few seconds, he had forgotten about the pounding in his skull and the blood still soaking through the loose tourniquet around his calf. All of his thoughts were trained on the pages that sped past his fingers.

He had reached the back half of the second drawer when he stopped, drawing out a familiar sheet of paper. It was the same list of 130 soldiers he had found beneath the golden Buddha. But in this list, there was a difference. One of the names was crossed off. Next to the name was a small, handwritten note:

Dopamine inhibitor deficiency, due to IV malfunction. Began cardiac convulsions shortly after 2 A.M. en route to in-house demonstration. Drone escaped custody shortly afterward.

Mulder rocked back on his feet, rereading the words. He thought back to the three men who had assaulted him. He pictured their overdilated eyes, their faraway stares. *Drone* was a fitting description. He remembered the tail end of the conversation he had heard, just before he had lost consciousness. Kyle had mentioned something about sending a drone after Scully. The memory sent shards of fear down Mulder's spine—but then he remembered the last part of the conversation. Kyle had said that the drone—the 'first-stage drone'—had been unable to complete the mission. Then the other man had mentioned something about a final stage—and a demonstration. A demonstration that was going to take place at a main laboratory . . .

Mulder turned back to the file cabinet. Near the back of the same drawer, his fingers hit a thick sheaf of pages. As he lifted the sheaf free, he saw that the front page was another copy of the familiar list. But as he turned the pages, his pulse quickened. The list did not end at 130 names: It was sixteen pages long. Mulder quickly did the calculations. *Over two thousand soldiers.* All designated as napalm-burn victims brought to Alkut between 1970 and 1973. It was unthinkable. Two thousand men who should have died more than twenty-five years ago. His mind whirling, Mulder opened the last drawer in the filing cabinet. The drawer was filled with photocopies of MRI scans. He pulled a handful free, leafing through them. The scans were cross sections of human brains, similar to the scans Scully had taken of Perry Stanton. Mulder was no expert, but he remembered what Scully had shown him, and he noticed some obvious similarities. As in Stanton's and the prisoners' MRIs, the brains in the scans had enlarged hypothalamuses. But as far as Mulder could tell, there were no polyps surrounding the augmented glands—

"Mulder!"

Mulder nearly dropped the scans as he whirled on his heels. He saw Scully rushing across the chamber. She had her gun out, and her eyes were scanning the room. Mulder tried to stand, but a rush of dizziness knocked him back to a crouch. In his excitement at finding the file cabinet, he had forgotten about the abuses his body had suffered. He leaned against the cabinet as Scully dropped to his side. She took in the hospital smock, then saw the bloodied tourniquet around his calf.

She quickly slid her gun back into its holster and put the back of her hand against his neck, checking his pulse. Her hand felt warm and reassuring. Mulder tried to smile. His head was pounding worse than before. But he wasn't going to give in to the pain. They were too close to solving their case. "I'm fine. A little elective surgery, that's all."

"Elective?" Scully asked, as her fingers probed beneath the edge of the makeshift tourniquet.

"As you can imagine, my vote was in the minority."

Scully's concern abated slightly as she discerned that the wound was minor. Then she shifted her attention to the small puncture where he had pulled out the IV wire. The anxiety returned to her face. "Do you know what you were given?

"Over there, by the stretcher. The yellowish liquid. I think it was some sort of dopamine inhibitor."

Scully raised her eyebrows. "That would explain your sluggishness. But what makes you think that?"

Mulder showed her the first list, with the handwritten notation. "According to this, one of the transplant patients died from a lack of dopamine inhibitor. I believe all the transplant recipients have to get periodic infusions of the inhibitor—to keep them from going psychotic."

Scully stared at him. "All the transplant recipients. Are you implying—"

"They tried to transplant skin onto my calf. Thankfully, the procedure was a failure. But they didn't know that—and hooked me up to the inhibitor." Mulder had made enormous jumps to come to the conclusion—but he knew he was on the right track. The blue-eyed man had tried to transplant skin onto his body—to turn him into a drone. They had left him with a dopamine-inhibitor drip. As Scully had explained back when she had first seen Perry Stanton's MRIs, dopamine was a neurotransmitter related to psychotic violence. Excess dopamine might also have explained the polyps surrounding Perry Stanton's hypothalamus.

Mulder handed Scully the MRI scans, and watched as she leafed through them. "The hypothalamuses are enlarged," she said, "like Stanton's. And look at this. The motor cortex has nearly doubled in size—while the amygdala has become almost nonexistent."

Mulder raised his eyebrows, confused. "The motor cortex and the amygdala?"

"The motor cortex is the part of the brain associated with involuntary reflex and motor control," Scully explained, still staring at the MRIs. "The amygdala is associated with personality and thought. If these MRIs are real, then the people whose brains have been photographed would be almost automatons—"

"Drones," Mulder interrupted. For some reason, Scully wasn't as shocked by the term as Mulder would have expected. Mulder shifted against the file cabinet. "They can follow simple commands—they can be controlled. Unless they don't get their dopamine inhibitor—and turn out like Perry Stanton."

Scully paused, still looking at the MRIs. "If your list is to be believed, our John Doe arrived here in Alkut—along with one hundred twenty-nine others—more than twenty-five years ago, burned almost to death. You're saying that all these men have been turned into drones?"

Mulder paused. He knew how insane it sounded. But he had his own experience to go from. They had tried to put the skin on him—*to transform him.* "That's just the beginning."

He showed her the list of two thousand names. Her eyes widened as she flipped through the pages. Two thousand men stolen from their families, turned into guinea pigs. Scully shook her head. "Impossible. The logistics alone would be incredible. These men would have to be kept in an intensive care facility. Someplace really big—with enough financing to last more than two decades. And for what purpose? Two thousand mindless drones—what's the point?"

Mulder slowly struggled to his feet, using Scully's arm for balance. "I don't think the drones are the final product. They were the first stage, the prototype. Paladin must be planning to create something much more valuable."

Scully exhaled. They had been through this before. She knew that death certificates could be faked—but Mulder had no real evidence that Paladin was still alive. Mulder thought about describing the blue-eyed man—but the surgical mask had hidden most of his features.

For the moment, Scully let the argument go and gestured

toward the open chamber. "So you're convinced that Paladin's search for synthetic skin led to all of this."

Mulder paused. He had been developing a theory since his trip to the temple—but he knew that Scully would never buy into it. Still, he felt the need to tell her his thoughts. "It's not synthetic. It's scavenged."

He started across the chamber. Scully followed alongside. "What do you mean?"

"Trowbridge told us that Paladin was a devoted student of Thai mythology. I think Paladin knew about the Skin Eater before he ever came to Alkut. He went looking for the creature— and has been using its skin as the source of his transplants." To Mulder, it made perfect sense. Skin was the source of the Skin Eater's power. Skin was also the source of Perry Stanton's invulnerability, and his strength. Paladin had wandered in the mountains surrounding Alkut—and had found a way to make miracles.

Scully stopped near the row of computer screens. She stared, silently, at the unnatural epidermal cells migrating across the swirls of red. Finally, she shook her head. "It has to be synthetic, Mulder. Some sort of chemical structure that interacts with the patient's bloodstream, spreading into the muscle-control centers of the brain. An extremely elastic and inviolable substance—except to electricity. Electricity passes right through the skin into the nervous system itself, setting off a cardiac reaction."

Mulder raised his eyebrows. Stanton and the John Doe had both died from electric shocks. But Scully had not accepted the connection before.

"I had an encounter with one of these men," Scully explained. "In my hotel room. He went into cardiac arrest after shoving a hypodermic needle into a light socket."

Mulder nodded. Now he understood why she had been

willing to accept his premise—if not his conclusions.

"If these men are just the beginning," Scully continued, "what's next?"

Mulder wasn't sure. But the sinking feeling in his gut told him where they would have to go to find out. "If Emile Paladin is experimenting on two thousand missing soldiers, he needs a private, secluded place to work. A place where no one would dare bother him."

Scully exhaled at his obvious attempt at melodrama. But Mulder was sure she was thinking along the same lines. As soon as he recovered his balance, they would be heading into the mountains that surrounded Alkut.

Searching for a secret intensive care unit—and a mythological lair.

25

 Scully sprawled next to Mulder against the fallen evergreen trunk, watching in awe as the three Thai guides hacked at the underbrush with their huge, curved machetes. All three men were bare to the waist, and their sinewy bodies glowed in the sweltering heat. A few feet away, the emaciated teenage monk guided their progress with abrupt flicks of his bony hand; even after seven hours of trekking upward through the dense tropical forest, he and the hired guides showed no sign of tiring. The sky had gone from orange to gray nearly an hour ago, and still they pushed forward, refusing to give up on the promise of reaching the mountain base before darkness set in.

"Very close," the teenage monk called over his shoulder, as he checked the sky with his eyes. "Trail ends over next hill."

Scully contained her enthusiasm. Malku had been making similar statements for the past three miles. What the teenage monk described as hills were actually small mountains covered in densely packed broadleaf evergreens, oak, laurel, and dipterocarps, a native Southeast Asian tree. And as far as Scully could tell, the "trail" was little more than a handful of disconnected breaks in the underbrush, separated by lush green barriers of tropical plant life.

Mulder noticed the skeptical expression on Scully's face, as he slipped off one of his combat boots and shook stones the size of marbles to the ground. A cloud of mosquitoes buzzed around his face, and he blinked rapidly, struggling to keep the irritating insects out of his eyes. "He knows where he's going, Scully. It's his religion, after all."

Scully glanced skeptically at her partner. It was a strange sight—Mulder in military camouflage, with combat boots and an assault rifle slung over his right shoulder. They had found the uniform and rifle at a shop next door to the town hall. Like the Jeep, the items were souvenirs of the Vietnam War—and both had been kept in surprisingly good shape. The uniform was frayed at the edges, and there were three quarter-sized holes in the lower back—but it fit Mulder's frame. He had balked at wearing the uniform until the shop owner had promised him that the original owner had survived his wounds.

The automatic rifle was a much easier decision. Mulder's gun had vanished with his clothes, and they did not have time to navigate the necessary channels in search of a replacement. Mulder's FBI training covered most models of assault rifles, including the CAR-15 slung over his shoulder. Basically, it was a shorter, carbine version of the M-16, chambered in 5.56 mm. The gun had come fitted with a single box magazine containing twenty rounds. The shopkeeper had done a good job keeping the machine oiled and clean, and it seemed battle-ready. A brutal weapon; surely capable of cutting through even the most durable synthetic skin.

"I don't share your confidence," Scully finally responded, focusing on the thin young monk. His jutting chin and narrow eyes made him look like some sort of plucked bird. "Even if the place we're looking for does exist, there are literally thousands of caves at the foot of See Dum Kao."

Mulder shrugged, pulling his boot back over his foot. He winced as the motion tweaked the edge of the fresh bandage around his calf. "You saw the map Ganon showed me in the temple. Malku has spent years memorizing its twists and turns. His whole life has been dedicated to understanding the legend of the Skin Eater. The cave is at the end of this trail."

Scully tightened the clasp holding her hair. It had been a struggle holding back her reservations when Mulder had brought her to Ganon and the Skin Eater temple. When the ancient monk had instructed his young apprentice to guide the agents to the legendary home of the Skin Eater, she had remained silent for one simple reason: The legendary mountain lair was their best bet for locating a private hospital large enough to hold two thousand burned soldiers. The myth was a good cover for unethical, radical experimentation. Emile Paladin could have set up some sort of private hospital during the war—and transferred control to Fibrol after his death. The company could have provided the funding necessary to keep the hospital functioning, while someone else—perhaps Julian Kyle—continued the transplant research.

But in no way did Scully give credence to the fairy tale itself. She had seen Allan and Rina Trowbridges' bodies. She had read Emile Paladin's death certificate. And she had found nothing in the underground laboratory that remotely suggested a connection to some sort of skin-eating beast. The skin sample that had been transplanted onto Mulder's calf had disintegrated into dust—and during microscopic analysis, the dust itself had decomposed beyond the molecular level, making any conclusions impossible. When Scully and Mulder had returned to the hotel before setting off for the mountains, they had found no trace of the electrocuted corpse. Scully assumed that the body had been discovered by the owner of the hotel and carted off along with the Trowbridges. She had unsuccessfully tried to track the body down by phone, and had finally accepted the obvious: another autopsy that would never take place.

All of the evidence pointed to a medical conspiracy: transplant experimentation with some sort of nefarious purpose, one valuable enough to kill for—and to spur a cover-up of violence and misdirection. In retrospect, Scully realized that their entire case had been watched, and to some extent guided, by sources unknown. From the missing John Doe to the outbreak of encephalitis lethargica, they had been steered away from the simple truth. In that, Mulder had been completely on target. The skin Perry Stanton had received was the source of his murderous rampage. But Scully was equally convinced that the source of that skin was science, not myth. And the people behind the skin were criminals: accessories to murder, conspirators who had at the very least falsified Vietnam War records—and at worst, kidnapped and experimented on American soldiers.

"Mulder, it's important that we keep focus. We're here to conduct a limited search of the area, to see if we can find traces of a major intensive care clinic or a laboratory. We're searching for criminal suspects—not monsters."

Mulder's response was cut off by a terrified shout that rang out from one of the machete-wielding guides. Mulder leapt to his feet, the assault rifle spinning expertly to his hands. Scully's Smith & Wesson seemed minuscule by comparison. The shouting changed to rhythmic chanting as the three guides backed away from the cleared underbrush. Scully moved between Mulder and the emaciated monk, her gaze shifting to the ground.

The skeleton was half-lodged in mud, curled in a fetal position. The bones were yellowish, obviously weeks old, and the skull was partially destroyed. Scully noticed the bowed shape of the spine and the short limbs. The skeleton wasn't human. "A gibbon. Dead at least a week."

"And picked clean," Mulder commented.

"By wildlife, yes. See the tracks in the mud over there? Cleft front hooves. Most likely a wild boar. Fierce animals. They're easily big enough to kill a gibbon."

Mulder dropped to one knee, looking over the skeleton. Malku was talking in quiet tones to the three other Thais, who had retreated a good ten feet back. One of them had slung his backpack full of camping supplies over his shoulders.

"Wild boars don't skin bodies," Mulder said.

"But jackals do," Scully responded. "There are at least two species indigenous to this area. Not to mention a number of feline carnivores, wolves, and flesh-eating insects."

Mulder nodded. They would need a zoologist to determine what had really happened to the gibbon. Mulder rose to his feet, then turned back toward the guides. Malku was pleading in a high-pitched voice, but the three guides were all shaking their heads. It was plainly obvious what was going on.

"They go back," Malku finally explained, his eyes sad. "Back to Alkut. They say I must lead them."

Scully glanced at Mulder, then at the underbrush. There was a break in the green, about the size of a person, extending beneath a thick canopy of branches. There was no telling how far the break continued. "I guess that doesn't give us much of a choice."

Mulder looked past her. "Malku, how much further is the base of the mountain?"

"Not far. Just over hill."

"Mulder," Scully said, "this trail could continue for miles. It's going to be dark, and we don't know the area."

"Before I became unconscious, I heard Kyle and the other man talking about the upcoming demonstration. It's happening now, Scully. We can't head back to town."

Mulder pointed to one of the packs lying next to the fallen trunk. "We can carry what we need. Malku will come back for us. Right, Malku?"

The young monk bobbed his head. Scully bit her lower lip, thinking. She did not like the idea of heading farther into the forest on their own, especially so close to nightfall. But Mulder was right—if they didn't reach the mountain soon, there was no point in reaching it at all. She took a deep breath, tasting the steaming, wet air. "Another hour, Mulder. If we don't reach the mountain, we turn back."

"The key is in the wrist," Mulder grunted, bringing his machete down in a vicious arc. "Don't let the weight of the blade control your swing. Like golf, only this sucker will take your head off if you mistime your follow-through."

Scully swung her own machete, severing a branch almost half her length. Her body was slick with sweat, and her shoulders ached beneath the weight of the heavy assault rifle. Mulder was carrying the backpack containing enough rations for two days in the forest. Overkill—Scully hoped. It had been only forty minutes since Malku and the guides had turned back, and already the forest felt as if it was closing in on her, an enveloping crush of nature. Her ears were ringing with the strange whistles and calls of tropical birds and monkeys, and she no longer noticed the carpet of blood-sucking insects stuck to most of her exposed skin.

"It's getting pretty dark," she commented, as she stepped over the freshly cut branch and went to work on the next obstacle, a thick bush nearly twice her height. The effort seemed futile, and she was more than ready to turn back. All she could think about was a cool shower and a flight back to Washington. "We'll have to make camp soon—and wait for Malku to return. Unless you think we can find our way back ourselves."

Mulder moved alongside, slashing deep into the fingers of green. "I'm not ready to give up yet."

"It's not a matter of giving up," Scully said, chopping into the bush with frustrated swipes. "It's a matter of being reasonable—shit."

Scully watched as the machete slipped out from her sweaty fingers and somersaulted through a breach in the thick bush. The blade quickly disappeared from view, and a second later there was the loud clatter of metal against stone. Mulder's face brightened. "That sounded promising."

Scully did not argue. She delicately stepped after the machete, working her way between the minced branches. To her surprise, the other side of the bush opened into a narrow rock canyon leading steadily upward. The canyon was little more than shoulder wide, running between twenty-foot-high rock walls. It was impossible to tell if the canyon had been purposefully carved into the rocks or was a feat of evolution. The rock walls were rough, with sharp, jutting protuberances and clinging green vines. Ten feet ahead, the canyon twisted tightly to the right, making it impossible to see beyond a few feet—but it seemed the agents might have finally reached the edge of the forest.

"It's a pretty tight fit," Scully said. "We'll have to go one at a time."

It was an unpleasant thought—but they had come this far already. Scully slid the rifle off her shoulder and held it lightly in her hands. She had not used anything as powerful as the carbine since her days at Quantico, but she was mentally prepared to fire if it became necessary.

She quietly worked her way forward, Mulder a step behind. The rocks grew steeper on either side, until she could no longer see anything but the narrow incline ahead of her. She found herself turning sideways to fit through the walls, and every few seconds she felt a sharp pinch as she brushed against the jagged rock. She was getting scraped and bruised by the forward progress—and from Mulder's cursing behind her, she knew he was suffering as well.

"I'm beginning to know what a kidney stone feels like," he whispered, yanking off the heavy backpack to make more room for his body. Scully silenced him with her hand as she came to an abrupt turn in the canyon. The walls finally opened up into a brief, rock-strewn plain, stretching upward in a gentle slope. The ground was reddish brown, a combination of packed forest mud and thin gravel. Other than a few knee-high bushes, the ground was clear of significant obstructions. It was strange seeing so much empty space after the long trip through the tropical forest.

Just on the other side of the cleared, reddish plain, Scully saw sheer rock cliffs rising almost straight up, disappearing into the charcoal sky. The cliffs seemed staggeringly large, and she knew her and Mulder's forward progress was about to end. They had reached the base of See Dum Kao.

"Scully," Mulder whispered, his cheek almost touching hers. "Over there."

He gestured toward a huge black oval carved directly into the sheer cliff, about thirty yards away. It was the mouth of a vast cave, exactly as Ganon had described. *A foreboding sight.* The opening was at least twenty feet high, with a span nearly twice as wide. Twisting green vines hung down across the cave entrance like a living portcullis.

"It looks deserted," Scully commented.

"There's got to be another entrance," Mulder explained. "There's no way they move supplies back and forth the way we just came."

"Well," Scully said, shaking sweat out of her eyes. "Let's take a look."

She started forward, casting a glance at the sky. In a few more minutes they would be in total darkness. Isolated in the middle of nowhere, waiting for Malku to lead them back to Alkut. It was not a pleasant thought. On the bright side, at least night would bring relief from the overwhelming heat. If the cave was as deserted as it looked, they would have a place to camp out and wait.

They made short work of the rocky glade, angling along the sheer cliff toward the opening. See Dum Kao seemed to rise straight upward forever to Scully's right, a dagger stabbed deep into the dark skin of the sky. She wondered how many thousands of caves pockmarked the ancient mountain—and how many miles of subterranean caverns spread out like a hollow circulatory system beneath the stone.

She slowed as she reached the edge of the opening. One of the vines hung down just inches from her body, and she reached out, gently touching the thick green rope. Its outer layer was rough, speckled with tiny prickers like an elongated cactus. She looked up, searching for the plant's center, but she could no longer see the arched top of the cave entrance. She carefully unslung the automatic rifle and handed it to Mulder. Then she withdrew her handgun.

Without a word, Mulder slid between two of the vines and into the dark cave. Scully followed, noting how the air seemed to change instantly. The temperature dropped by at least ten degrees, while the humidity seemed to increase, causing an involuntary shiver to move down Scully's back. A dank, mossy smell filled her nostrils, and she fought the urge to cough. She knew there was a danger of inhaling poisonous gases—carbon monoxide, methane, even cyanotic compounds resulting from natural decomposition. But she hoped the wide opening kept fresh air circulating enough to provide sufficient oxygenation.

Beyond the entrance, the cave opened up into an oval chamber, similar in size to the laboratory beneath the church. Huge stalagmites rose up at random intervals across the red-mud floor, sparkling with crystal deposits. Some of the stalagmites were nearly fifteen feet tall—thousands, if not millions, of years old. The ceiling was shrouded in darkness, but Scully could make out the points of similar stalactites hanging down like dulled fangs. Directly across the room was another arched opening, leading deeper into the mountain. A yellowish light trickled across the stone floor, coming from somewhere beyond the second entrance. Scully could not tell for sure—but the light seemed artificial. Still, it was possible that some sort of natural aperture was directing reflected light through the cavern. Perhaps the moon had broken through the clouds, and its light was funneling through fissures in the surrounding stone.

Mulder touched her shoulder, pointing past one of the larger stalagmites to a cleared-out area by the far wall. A glint of reflected light caught her eye, and she held her breath. There was a large, rectangular object at the edge of the chamber. From the distance, it seemed to be made of glass.

Mulder advanced, the automatic rifle cradled in his arms. Scully weaved behind him, circumnavigating a huge stalagmite. As she moved closer to the reflection point, she saw an enormous glass tank running waist high along the wall. The tank was at least twelve feet long, perhaps four feet wide. A series of rubber tubes twisted out of the bottom of the tank, disappearing into holes drilled straight into the stone wall.

Scully's thoughts swirled as she stood next to Mulder, peering into the tank. It was half-filled with transparent liquid, and a strong scent wafted in Scully's nostrils. Salty and familiar. It reminded her of the many thousands of hours she had spent in bio labs during college, medical school, and beyond.

"Ringer's solution," she said, softly. "It's a biochemical solution used to keep organic cells alive. Tissue cultures, bacteria—"

"Transplant materials?" Mulder asked.

Scully shrugged. She was stunned by the sight of the tank. Now there was no doubt—the enormous mountain cave was the site of some sort of medical research. The long path from New York had led to this place in the mountains of Thailand—through the guidance of a religious cult and an ancient fairy tale. Scully reminded herself—there was logic behind it all. The myth of the Skin Eater was a cover story, much like the outbreak of encephalitis lethargica. "It's possible synthetic skin was kept in this tank."

"Maybe just the family pet," Mulder commented, reaching into the tank and touching the liquid inside. He took out his hand and shook the droplets toward the ground. Then he started toward the inner entrance. Scully followed, her nerves on edge. As they moved closer to the yellowish light, unnatural, vaguely mechanical sounds drifted into her ears. Soon the sounds reached a recognizable volume. She clearly made out the rhythmic pumping of respiratory ventilators, mingling with the hiss of liquid infusers and the beep of computer processors. She cautioned Mulder with her hand as they reached the entrance, and they spread out to either side, crouching low.

The inner room was at least four times as large as the initial chamber—massive and naturally domed, nearly the size of a football field. It was the largest underground cavern Scully had ever seen. Soft yellow light poured down from more than a dozen enormous spotlights hanging from steel poles suspended along the walls. And beginning just a few feet in front of Scully, stretching as far as her eyes could see—row after row of empty chrome hospital stretchers. The stretchers seemed to go on forever, parallel rows extending from one end of the cavern to the other.

"They're not here," Mulder whispered, slowly moving between the stretchers. "These stretchers are all empty—"

He paused midsentence. Then he pointed up ahead. There was a group of stretchers—between twenty and thirty—separated from the chrome sea, situated near the far end of the cavern. Each of the segregated stretchers was covered by a milky white oxygen tank.

Mulder rushed ahead, Scully a few feet behind. Their pace slowed as they reached the first oxygen tent. At the head of each tent stood a semicircle of medical carts; Scully recognized respirators and cardiac machines—but some of the other devices were foreign to her, and there were numerous infusion pumps attached to vessels full of unidentifiable chemicals. Tubes ran from the carts to valves attached directly to the plastic oxygen tents.

Scully followed Mulder through the maze of oxygen tents, counting as she went. Her approximation had been accurate; there were twenty-five tented stretchers. She took a deep breath and approached the closest plastic tent. She could hear the rhythm of the oxygen being pumped through the tubing—creating a pristine, sterile environment inside. She searched the outside of the plastic tent—and found a triangular flap held down by a steel zipper. She called Mulder over, and carefully undid the flap.

"My God," she whispered, as she stared through the thin transparent plastic viewplate beneath the flap. She was looking at a horribly burned face and upper torso. Nearly every inch of skin had been seared away, and in many places she could see straight through to the muscle and bone beneath. The patient was a patchwork of black, white, and red, with charred regions, exposed subcutaneous fat, and pulsing veins and arteries revealed to the sterile air. Both eyes were burned away, leaving blank sockets, and the patient's mouth was wide-open—and missing all of its teeth.

But amazingly—the patient seemed to be still alive. Scully could see the mechanical rise and fall of his chest. She could watch the blood pumping through the body's circulatory system. Still alive—in a sense. More an organic machine than a human being. Blood pumping, lungs working, but brain function? Doubtful, if not impossible.

"This one's in the same condition," Mulder called to her from a few feet away. He had opened a similar flap on another oxygen tank. As Scully watched, he moved from stretcher to stretcher, carefully unzipping the flaps. "Twenty-five of them, all in similar states. The rest of the two thousand must have been moved, maybe to other holding areas."

Scully shifted her eyes to the semicircle of medical carts at the head of the stretcher. She listened to the symphony of life-support machinery. "We don't know that these twenty-five patients are from the list. And I'm not even sure there's any way to identify this man. No fingerprints, no teeth."

Mulder had paused by one of the stretchers. He peered down, then continued to the next. "None of these men has teeth—for that precise reason. But there's no doubt in my mind. These are Paladin's guinea pigs. And the rest are out there, somewhere. Waiting for the next phase."

Scully tore herself away from the stretcher and followed

Mulder through the chamber. She thought about the man who had accosted her in her hotel bedroom. Had he once been like one of these patients, a skinless vegetable kept alive by tubes? It seemed impossible. The changes in Perry Stanton—in the MRIs she had seen in the basement of the church—these were changes she could fathom. Chemicals affecting brain structure, neurotransmitters affecting behavior, synthetic skin as a method of transmission. But Mulder was suggesting something completely different. *The raising of the dead.*

"No," Scully finally said. "These burns can't be healed. Not to that degree. Medicine isn't magic."

Suddenly, Mulder grabbed her arm and yanked her to the side. She gasped, nearly losing her footing. Mulder was pointing straight ahead. They were barely twenty yards from the back wall of the enormous chamber. A double door had been cut directly into the stone, and there was a circular viewing window set waist high in one of the doors, a few feet in diameter. Bright light poured through the window, and Scully could see movement on the other side.

"Over there," Mulder mouthed, pointing toward a pair of huge machines a few yards from the doors. Scully identified them as autoclaves: enormous steam sterilizers, each about the size of a small closet, with a transparent Plexiglas face. One of the autoclaves was open, its digital display glowing red, indicating that it was set on automatic and ready for operation. The other looked as if it had been recently used; Scully could see traces of the superheated steam on the inside of the glass, and there were racks of syringes and scalpels glistening inside.

She crouched next to Mulder behind the second autoclave, craning her neck for a better angle through the viewing window.

"Looks like an operating theater," she whispered.

"Theater's the right word," Mulder responded. "Do you see the cameras?"

Scully nodded. From her angle, she could see at least three video cameras on tripods focused on the raised operating table on the other side of the window. A tall, thin man in surgical garb was speaking into one of the cameras, his face covered by a sterile white mask. Another man—squat, square, in similar surgical clothes—was hovering closer to the operating table. In his hands was an oversize plastic cooler, partially opened.

"Julian Kyle," Scully commented, snapping the safety off her Smith & Wesson. She didn't know what sort of surgery was going on in the other room, but she was ready to make an arrest. There were twenty-five burned patients on life support in a cave. *She certainly considered that probable cause.* "What do you suppose the cameras are for?"

"It's a satellite link," Mulder responded. His fingers had tightened against his automatic rifle. He was also preparing for the confrontation. "I heard them talking about it before I lost consciousness. They're demonstrating their procedure—probably to interested buyers."

"Do-it-yourself drones?" Scully asked. She still found the idea implausible. Nobody would go to this much trouble for mindless drones. Trained soldiers could fight circles around men who couldn't think. The drone who had accosted her was a perfect example. He had been unable to react to her surprise attack. How much money could an army of drones be worth?

"As I said before," Mulder responded, "the drones were just the first step. The procedure has been perfected—and the next stage is in that room."

Mulder's whisper had changed to an angry hiss. His objectivity was long gone. Looking at the twenty-five oxygen tents clustered together in the room like white ripples in a tormented ocean, Scully felt her own objectivity waver. She wanted answers as badly as her partner.

She nodded, and Mulder slid forward. Scully followed a step behind, her focus trained on the double doors. Another few seconds, and it would all be over.

26

 Quo Tien's face suddenly drained of color as he watched the two agents sweep out from behind the autoclave. He was standing twenty feet away, in the dark entrance to a secondary tunnel leading off from the main chamber. He could not believe the sight in front of him. The male agent—Fox Mulder, whose flesh Tien had almost tasted—had somehow escaped the effects of the transplant procedure. Now he and his partner were here, in Tien's playground—seconds away from ruining everything.

Tien's surprise rapidly turned to rage. This was his home. The agents' very presence was an abomination. This time, Uncle Julian would not get in the way.

Tien slid forward, his hands breaking free of his long sleeves. He had just returned from securing the last of the first-stage drones; in his left hand he held a compact stun gun, which had become a requirement since the debacle involving the drone in New York. *Better to kill a drone than let it escape.* His right hand embraced the hilt of his straight razor. The two agents were heavily armed—but Tien knew the razor and the stun gun would be enough.

The hunger screamed in his ears as he quickly closed the distance between them.

27

Scully saw the sudden flash of movement and jerked her head to the side. The thin young man was sprinting toward them, his lithe body cutting between the oxygen tents with amazing agility. His face was a mask of rage and violence, his eyes narrowed to black points. He looked more snake than human, his hands rising like fangs. Scully saw the sharp razor blade flashing under the yellow spotlights, then the stun gun—pointing right at her. She didn't have time to get her gun around, didn't even have time to scream. Instead, she did the only thing she could think of. She reached out and grabbed Mulder's shoulder.

The bolt of electricity hit her in the side, and there was an enormous popping in her ears. Her body lifted a few inches off the ground, and her muscles spasmed, sending her careening into Mulder. He jerked beneath her hand as half the electricity transferred to his body. The automatic rifle whirled out of his hands, clattering beneath a stretcher a few feet away. Together, they slammed into the stone wall, just inches from the double doors. Scully's skin felt as if it was on fire, her head spinning, black spots ricocheting across the plane of her vision. She felt Mulder roll free from beneath her, crawling toward his gun.

Her cheek touched the floor, and the room turned to liquid in front of her eyes. She blinked rapidly, struggling to remain conscious. She had avoided the full effect of the stun gun by grabbing Mulder—and she had warned him with the same stroke. But she had partially incapacitated them both. She managed to get her hands in front of her, lifting her face off the ground. She saw Mulder a few feet away, his hands inches from the rifle. Then she saw a long dark shape land on top of him, a shadow come to life. The shadow dragged Mulder back from the gun and spun him onto his back.

Scully shook her head, her vision clearing. The shadow flickered into three dimensions. It was the young man, straddling Mulder around his waist, the razor blade rising above Mulder's face. *Christ.* Scully clenched her jaw and launched herself forward. She slammed into the young man's back, knocking him off Mulder with her weight. Even before they hit the ground, the young man had twisted out of her grip. The back of his left hand caught the side of Scully's jaw, and she spun across the floor, crashing into a semicircle of medical carts. She tasted blood and felt the sharp pain of a pulled muscle daggering down her right side. She was lying against the legs of one of the occupied stretchers, staring up at the white-plastic oxygen tent. One of the carts had collapsed on top of her, and a cardiac machine was lying shattered next to her shoulder. A long plastic tube had yanked free from the machine, and Scully saw a sharp steel wire sticking out of the end of the tube. A trochar, used to insert an emergency cardiac balloon into a patient. Relief filled her as she realized that the machine had not been attached to the burn victim in the oxygen tent, that it was there in case of an emergency. Then her eyes focused on the trochar. The hollow steel wire was eight inches long, with an extremely sharp point.

Scully grabbed the trochar, yanking it free from the plastic tube. The sharp pain in her side sent tears to her eyes, as she struggled into a crouch. She spit blood, searching for Mulder and the young man.

She spotted them directly in front of the two autoclaves. Mulder was on his knees, his hands clenched around the Amerasian's wrists. There was blood pouring from a gash in Mulder's cheek, more blood from a deep cut in his left arm. The Amerasian clearly had the upper hand. The bloody razor blade was moving steadily toward Mulder's throat. The Amerasian's face was perfectly calm, the surface of a lake right before a storm. His lips twitched upward at the edges, a strangely erotic smile.

Scully clenched her hand around the trochar and hurtled forward. The Amerasian looked up at the last second, his eyes going wide. He tried to twist his body out of the way, but Mulder held on tight to his wrists, limiting his range of motion. The trochar caught the side of his shoulder and plunged through, ripping deep into his muscle, wounding him severely. A geyser of bright red blood sprayed Mulder's face, and he reeled back. The Amerasian lurched to his feet, his eyes wild. He staggered back, swinging the razor blade impotently through the air, his face draining as the blood fountained out of his deeply skewered shoulder. His feet tangled together, and he fell, crashing into the open autoclave. His weight sent the machine rocking backward, and the door swung shut.

There was a mechanical click, followed by a series of loud beeps. Scully's stomach dropped as she realized the machine was set on automatic. She lurched toward the control panel— but she was too late. She watched in horror as the Amerasian's body slumped against the transparent door, his knees buckling. Suddenly, a thunderous hiss erupted from the machine. Plumes of superheated steam exploded out of the half dozen sterilizing jets, hitting the young man from all four sides. His skin was instantly flayed from his body, tearing off in long, bloody strips. In less than a second he had been reduced to a skeleton shrouded in white steam.

Scully stared in shock, unable to turn away. Mulder staggered to his feet next to her, his hand over the wound on his left arm. "Karma," he said, simply. "Two thousand degrees of pure karma."

Scully looked at him. The blood flowed freely down his face from the cut in his cheek. Her own mouth ached, and she realized that one of her lower teeth was loose. "Was that Emile Paladin's son?"

Before Mulder could answer, there was the sound of a swinging door behind them. Scully turned, and saw Julian Kyle staring at them from in front of the double doors. He had the plastic cooler in his hands, and there was a shocked look on his face.

"Stay where you are," Mulder shouted, but Kyle was already sprinting across the chamber. Mulder ignored him, heading toward the double doors. The other man was presumably still inside the operating theater. "Scully, don't let him get away. He's got the skin!"

Scully thought about going after her gun, but decided she didn't have time to waste searching the chamber. Kyle was already near the secondary tunnel from where the Amerasian had entered the room. Scully raced after him, ignoring the pain in her side. She heard Mulder hit the double doors behind her, and she knew he was also unarmed.

She wondered how far they'd get on karma alone.

28

 Mulder crashed through the twin doors shoulder first, bursting into the bright light. His boots skidded against the floor as he narrowly avoided a video camera set atop a tripod. The raised operating table was ten feet away, surrounded by surgical equipment. Anesthetic tanks stood by the head of the table, next to a respirator pump and two enormous canisters of oxygen. On the other side of the table, Mulder recognized the articulated arm and cylindrical housing of a high-powered laser scalpel, similar to the device he had seen used during the tattoo removal in the surgical ward at Jamaica Hospital. Next to the laser apparatus stood a defibrillator cart, next to that a cardiac monitor. Bright green mountains raced across the monitor, the fierce cadence of an overstimulated heart. Each peak sent a high-pitched tone echoing off the walls.

The blue-eyed man in the surgical mask stood frozen beside the monitor, a serrated steel scalpel in his right hand. Three separate video cameras were trained over his shoulders toward the operating table, and Mulder saw a spaghetti-sea of wires looping behind the cameras to an enormous receiver plugged into a generator by the wall. The cameras whirred in a quiet symphony of invisible gears.

"Sorry to interrupt the show," Mulder said, breathing hard in the doorway.

The blue-eyed man remained still, a strange calm moving across his features. He gently lowered the scalpel. His eyes shifted to the patient on the table in front of him. Mulder followed his gaze.

The patient was a work in progress. His bare torso was split into two distinct sections; his abdomen was still covered in terrible burns, a mix of white, black, and ruby red. But his upper pectorals, shoulders, neck, and face had been delicately reconstructed. The new, yellowish skin was pulled taut against his muscles and bone, giving off a jaundiced glow. At the edges of each newly transplanted section, Mulder could make out the thin staples—and spread around the staples, tiny flecks of red powder. *The Dust*—the antibacterial substance that had first connected their investigation to Fibrol, and Emile Paladin.

Beneath the fresh skin, the patient's face was unnaturally smooth, the features icily still beneath the anesthesia mask. His eyes were wide-open, the same piercing blue as the surgeon by his side.

Mulder realized with a start that he recognized the patient's face. *Andrew Paladin.* He had found the recluse brother. He shifted his gaze back to the masked surgeon. The blue-eyed man moved slowly to one of the video cameras behind him, and hit a switch. The cameras stopped whirring. "You've disturbed a delicate procedure. This man could die because of you."

The voice was soft, almost melodic, tinged with confidence. He did not seem fazed by Mulder's presence.

"This man should have died a long time ago," Mulder responded, slowly moving around the operating table, his eyes flickering toward the scalpel. He could feel the warm blood still trickling down his jaw to his neck, staining the front of his camouflage. His wounded left arm hung uselessly at his side. "There are twenty-five just like him imprisoned in the next room. And there are close to two thousand more hidden somewhere, suffering the same horrid fate. Tortured souls, separated from their families for more than twenty-five years."

The blue-eyed man took a step back from the operating table, the scalpel poised expertly in his gloved hand. "Those men are alive because of me. My skin will give them a second chance—a way out from the torture."

Mulder shook his head, anger filling him. "You mean turn them into slaves—drones?"

The blue-eyed man backed between the two oxygen tanks as Mulder skirted the bottom corner of the operating table.

"No," Mulder continued, his anger turning his voice sharp. "That was just the first stage. Incapable of individual thought—willing, unthinking servants, following your orders. But the next stage—it's something much more advanced, isn't it? Much more *valuable*."

"This is beyond you," the blue-eyed man said, his voice indifferent, even clinical. "You can't possibly begin to understand."

Mulder felt his anger multiply. "I know that you've kept these men alive for the past twenty-five years. Medically, that seems impossible. So it must be the skin itself—or perhaps chemicals within the skin, that has made this longevity possible. You've used the skin to alter these men—to prepare them. For this *demonstration*."

Mulder paused, looking at the patient on the stretcher. Then he glanced at the cameras, then at the receiver by the wall. He assumed it was connected by a fiber-optic link to a satellite dish somewhere high in the mountains. "Soldiers—intelligent, invulnerable soldiers. That's what you're trying to create, isn't it? And you intend to sell them—to the military? To another government? Who's on the other end of the cameras?"

The blue-eyed man's face tensed as his left hand suddenly slipped into his coat pocket. When it reappeared, he was holding a small-caliber handgun. Mulder's chest constricted, and he took a step back. The cold glint in the man's eyes scared him almost as much as the gun.

"That's enough," he said, quietly.

It was more than a statement—it was a command. Looking at the man's face, at the intensity of his gaze, Mulder was struck by a sudden thought: This man was nothing like Julian Kyle. He might have worn a green uniform—but he had never been hard-line military. He was arrogant, egotistical, controlling; certainly, he was not a man who followed orders. His motivation came from within, from his own obsessions, his own unquenchable ego. Mulder glanced back at the cameras, at the operating table—and he realized it didn't make sense.

"It's not about money at all," he finally said. "The men who are funding you might think that's what you're after—but that's not it. You're chasing something else. Something much more powerful than money."

He thought about the twenty-five burn victims in the vast chamber, kept alive for twenty-five years. Then he thought about the first-stage drones—men who should have died during the Vietnam War, men who still appeared as young as they had the day they were injured. He realized that he and Scully had missed the point from the very beginning.

"Immortality," he whispered, his eyes widening. "Invulnerable soldiers are just the beginning. The skin is ageless. Timeless. Immortal—like the Skin Eater itself. That's what you're after, isn't it? Immortality—"

Mulder ducked to the left just as the gun went off. He felt something slam into his right shoulder, and he was whirled off his feet. He hit the floor, rolling as fast as his wounded body could manage. A second shot exploded against the floor by his feet, sending up a plume of shattered stone. Mulder scrambled the other way, his mind churning as he partially concealed himself beneath the raised operating table. He couldn't tell how badly he'd been shot, but a dull ache was moving through his shoulder, mingling with the pain from his slashed left arm. He could hear the blue-eyed man circling the operating table toward him, and he crawled in the opposite direction, struggling against the growing sense of panic. He had grossly misjudged the situation. He had let his adrenaline drive him carelessly forward. He had not counted on the hubris of a man who had turned a myth into a miracle. *A man who had spent his adult life searching for a way to beat death.*

"Two thousand regenerating sources of immortality," Mulder said, his voice low. "Including your own brother."

There was an audible cough, and Mulder's shoulders trembled. He had been correct all along. Emile Paladin was the man behind the surgical mask. Mulder leaned back against the operating table, the pain from his gunshot wound sapping his energy. Paladin's hubris was numbing—his accomplishments, overwhelming. Two thousand invulnerable soldiers, each to become a regenerating source of the transforming skin. A demonstration—and presumably, a sale of the product—to unknown forces within the Defense Department, men who had funded Paladin up until this point. Tinkering with the human species, an experiment that meddled with evolution itself—it was abominable. But there was nothing Mulder could do. He felt his head falling forward—when he noticed a rounded pedal just a few inches from his right foot. He followed the pedal to its cylindrical root, and realized he was lying a few feet from the base of the laser scalpel.

His heart slammed in his chest, the adrenaline rocking his body awake. He heard Paladin circling around the head of the operating table. He closed his eyes, imagining the man's position. He pictured the articulated arm with the attached laser, the way it pointed at a slightly upward angle. He set his jaw, tensing his aching muscles, forcing his body to coil inward. He counted the seconds, listening as the footsteps moved closer and closer and closer . . .

Suddenly, Mulder leapt out from under the operating table and rose to his full height. Paladin reared back, stunned, the gun sweeping upward. Before Paladin could pull the trigger, Mulder slapped at the steel arm with his open right hand. The mechanical arm sprang forward on its hinged springs, spinning wildly away from the cylinder. At the same moment, Mulder's foot came down hard on the control pedal and there was a loud, electric snap, like a leather belt pulled tight. The red guiding light flickered out toward a spot a few inches past the blue-eyed man's shoulder. Mulder's eyes went wide as he watched the light land directly on the rubber gasket at the top of one of the oversized oxygen tanks by the head of the operating table. Christ, he thought to himself. *Another miscalculation.* There was a moment of frozen time—followed by a blinding flash of white light.

Mulder was thrown backward as the oxygen tank exploded. A searing heat licked his face as a sphere of flame billowed out from the eruption point, instantly consuming Paladin from behind. The fiery sphere continued to expand, enveloping the operating table, licking at the canisters of anesthetic gas. Mulder crashed back into the wall, covering his head with his hands as a second explosion rocked the operating room. Metal shrapnel tore through the air, chunks of stone and steel pummeling the walls and floor. Something hit Mulder in the stomach, driving the air out of him. He doubled forward, gasping, the heat singeing the hairs on the back of his neck.

And just as suddenly, the heat evaporated as the oxygen

burned out. Mulder staggered to his feet, staring at the devastated room. Medical machinery lay strewn against the walls, most of the devices charred beyond recognition. The video cameras lay mangled in the corners, lenses melted into crystal pools against the floor. The operating table itself had split down the middle—and Andrew Paladin was nothing more than a curled, blackened shape. The anesthetic gas inside his lungs had obviously ignited, engulfing him from the inside.

Mulder stumbled forward, his eyes searching for the man who had started it all. He stepped over the smoking remains of the cardiac monitor, wincing as the motion exacerbated the pain in his right shoulder. Still moving forward, he pulled open the buttons of his shirt and slid the material gently away from the wound. Relief filled him as he surveyed the slash of blood; the bullet had only nicked him, cutting through his skin but missing the muscle and bone beneath. His gaze moved back to the floor—and he stopped dead, his heart pounding in his chest.

"Mulder?" he heard from the entrance to the devastated operating room. "My God. What the hell happened in here?"

Mulder stared down at the blackened, mangled thing on the floor by his feet. "Emile Paladin. Though you'll have to take my word for it. There's even less of him to autopsy, this time around."

Mulder looked up. Scully was gingerly touching a burned corner of the operating table. There was dried blood on her lower lip, and her red hair was matted with sweat.

"What about Julian Kyle? And the cooler of skin?"

Scully shook her head. "Kyle got away. The tunnels go on for miles into the base of the mountain. It could take days to search them all. We need to get back to Alkut and call Washington, then bring in Van Epps and the military."

"The military," Mulder repeated. He glanced at the ruined

video cameras. Despite the horror he had just witnessed, an ironic smile inadvertently touched his lips. "The military may be less than helpful."

Scully shrugged. It was not the first time Mulder had made such a statement. Mulder sighed, frustration and fatigue tugging at his insides. The case was over—but they had little more evidence than when they had started. He knew it would be next to impossible to match the twenty-five soldiers with any of the names on the list. And by the time the military got involved, he doubted there would be any evidence of the 130 first-stage drones, or any trace of the rest of the two thousand burn victims. Without Kyle and the drones there was no remaining evidence of Emile Paladin's miracle skin—and no definitive proof of its source.

Scully seemed to have come to the same conclusion. She moved carefully into the room, her eyes focused on Mulder's shoulder wound. In many ways, she was a doctor first, a federal agent second. "We may never know the truth behind Paladin's synthetic skin. But we've put an end to his experiments."

Mulder wondered if it was true. Kyle had escaped with the synthetic skin. And the rest of the two thousand guinea pigs were still out there, somewhere. It was possible he could start again. Still, Julian Kyle wasn't Emile Paladin. It wasn't his experiment—and it wasn't his obsession.

Mulder sighed, letting Scully's expert fingers probe his bared shoulder. "Another case without closure, Scully. Without any hard evidence to take back with us."

Scully finished with his shoulder and stepped away, watching him rebutton his shirt. "Actually, on my way back to the chamber, I did find something. But I'm not sure what it means."

Mulder looked at her eyes. There was something there,

deep beneath the green. Something was bothering her. Mulder felt the fatigue disappear from his body.

"Show me."

Twenty minutes later, Mulder stood next to Scully in a small alcove near the center of the network of tunnels, staring up at two objects embedded in the stone wall. Mulder could feel his heart pounding in his chest.

Finally, Scully broke the silence. "I can think of a number of plausible explanations."

Mulder didn't respond. To him, no explanations were needed. Scully could break the objects down to their molecular level, stare at them under an electron microscope, bathe them in an acid bath or weigh them on an atomic scale. She could subject them to every possible abuse in her scientific arsenal, and it wouldn't make any difference. To Mulder, the objects were an explanation in themselves. Their meaning was as terrifying, abrupt, and obvious as their appearance.

Mulder shivered, then slowly turned away. Scully remained behind, staring uneasily at the pair of crisscrossing, razor-sharp tusks.

29

Scully leaned back against the chain-link fence and shut her eyes. Even through her eyelids, she could see the lights: a caravan of flashing red and blue, a Christmas tree on its side stretching more than fifty yards beyond the edge of the cordoned-off runway. Although the sirens had been silenced because of the late hour and the proximity to Dulles International's main terminal, sound filled the night air: the rumble of diesel emergency vehicles, the shouts of medical personnel, the shrill squeal of steel stretcher wheels against pavement.

"It's like watching some sort of macabre carnival," Mulder commented from a few feet away. He was also leaning against the fence, his bandaged right arm resting in a sling against his chest. The razor wound on his cheek was covered by two strips of gauze, there was an Ace bandage around his left forearm and heavy bags under his eyes. His stooped shoulders showed the effects of twenty hours in a plane and another ten in debriefing at FBI headquarters. "From here, it seems like a lot more than twenty-five ambulances."

Scully opened her eyes, watching the colored lights play across her partner's battered cheeks. She wondered if she looked as worn as Mulder. Her jaw still ached from Tien's backhand blow, and her eyesight had begun to blur from exhaustion. She had napped briefly on the plane, and had showered and changed at her apartment; but she knew it would take at least another week to recover fully from the rigorous case. It didn't help that there were still so many questions left unanswered. Sadly, lack of closure was not unfamiliar territory.

She rubbed the back of her hand across her eyes, clearing her vision. A hundred yards down the runway, beyond the ambulances, she could just make out the Boeing 727. A dozen high-intensity spotlights surrounded the curved fuselage of the plane, illuminating the military markings on the tail and wings. Both the front and back hatches of the plane were open, and bright orange mechanical hoists squatted beneath the openings, surrounded by medical technicians in light blue military uniforms. Scully watched as one of the hoists smoothly lowered a pair of stretchers from the front hatchway. Once the hoist had reached the ground, the medics spirited the stretchers to one of the waiting ambulances. Then the hoist rose back to the hatchway, ready for another pair.

Skinner had estimated that it would take only two hours to remove the patients from the specially outfitted plane. The expense of transporting the twenty-five burn victims—and for the years of medical care that would come next—fell squarely on the taxpayers. A VA hospital in Maryland had already been outfitted with the necessary life-support machinery, and a staff of full-time convalescent nurses had been hired. Frankly, Scully had been pleasantly surprised by the military's swift response to the situation. The first recon teams had arrived in Alkut only hours after she and Mulder had contacted Washington; led by Timothy Van Epps, three squadrons of Marines had quickly prepared the scene for transport. Meanwhile, Skinner had worked through the red tape in Washington, using Mulder and Scully's case report as a guideline for the upcoming analysis and management of the situation. Six hours later, the two agents were in an ambulance on their way to Bangkok. Scully had insisted that one of the burn victims be transported with her—perhaps in response to Mulder's growing paranoia at the military's swift presence.

The long journey to Bangkok had given Scully the opportunity to evaluate the patient firsthand. On closer inspection, the longevity of the napalm-burn victims seemed less miraculous than tragic. As she had suspected, the patient was in a vegetative state, in complete organ failure, kept alive by mechanical intrusion. Despite what Mulder had hypothesized, from a medical perspective there was no chance the patient would ever recover.

Still, Scully *had* discovered evidence that the patient's cellular structure had been infused with an unknown chemical—a strange, carbon-based molecule Scully had never seen before. The unknown chemical displayed two amazing characteristics: the ability to strengthen cell walls and to stave off fibroblast deterioration. Scully could only assume that the chemical was another synthetic breakthrough, like the red antibiotic dust. According to Mulder's theory, the chemical had "prepared" the patients for Paladin's radical transplant procedure. It would take years of further analysis to determine fully if that was true.

In the meantime, the military was considering her and Mulder's request for a regional search for the rest of the two thousand Vietnam casualties. Scully was pessimistic about the likelihood of a major operation ever taking place—after all, there wasn't any real evidence that the burn victims were still alive, nor was there much hope of tracking them down after so many years. Still, she could envision quiet diplomatic inquiries being circulated throughout Southeast Asia, and perhaps even a more wide-scale search of the mountains around Alkut.

She was more optimistic about the current efforts being made to match the twenty-five recovered patients to the list of casualties. Without teeth and distinguishing features, it would be difficult—but not impossible. DNA samples would be matched to blood taken from the casualties' surviving family members, and identities would be confirmed. The only obstacles were time and money, and the U.S. military had plenty of both.

"Isn't that Skinner?" Mulder interrupted, gesturing with his good arm. Scully saw a tall man separate from a group of uniformed officers fifty yards away, just beyond the rear ambulance. She easily identified the assistant director's broad shoulders and distinctive gait. Skinner was moving down the runway toward them, a heavy clipboard in his hands; Scully recognized the case file she and Mulder had prepared on the flight back to Washington.

"Maybe there's been some progress in the search for Julian Kyle," she said, hopefully. She and Mulder had sent out an international APB on the fugitive scientist, and had transferred his stats to Interpol and the Southeast Asian division of the CIA. Still, despite her hopes, she doubted Kyle would be apprehended anytime soon. Kyle was ex-military, and assuredly had the resources to hide in Asia indefinitely.

"I wouldn't hold my breath," Mulder commented, putting voice to Scully's thoughts. "From what the search teams reported after hitting Fibrol, I'd say Kyle planned for this contingency a long time ago."

Scully sighed, straightening her slacks as she pushed off

the fence. Mulder's sentiments were accurate; there was little hope of finding Kyle or, for that matter, any evidence of a connection between Paladin's work and Fibrol International.

Three FBI search teams had descended on Fibrol's main complex just hours after Scully and Mulder had reported their findings to Skinner. Every office and laboratory had been thoroughly searched, every file cabinet and computer processor scoured for evidence. No links to Paladin or his experiments were found. Nothing to indict either Fibrol or Julian Kyle, and no indication that anyone at the company had previous knowledge of Emile Paladin's faked death or continued existence. Fibrol's board of directors had stood up to twelve hours of direct questioning—and not one member of the executive staff had shown evidence of the slightest deception, or any knowledge of Kyle's possible whereabouts. Paladin and Kyle had obviously been working alone. If, as Mulder maintained, they had been funded by sources within the Defense Department, the paper trail had long since vanished.

Still, the raid on Fibrol had not been a total waste of time. While going through Julian Kyle's office, the search team had found an unlabeled phone number in a locked drawer in his desk. The number had been traced to a studio apartment in Chelsea. The apartment had been deserted for at least a week, but the forensic specialists had found a number of hair and skin samples in the sink and shower drains matching similar samples taken from the cave at the base of See Dum Kao.

According to preliminary DNA matches, the apartment had belonged to Quo Tien, Emile Paladin's son. Twenty minutes after the search team began to scour the apartment, they made a chilling discovery. Beneath a hinged tile in the apartment's

THE X-FILES

bathroom, they had found a small vial of clear liquid and two specially manufactured, spring-loaded miniature syringes. Scully had recognized the description of the syringes from a *New England Journal of Medicine* article on microsurgery; they had been designed for intercapillary intrusions during microscopic surgical procedures. That in mind, she was not surprised when the clear liquid in the vial was identified as a rare viral sample suspended in a supercooled chemical base. The search team had solved the mystery of the encephalitis lethargica outbreak.

"Kyle's long gone," Mulder continued, as he and Scully started toward the runway, intending to meet Skinner halfway. "And he took Paladin's skin with him. We're left with twenty-five unknown soldiers, a trail of brutal murders, a medically exonerated Perry Stanton—and, of course, a pair of tusks. In retrospect, I guess it's a pretty good ending to a three-hundred-year-old myth."

Scully avoided looking at her partner. They had been over the subject a dozen times. The tusks had been transported to the FBI headquarters along with Scully and Mulder's case file. Preliminary molecular dating had placed the age of the objects at approximately three hundred years—a fact that, on its own, was inconclusive. Elephants and wild boar were indigenous to the region, now as well as three hundred years ago. Although DNA analysis had not yet found a species match, there was a good chance the tusks belonged to a strain of elephant or boar that had since gone extinct.

"Maybe that's what Skinner wants to talk about," Scully finally responded, her voice low. They were now only a dozen yards from the assistant director, closing fast. "Maybe he wants to donate the tusks to a museum. Or better yet, sell them to pay for our little excursion."

"I'd rather mount them on the wall of my office," Mulder

260

said. "A memento of our romantic journey to Southeast Asia. What do you say, Scully? We could split the pair."

"Thanks," Scully responded, her face stiffening as they met Skinner at the edge of the runway, "but I think they're more your style."